No, it couldn't be...

"Andy Montgomery, at your service," he announced, immediately focusing on the injured fox cub.

His voice still sounded so familiar after all this time; deeper, perhaps, but with that same bright, melodic lilt. Relieved to have a second to pull herself together, Ellie concentrated on breathing steadily as he ran his skilled fingers over the little animal's unresisting body.

"Right," he said eventually, jumping up. "We'd better get it to the center as quick as we can."

Ellie hesitated, steeling herself for the inevitable. It must have been almost six years since she'd last seen Andy...six years since he'd broken her heart. The heavy anger she'd clung to since that day kicked in, and she stood slowly.

"Of all the vets in the world, Andy Montgomery?" She hardened her gaze as she met the eyes of the person she had once loved so much. "What a coincidence. I'm glad you finally qualified—I wondered if you would."

She had the momentary satisfaction of seeing his tall frame freeze. His face pale with shock.

Dear Reader,

Thank you for picking up my book, I do hope you enjoy it.

If you have previously read *The Country Vet* (the first book in this series), you will already be familiar with Little Dale, in the Lake District hills, and many of the characters that are also in *this* story. It is satisfying, I think, to see how people's lives develop after that first huge rush of falling in love.

I hope you can keep staying in touch with the lives of the characters you have come to know, not only human but animal, too, for as well as being in love with love, anyone who reads my books just has to love animals.

I feel very privileged to be able to write romance, to lose myself in love stories on a regular basis. Without love, our lives are empty. And hopefully you will be able to lose yourself in my love stories, too, to identify with the characters and experience that heady rush of falling in love again and again.

Life doesn't always stay perfect for long; embrace the best bits and live for today.

I would love to hear from you, either to hear your comments about my stories or to answer questions, and if you need advice about the love in your life, then I'd be very happy to try to help.

You can contact me at info@holmescalesridingcentre.co.uk.

Without readers, I cannot be a writer, so thank you for picking up my books.

Very best wishes to you all,

Eleanor

HEARTWARMING

A Place Called Home

—

Eleanor Jones

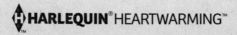

Recycling programs
for this product may
not exist in your area.

ISBN-13: 978-0-373-36712-2

A Place Called Home

Printed in U.S.A.

Eleanor Jones was brought up on a farm in the north of England and learned to love animals and the countryside from an early age. She has ridden all her life, and after marrying her husband at just eighteen years old and having two wonderful children, they set up a riding centre together. This is still thriving over thirty years later, doing hacks, treks and lessons for all ages and experiences. Her daughter competes at the national level, and she is now a partner in the business and brings her adorable three-year-old son to work with her every day. Eleanor's son is also married with two children, and they live nearby. Eleanor has been writing for what feels like her whole life. Her early handwritten novels still grace a dusty shelf in the back of a cupboard somewhere, but she was first published over fifteen years ago, when she wrote teenage pony mysteries.

Books by Eleanor Jones

HARLEQUIN HEARTWARMING

The Country Vet
Footprints in the Sand

HARLEQUIN EVERLASTING LOVE

A Heartbeat Away

Visit the Author Profile page
at Harlequin.com for more titles

I would like to dedicate this book to my husband, Peter, who has to put up with my head being in the clouds most of the time.

Acknowledgments

It has been over five years since I started writing for Harlequin, and I will be eternally grateful to Paula Eykelhof, both for spotting my first manuscript and for believing in me ever since. I must also thank my Heartwarming editor, Claire Caldwell, for all her help and for the wonderful job she, too, does in helping make my stories better.

CHAPTER ONE

ELLIE CLUNG TO her seat, fingers wrapped fiercely around soft cream leather as the hedgerow spun by her window in a blur of mottled greens. For a moment the fuzzy images brought her paintings sharply to mind... until the fast-moving vehicle hit a sharp bend in the road. Then all she could think of was survival.

She tightened her grip, fear rising as she watched Matt fighting for control. His jaw was set, his profile firmly etched, displaying his annoyance at having had to leave work midafternoon to come and pick her up. But if they were going to get back home in one piece, then she had to say something, no matter how angry he was.

"Come on, Matt... I'm sorry that my car broke down, but if you keep driving like a madman, you'll put us both into the hedge. If I'd known you were going to be like this,

I'd have gotten a ride into the village with the tow truck, then caught a bus or something."

"Don't be ridiculous. I could hardly leave you stranded in the middle of nowhere. You just don't understand…" Matt increased his speed as the road leveled out. "I'm putting together an important deal and I need to get back to the office."

"When *aren't* you putting together a deal?" groaned Ellie. "But if you keep up this speed, you're not going to be there to finalize it anyway—you're going to be in the hospital.

"I can handle this car with my eyes shut," Matt insisted, his voice softening as he mentioned his beloved BMW. "And what were you doing in this miserable place?"

"I told you yesterday I was going on a painting excursion today. There's a chance I might be able to show some of my pieces at an exhibition in a couple months, and I need more material."

Matt swung the wheel hard right, a sparkle of elation in his eyes as the powerful car responded.

"About that…" he began, concentrating all his attention on the road.

"What about it?"

The vehicle straightened out and he glanced across at her, a hint of amusement in the curve of his lips. "Your new paintings…"

Ellie frowned. Matt rarely took any notice of her work.

"No offense, Ellie, but are you really sure you're going the right way with it? All those faded blurry bits make the pictures look kind of strange. Why can't you just paint nice scenes with proper animals, if that's what you want to concentrate on?"

Respecting the fact that Matt had gone out of his way to pick her up, Ellie had been trying to stay reasonably calm. His derogatory comment about her work, however, made her blood boil. Plus, he knew nothing about art.

"I don't tell you how to do your deals," she retaliated. "So why don't you just keep your opinions on my painting to yourself. For your information, I'm taking a contemporary slant on animals and the countryside, and if you had any interest at all you would have noticed that I've been changing my style for a while."

Matt turned his attention back to the road, negotiating another tight curve in the narrow lane. The car swerved sideways, tires screaming and Ellie tightened her grip on the seat, wishing she was anywhere but here.

"Slow down, Matt!" she yelled.

"And maybe you should keep *your* opinions on my driving to yourself," Matt responded. "I'm perfectly in control."

"Until we hit a tree or a tractor or something. Are you trying to kill us both?"

As they cleared the corner, Ellie took a breath, leaning back. She and Matt may have been engaged for only a few months, but these days it felt more like a lifetime. They seemed to be pulling in different directions, arguing about anything and everything. Determinedly shrugging off her irritation, she tried again.

"Look, Matt…I know it's a pain for you having to come out here, and I do appreciate it…"

He cut her off midsentence. "No, Ellie, you have no clue how much of a pain it is for me to drop everything in the middle of a big deal. But I'm not so selfish that I'd leave you stranded. In fact…" He glanced across at her, his gray eyes cold as ice. "Sometimes I think you don't actually have much of a clue about anything to do with me."

"What!" Ellie froze. "*I* don't have much of a clue about *you*? You've got that the wrong way around. If you understood anything at all about me, you'd know that my *stupid* paintings are actually beginning to do quite well. In fact, Mel says…"

"And that's another thing," he blurted, pushing his foot down on the gas again. "I'm sick of you going on about this Mel bloke. I'm your fiancé, remember."

"How could I forget that? Clearly, though, you've forgotten that Mel is the owner of the gallery that might be exhibiting some of my paintings, and she just happens to be a woman."

For a fleeting instant, she detected a flicker of amusement in his face as her information sank in. He glanced across at her, his expression softening, but before she could respond, a bright flash of russet against the vivid green of the grass shoulder up ahead caught her attention.

"Watch out!"

His automatic reaction was to stand hard on the brakes. As if in slow motion, the car skidded out of control, sliding helplessly toward the terrified creature that was running in terror alongside the gray stone wall, desperate to escape the oncoming vehicle. To Ellie, it was as if time was temporarily suspended. The inevitable thud made her stomach turn, and suddenly she found her voice, screaming at him to stop, her door already half open. As the car came to a standstill, she leaped out, running back to where the animal now lay motionless in the dirt.

"Matt," she cried. "It's a fox cub, and it's hurt."

Dropping onto her knees, Ellie peered at the little creature. It looked so young, so vulnerable. She reached out to find a pulse, her heart lightening as she felt a fluttering against her fingers.

The black BMW reversed until it was next to her, and Matt'sface appeared in the window.

"Push it into the hedge and get in the car," he ordered. "It's just a fox. Vermin. It's obviously going to die, anyway."

For Ellie, it suddenly seemed so important to try and save the innocent creature.

"Just go, Matt," she told him. "Finish your deal. We knocked the poor little thing down, and the least I can do is to try to save its life."

Matt rolled his eyes. "Get in the car, Ellie, and don't be so soft. People hunt foxes, you know—we've probably done the local farmers a favor."

"No." She looked at him fiercely. "I mean it. Just go. I'll get a taxi or something."

For a moment, he stared back at her, then he shrugged, raising his eyebrows in mock despair. "All right, if that's what you want."

As she watched the big black car roar off up the lane, Ellie felt as if Matt was driving right out of her life...and she really didn't care. When she'd first met him, while she was working in a bar to fund her painting career, he had seemed so different; mature and fun and very far away from the place she was trying to forget...and the heartbreak it represented. But as she sat at the side of the deserted lane, feeling more alone than she had since she first came to the city, a heavy longing for that place and all it stood for came creeping out, saturating her in painful memories.

Containing a sob, Ellie turned her attention to the motionless fox cub. Its heart still beat softly as it clung on to life. She couldn't let it die. She had to find a vet...but where was she? She glanced around, spotting a road sign. Tarnside. Her fingers shook as she scrolled through her cell phone, searching for vets in the area and tapping out the number of the first one she saw.

The receptionist's voice was clear and calm. "Hello, Tarnside Veterinary Center. How can I help you?"

Ellie mumbled her message. "I need a vet at once. I've found an injured fox in the side of the lane, near the sign for Tarnside, and it needs help urgently."

"Well you're not too far from Cravendale, the wild animal sanctuary. They should be able to help you. Perhaps you could get it into your car and…"

"I don't have a car…that's the whole point."

The receptionist hesitated. "Well, I suppose I could call them for you."

"I'll give you my number in case they can't find me," Ellie suggested, relief washing over her. "And please, tell them to hurry."

CROUCHING IN THE DIRT on the side of a road in the middle of nowhere, stroking the rough fur of a wild creature while waiting for help she could only hope would come, all felt vaguely surreal. The atmosphere reminded Ellie of everything she used to love as a child—clear, fresh air, animals and country aromas. These were the things she had tried to put out of her mind when she'd left home at nineteen for a new life in the city.

She had always been passionate about drawing and painting, so when she was offered a place at an art college in Manchester, it had seemed like the perfect opportunity to do something she loved and escape the heartache that had overtaken her life. In Manchester, she had carved out a completely different scene with new friends and new goals. And it had suited her for a while, given her a chance to distance herself from the pain that had turned her life upside down in a matter of months. In fact, if she was honest with herself, Matt had been a kind of escape, too. Suddenly, though, she was beginning to feel as if her plan was backfiring.

She stood, pacing impatiently, the memories she had unwittingly unleashed swirling around inside her head and bringing guilt and regret. Maybe she should have stayed at home for her dad—not that he wanted her there. He had totally shut her out after her mum's funeral, as if just looking at her was too painful for him.

The rumble of an engine brought Ellie's thoughts swiftly back to the present, and she raised a hand to shade her eyes from the afternoon sun, peering down the lane. A green 4X4 appeared—a utility vehicle, muddy and battered, totally functional. It stopped right beside her and a tall young man jumped out of the driver's seat. He had floppy blond hair, a wide-open smile and eyes she could die in. A sharp pang tore through Ellie's heart. No, it couldn't be… She turned away before he could recognize her, dropping back onto her knees beside the cub, trying to control her shaking hands.

"Andy Montgomery, at your service," he announced, immediately focusing on the injured fox. "Now let's see what we have here."

His voice still sounded so familiar after all this time; deeper, perhaps, but with that same bright, melodic lilt. Relieved to have a second to pull herself together, Ellie concentrated on breathing steadily as she watched him run his skilled fingers over the little animal's unresisting body.

"Right," he said eventually, jumping up.

"There's a nasty wound across its chest, but as far as I can tell, no broken bones. We'd better get it to the rescue centre as quick as we can."

Ellie hesitated, building herself up to the inevitable. It must have been almost six years since she'd last seen Andy... Six years since he'd broken her heart. The heavy anger she'd clung to back then kicked in, and she stood up slowly, running her hand through her cap of blond curls. Her hair had hung in a long blond mane down her back when she was dating Andy, she remembered, but that had been a part of the old Ellie Nelson.

"Of all the vets in the world, Andy Montgomery?" She steeled her gaze as she met the eyes of the person she had once loved so much. "What a coincidence. I'm glad you finally qualified—I wondered if you would."

She had the momentary satisfaction of seeing his tall frame freeze. His face paled with shock.

"Ellie?" he breathed, as if unable to believe his eyes.

"That's me," she responded, trying to ignore the wild hammering under her rib cage.

It must be just the shock of running into him so unexpectedly.

"You wouldn't have been my first choice," she told him, her voice forcedly calm and casual. "But you're here now, so I guess I'm just going to have to put up with you. Come on, let's see to this poor little fox."

Andy shifted quickly back into professional mode, carefully lifting the limp form off the road.

"If you could open the back door for me, please…"

Ellie rushed to do his bidding, watching as he placed the cub in a mesh cage.

"It may look vulnerable," he told her. "But we can't forget that it's a wild creature. If it wakes up, it could panic."

They traveled in silence, Ellie desperately trying to nurture the anger that had kept her going when her whole world had turned upside down. Andy just stared at the road ahead.

It had been years since that awful day when he'd told her he'd met someone else, Ellie reminded herself. So why did it suddenly feel like yesterday?

"So…how have you been?" Andy's voice cut through the stifling atmosphere.

"Fine."

"I was so sorry to hear about your mother…"

She wanted to shout at him, to tell him that if he'd been there to support her through the black days after her mum was diagnosed with terminal cancer, perhaps it would have been easier to bear. Instead, she just stared at her hands, trying to control the rush of emotion that still tore her apart every time she thought about her mother.

The silence fell again, awkward and unbreachable.

"Ah, this is it," Andy said with obvious relief as the sign for Cravendale Animal Sanctuary appeared. "I'm only a volunteer here, so it's lucky I was around when we got the call. We don't have a resident vet. Now let's get the poor thing in as quick as we can."

Ellie hung back as he gently lifted the fox cub's cage and headed for the side door of a low stone building. What to do now? She'd just have to call a taxi.

"Come on, then," Andy said, looking back at her. "Do you want to see this through or not?"

"Oh…yes, please," she mumbled, hurrying to catch up.

THE MAKESHIFT CLINIC was utilitarian, but it had an ad hoc feel, with well-used equipment and mismatched decor.

Noting Ellie's scrutiny of the place, Andy shrugged. "Most of the fixtures and fittings are from the clinic where I work. You'll know it, of course—Low Fell in Little Dale."

"What?" Ellie looked at him in surprise. "You mean you're back home again? But your family moved away."

"They may have moved on, but Little Dale will always be home to me…although I seem to spend almost as much time here these days. Anyway, when they renovated a few months ago, they let me pick what I wanted. Some of the equipment's a bit dated, but the donation was a lifeline for the center. Now, let's get this little guy onto the table and see what we can do for him."

Ellie was mesmerized by the way Andy dealt with the injured cub. After giving it a couple of shots, he set about cleaning and suturing the gaping wound.

"You know, some vets would have just put it to sleep," he remarked, finishing off the dressing with a satisfied smile.

"Well, then, it's lucky I picked you." Ellie smiled, but instantly regretted her own words.

He shot her an amused glance. "Thanks for that. Now I'll just give him a long-lasting antibiotic shot, and we'll get him into a cage before he decides to come to. Would you pass me that dog carrier behind you?"

He placed the fox gently back into the cage, fastening the latch.

"I think you might get a shock when our little guy recovers consciousness. He may seem cute, but I think we'll find he can be pretty vicious when he gets all his faculties back. He'll be scared, too, and that can make animals lash out."

"Have you always done work with wild creatures?" Ellie asked, intrigued by Andy's obvious expertise.

He shook his head. "Not really, although at Low Fell we do get the occasional case brought in. It wasn't until I came across this place that I really started working with them. To be honest, it's become a bit of a passion of mine. Paula, the woman who runs Cravendale, has such high hopes for it. She works so hard to get funding."

Ellie nodded. "So it's a charity?"

"Paula started it up by herself, using her own money, but she managed to get charity status a couple of years ago, which means she can run fund-raisers and all other activities to get enough money to keep it going. People even pay to adopt pets."

"What, you mean take a wild animal home?"

"No, they just pay a small fee to board and feed an animal, and she sends pictures and letters about how it's doing. Some people come to visit, too. It can be anything from a hedgehog to a badger or even a snake. When, or if, it recovers and gets released, the money stops, but Paula usually has another animal available for them to take an interest in."

"She sounds like quite a businesswoman, this Paula of yours," Ellie said, wondering about the woman's relationship with Andy.

Andy smiled, carefully picking up the cage. "Not really, she just does what she has to do for the animals. She should be here soon, so you'll probably get to meet her. We'll just get this guy settled."

"Will he stay here for long?" Ellie asked, uncomfortably aware how close she was to her ex as she followed him along a narrow corridor.

"Probably not," he said. "We'll let him recuperate for a while, and when he's better, someone will take him back to where you found him and set him free."

When they reached a long, narrow indoor enclosure obviously converted from an old farm building, Ellie peered into the cage, surprised to see the little fox already groggily trying to stand, its sharp white fangs bared back from pale pink gums.

"He's on his feet," she cried, holding back a sudden rush of tears as relief flooded in. "He really is going to be okay, isn't he?"

Andy nodded, putting the cage down in the center of a large pen and opening the door. "Hopefully he'll be good as new in no time."

They watched the terrified fox cub take its first cautious steps out into the open. It turned to stare at them, yellow eyes gleaming with fright and ferocity.

"It's hard to tell if he's angry or scared stiff," whispered Ellie.

"There's not much difference between fear and ferocity in the animal kingdom," Andy said. "Ferocity is often born through fear. We'd better leave him alone to settle down."

Carried away as she'd been by the fox

cub's plight, it wasn't until they were back outside in the afternoon sunshine that Ellie took full stock of her situation. She was in the middle of nowhere with the ex-boyfriend she professed to hate, with no means of getting home.

"Well," she said, her tone curt and distant. "I suppose I need to thank you for your help. Do I owe you anything?"

Andy raised his hands. "Of course not. It's a wild creature, and it was my duty to help. It's what we do here."

Warmth flowed through Ellie's veins. "My fiancé told me it was vermin and that I should leave it to die."

Andy sighed. "There are farmers around here who would have said exactly the same thing."

"Especially chicken farmers," Ellie said, smiling.

"So did he leave you behind?"

She found herself jumping straight to Matt's defense. "He had to get back to work."

"But he is coming back for you, right?"

"I'll probably just get a taxi, at least to the train station. He'll be tied up until late."

"I can drop you off somewhere, if you

like," Andy offered. "Where do you live now, anyway?"

Every fiber of Ellie's being recoiled from spending time with Andy. They were over a long time ago, totally finished, and being near him brought out too many painful memories.

"The outskirts of Manchester," she told him. "But you don't need to drive me. If you could just give me the number for a cab…"

He looked down at her, a familiar twinkle in his soft brown eyes.

"You're a city girl now? Well, I would never have imagined that. And with a fiancé who works in an office."

"I went to art school in Manchester." She bristled. "And now I'm an artist… Well, a wannabe artist, really. I have a part-time job, as well. My first exhibition is coming up soon, though. At least, I hope so."

"You always did used to be painting or drawing something—usually animals, I remember. I'm glad you've made a success of it. What do you paint now?"

"Still mainly animals and the countryside, but lately I've been trying out a more contemporary style."

"That settles it," Andy said, walking toward the door. "You *are* still a country girl at heart. Come on, you may as well get a ride with me." He paused. "You can't bear grudges forever, Ell…and it *was* a long time ago."

Ellie ignored his familiar shortening of her name. "I don't bear a grudge," she insisted. "What happened between us was only a teenage fling, anyway wasn't it?"

Andy nodded. "I guess it was," he said. For the briefest moment, her eyes met his and glanced away. How could he believe that? He may have met someone else and revealed himself as the liar and cheat he really was, but how could either of them be so dismissive of what they once had? Her anger came back full force. Andy Montgomery owed her big-time.

"Okay," she agreed. "I will take you up on your offer of a ride. Sure your wife won't be jealous, though?"

"Young, free and single, that's me," he told her, fumbling in his pocket for his keys.

"So she dumped you, then. After all that?" She couldn't help the barbed retort.

He laughed lightly. "Actually, no, I dumped

her. To be honest, that relationship didn't mean much..."

The breath froze in Ellie's throat and was replaced almost instantly by a hot rush of anger. She had almost come to terms with the fact that Andy had fallen in love with someone else, but to find out that the whole thing had meant so little to him seemed somehow worse.

Oblivious to her reaction, he shot her a broad smile. "I *was* married, though...for a while."

She raised her eyebrows, smothering her turbulent emotions. What did she care? Andy Montgomery was just a piece of her past. "And I take it that didn't work out, either?"

"I guess I'm not the marrying kind. When is *your* wedding, anyway? Have you set a date?"

Ellie hesitated, her heart racing. Had they set a date? Had they ever even discussed a wedding? Her mind slid back to the night Matt had proposed. They had been seeing each other for just a few weeks; he was exciting and fun and so sure of himself. "Let's get engaged," he had cried in front of all his friends, and Ellie had felt a new door opening in her life. A door, she suddenly realized, that hadn't actually opened after all. Come to think of it, neither of them *had* discussed marriage again after that, apart from the ring. She felt for the diamond on the third finger of her left hand, rubbing it gently. Was that what it had all been about then? The engagement? Did Matt really want to take their relationship to the next level? Did she? Slotting her confusing thoughts into the back of her mind, she looked up at Andy. What right had he to make her question her intentions?

"No," she said. "Not yet."

He stopped beside his battered green truck, holding her gaze for an endless moment.

"Make sure he's the right one, Ell," he said quietly.

Anger brought a flush to Ellie's face. "And what gives you the right to offer me advice?"

He shrugged. "Just saying."

"Don't bother. You already messed my life up enough without trying to interfere in it now."

He flashed her another one of his everready smiles. "So you're still angry with me? It's been what—five, six years? Well, I suppose any emotion is better than none."

"Don't kid yourself, Andy." She yanked open the passenger door, not wanting him to see how much he'd rattled her. "I was well over you years ago. You just make me remember home, that's all."

Before Ellie had a chance to climb into the truck, a small blue car drove up next to them.

"Paula's back," Andy said. "Come on, you'll have to say hello at least."

Slamming the door shut again, Ellie followed reluctantly.

Paula Carr was one of the most dazzling women Ellie had ever met. She wasn't classically beautiful, but she radiated an inner warmth.

Paula hurried toward them, and when Andy reached down to give her a peck on the cheek, she smiled, squeezing his forearm. Her fair, shoulder-length hair shone in the sun, and her eyes were glowing. *She's in love with him*, Ellie realized suddenly. She pushed away the knot in her stomach. What did she care? Andy Montgomery meant nothing to her anymore, and she felt sorry for any woman who came his way. It was obvious that he never stayed with anyone for too long, not even the woman he married.

"Paula, meet Ellie," said Andy, placing a firm hand on her shoulder. Ellie sidestepped, uncomfortable with his touch.

"She found the fox I called to tell you about, on the side of the road."

"I've got to confess," Ellie said, "I didn't exactly find it. My fiancé's car clipped it. I feel terrible."

Paula smiled, all-forgiving. "These things happen. At least you bothered to call for a vet—it sounds like you saved its life. Come on, then, show me the poor little thing."

On the way back to the enclosure, Paula and Andy fell into a conversation about some creature or another, totally on the same wavelength. *Totally suited for each other*, Ellie thought. Unlike her and Matt? The idea niggled uncomfortably.

The cub was curled up in a dark corner, as settled as it could be in its new environment.

"We'll have to keep an eye on it now," said Paula, confirming what Andy had said earlier. "And perhaps before too long it can be released. Thanks again, Ellie, for saving it."

Ellie squirmed. "Well, it was kind of my fault...our fault...so it was the least I could do."

Paula shook her head. "Accidents happen

to everyone. There's no use in laying blame. It's how you deal with the aftermath that really matters."

"Right, then," Andy interrupted. "I'm off to give Ellie a ride somewhere. I'll be back in the morning, Paula, and in the meantime, call if you need me."

"You're a godsend, Andy." Paula smiled. "I'll go and get some food for the new arrival." She stood in the doorway as they walked away.

"Aren't you going to say goodbye to her?" Ellie asked, nudging Andy's arm.

He frowned, raising one hand in farewell without looking back. "I'm in and out of here all the time, and Paula doesn't need all the niceties. I'll check on your fox in the morning, so if you give me your number I can let you know how it's doing."

Ellie paused. This would open contact between her and Andy again…contact she'd relinquished long ago.

Andy pulled his cell phone from the pocket of his jeans.

"No…" she heard herself saying. "It's okay. I don't need to bother you. The number for

Cravendale is there on the sign. I can phone and ask Paula how it's doing."

Was that disappointment she could see in his face?

"Suit yourself," he said, his voice distant. The voice of a stranger, thought Ellie, when he had once been her whole world. How could that happen?

CHAPTER TWO

ANDY DROVE ON AUTOMATIC, hunched forward over the wheel, staring straight ahead. He'd always had that habit of slipping totally into his own thoughts while he was driving, Ellie recalled, thinking of all the other times she'd sat beside him like this. That seemed like a lifetime ago, and yet it still felt so familiar.

It was true that he reminded her of home, and as they drove along narrow country lanes the memories she had kept locked away seeped from their confines, real and raw. The landscape around her didn't have the same rugged beauty as her native Lake District, which was over fifty miles away, but the colors, sounds and smells were the same. Suddenly, she was consumed by a longing for the place she used to call home. Hope Farm in the Lakeland hills, near the village of Little Dale. It had been weeks since she'd spoken to her dad; she would call him tonight, she

decided, just to make sure he was okay—
even if he only answered in monosyllables.

"So where should I drop you?" Andy
asked. "Hey, there...not asleep, are you?"

Ellie jerked herself out of her reverie. "No,
of course not. Sorry, I was just thinking."

"Nice thoughts, I hope."

"Yes..." A half smile flitted across her
face. "I guess they were."

He raised his eyebrows. "So am I in them?"

She stiffened. "Oh, please. You left my
thoughts a long time ago."

"Are you sure about that?"

"Dead sure. You let me down when I
needed you most, Andy, so don't expect me
to be all sweetness and light just because you
reappeared in my life after six years to save
the fox."

Andy turned his attention abruptly back to
the road ahead, brow furrowed and fingers
gripping the wheel. They drove in silence
for a while, the air between them heavy and
awkward.

"You can drop me at a bus stop if you
like," Ellie said eventually.

He flashed her a wry grin.

"You might think I'm a total waste of
space, but I do owe you, in a way."

"You owe me nothing," she said quietly, though she was secretly relieved at not being abandoned.

"Oh, yes I do," he insisted, smiling his painfully familiar, lopsided smile.

Back when they were together, that smile would have been quickly followed by a kiss. She shuddered, imagining the feel of his lips on hers.

"I owe you for helping the fox," he said. "And for breaking your heart, of course."

Ellie stared out the window, seeing nothing, anger bubbling inside her as the memories seeped away. How dare he make light of the event that had colored her teenage years…and her whole adult life? At the time, it had felt as if his breaking up with her and the shock discovery that her mother hadn't long to live were painfully intertwined, as if it was all his fault. Now she knew better, but the pain still remained.

"Don't give yourself so much credit, Andy Montgomery," she snapped. "How could you even think that you broke my heart? We were just two kids having fun. It would never have gone anywhere."

"Wouldn't it?"

"Obviously not, or we wouldn't be here now, would we?"

He stared at the road, his expression serious for once.

"I've always regretted it, you know. We just met too soon, and…"

"And you got bored," she finished for him. "Just like you got bored with your wife and probably all the other girlfriends you've had along the way."

"No, I—"

"Look, Andy," Ellie said, cutting off his attempt at an apology—or was it an excuse? "Just leave the past in the past. There have been a lot of worse things in my life than getting dumped by my teenage crush."

He glanced across at her. "I know. And I'm sorry about your mum… I really regret not being there for you."

The memories Ellie never allowed herself to face suddenly broke free; all the emotion of those terrible days when she watched helplessly as her mother lost her fight with death swirled around inside her, dark and suffocating.

"It was so quick," she cried, struggling to hold back tears. "She'd had that pain in her back for ages. I told her and told her to see a doctor, and when she did… When she did, it was already too late."

"It must have been a terrible time…for all of you."

Andy's voice was warm and caring, reminding her just how much she'd needed him during her mother's decline. Reminding her of how lost she'd felt without him. Suddenly, his presence felt stifling.

"Here," she cried. "Stop here, Andy. This is fine."

"But…" he objected, touching the brakes.

"It's fine," she repeated, fumbling for her bags. She was already scrambling out of the vehicle as he pulled up to the curb.

Andy reached out to take her arm, but she wriggled from his grasp. "Thanks for the ride, and for helping the fox," she mumbled, already walking away. "I'll see you."

When she heard his door slam, Ellie couldn't help but look back. He was standing on the pavement, long fingers pushed through his thick blond hair, tall and lanky and totally out of place in the suburbs of the city, watching in bewilderment as she raced off down the street. His voice followed after her like an echo from the past.

"Ellie...Ellie..."

For a heart-stopping moment, she wanted to turn and run back, to share all her agony with him. But it was way too late for that. Andy Montgomery was out for just one person—himself. She knew that all too well.

Ellie ran for what felt like miles, as if she could run away from all the things Andy had made her remember. Her phone rang just as she saw a familiar landmark, and she stopped, breathing heavily. Was it him? No, it couldn't be, she realized with relief. She hadn't given him her number.

Matt's name flashed on the screen.

Ellie took another deep breath and answered. "Yes?"

"You okay?"

"No thanks to you."

"Do you want me to come get you?"

"I take it your deal worked out?"

Matt paused. "Kind of. Do you want me to pick you up or not?"

"No, thanks. I'm nearly home."

"Then I'll come by at seven-thirty and take you out to dinner."

There was no point in trying to put him

off, and Ellie was too tired to resist, anyway. "See you then."

"Oh, and Ellie?"

"Yes?"

"I'm sorry for abandoning you."

Flicking off her phone, she stepped back into the present, determinedly trying to shake off the events of the afternoon.

Her phone rang again, buzzing against her hip as she was finally climbing the stairs to her apartment. With a sigh, she retrieved it from her jacket pocket, wishing she had passed on Matt's dinner offer.

"Hello?" she responded, tucking the phone in between her shoulder and her chin as she fumbled to unlock the door.

It was Matt again, his voice high-pitched and urgent. As always, he was living life in a rush. "You home yet?"

Her heart lifted. "Don't tell me. You've changed your mind."

He laughed. "No, nothing like that. I just wanted to make sure you knew what time I was picking you up."

"Seven-thirty, right?"

"Yes, and wear something nice."

"Don't I always," she retorted.

As ELLIE BURROWED through her closet for
an outfit, she realized she hadn't called her
dad, as she'd told herself she would. She was
going to Hope Farm next weekend, she decided, no matter what he said. Seeing Andy
again had brought the past sharply back into
focus. For the first time since leaving home,
she felt as if she was finally ready to face
those memories and maybe even make peace
with all that had happened. She didn't dare
give herself enough time to change her mind.

"Sorry, Mum," she whispered, holding
back tears. She had let down her mum's memory. Badly. She should have stayed home and
supported her dad, she understood that now,
or at least kept in better touch with him…
whether he wanted her to or not.

Ellie took a short black skirt and lacy top
from their hangers and let her mind slip
back to the difficult days after her mother's
funeral. She had been just a teenager back
then; her dad was the adult. Now, though,
she was an adult. She'd made her own way
in the world for almost six years, ever since
she said goodbye to her grieving father and
drove away from Hope Farm. Maybe that
was the day she'd grown up—or perhaps that

had happened when she'd held her mother's hand as her life slipped away. The hustle and bustle of a totally new life had seemed to help her through her own grief, but now she wasn't so sure. Maybe this life she'd made for herself wasn't really a new beginning… Maybe it was a hiding place.

Ellie stepped into the shower, and as the water ran soothingly over her aching limbs, she let out a sigh. The safe little world she had set up for herself felt as if it was crumbling around her.

CHAPTER THREE

THE RESTAURANT MATT had chosen was suave and sophisticated.

"I wish you'd told me we were coming here—I would have worn something classier," Ellie groaned as they pulled up outside. She checked her reflection, fluffing up her short blond curls.

"You look fine," he insisted. "And you'll be far more likely to charm my client dressed like that."

"You're not seriously telling me this is a business dinner, Matt. I thought you were trying to make amends for abandoning me this afternoon."

"I am, kind of. I'm killing two birds with one stone, so to speak."

Her irritation suddenly faded, and was replaced with amusement. Was that why she was with Matt? she wondered. Because she didn't need to take him too seriously? It occurred to her that their whole engagement might be a sham. If they were both honest, neither of them actually wanted to get married…or even move in together. The thought left her feeling vaguely uncomfortable, and when Andy's warm grin flashed into her mind, she quickly stifled the emotions it conjured, turning her attention back to the present.

"Ever the opportunist, eh, Matt?" She laughed, trying to sound lighthearted.

"Have to be." He grinned, holding out his arm.

As she curled her fingers around the expensive material of his suit jacket, she lifted her chin, silently cursing Andy Montgomery for coming back into her life; hopefully their paths wouldn't cross again for a while…or ever. He conjured up way too many painful memories. Life with Matt was lighthearted, and she liked lighthearted right now.

DETERMINED TO ENJOY the evening, Ellie tried her best to make conversation with Matt's middle-aged client, Jack Noble. She was a bit self-conscious about the length of her skirt, but she didn't let on. She had been to so many of these dinners since she met Matt that sometimes she wondered if he was only with her to have a trophy on his arm, someone to flirt with his clients in order to weaken their resolve. Until recently it had just felt like a bit of fun; she'd been in control and that had made her feel good. Tonight, though, despite her outward show of joviality, she couldn't seem to find the right mood. It all seemed so shallow. Smiling at yet another of Jack's unfunny jokes, she was overcome with the feeling that her whole life was a sham, too. The only real, true thing in her life was her painting. She'd convinced herself that her relationship with Matt was fun and lighthearted, but suddenly it just felt false. A heavy ache began to throb in her temple.

"Look…" She put her hand to her head. "I'm really sorry, but I don't feel so well. I think I may have to go home."

She caught a glint of anger in Matt's gray eyes and grimaced.

"My head is killing me."

The client was more understanding.

"Perhaps you should take her home," he said to Matt. "We can do this some other time."

"No, honestly, I just need some fresh air,"

Ellie objected. "You two carry on. I'll call a cab."

"Why don't you try going outside for a bit, then, before you rush off," Matt suggested, eager to salvage what he could of the meeting.

Ellie was already on her feet. "It's just a headache, but I do think I'd better head home." She held out her hand to Jack, who seized it with plump fingers, pumping it up and down. "Nice to meet you," she said, smiling. "And I really am sorry about this."

"I'll call you later," Matt cut in, making his opinion clear.

The fresh evening air hit her as soon as she left the restaurant and she felt the pain in her head already beginning to recede. Rejecting her plan to call a taxi, she decided to walk the mile or so back to her apartment. By the time she got home, she would probably feel absolutely fine.

Setting off, she listened to the staccato sound of her heels on the pavement. She had become used to living in the city, with its constant buzz and bright lights, but tonight it felt oppressive. She found herself hankering once again for the quiet peace of the countryside. It was all Andy Montgomery's fault. He'd brought back memories and emotions she didn't want to feel, but now that he had, she couldn't ignore them. Reaching into her pocket for her cell phone, she dialed her dad's number, not really expecting an answer. When his deep voice with its strong Northern accent filled her ears, she was suddenly struck dumb.

"Who is this?"

As usual, he sounded irritable and less than pleased to be disturbed. Remembering how he used to be when her mum was alive, Ellie found her voice.

"Dad?"

"Ellie? Is that you?"

Was she just imagining the lift in his tone?

"Yes, it's me, your one and only daughter. How are you, Dad?""

He was quiet for a moment. "Business is good—new stallion's popular."

"But how are *you*?"

"I get by."

"Dad, I thought I might come see you next weekend, stay a night or two."

His response was immediate. "You don't need to."

"I want to," she said, meaning it. "So…
what's the new stallion's name?"

His voice brightened. Her dad never had
trouble talking about the horses. "We call
him Dennis, stud name Grand Design. He's
giving Blue a run for his money."

Ellie smiled, recalling how proud her parents had been of their first homebred sire,
Into the Blue. His first crop of foals had been
born the year before her mother was diagnosed, when everything in their world was
still rosy. Grief and homesickness split her
in two, and her need to see her dad and all
the animals grew stronger.

"I'll see you next weekend, Dad."

"Suit yourself. I don't need help, mind. I've
got by on my own for the last six years, so
what's different now?"

Ellie hesitated, pondering the question.
"Maybe *I'm* different, Dad…and perhaps
you are, too."

"I've got to go. Jake Munro's here to see
me."

Ellie wasn't surprised when the line went
dead. Nothing had changed there, then. Her
dad had never been good with emotion. It
hadn't mattered when she was small because

her mum had always had enough for both of them. But now it was just Ellie and her dad.

Taking in her surroundings, Ellie noticed how enclosed everything seemed. Cars and lights and tall, looming buildings. Images of a wide-open sky and rugged hills filled her mind. Her day out in the country and her run-in with Andy had triggered this trip down memory lane. She hadn't planned on it, but now she felt as if today had released some of her demons. The painful months before and immediately after her mother's death were difficult to face, but Hope Farm also held the memories of her childhood. For the first time in over five years, she wanted to go home.

To ELLIE'S SURPRISE, Matt wasn't too happy when she told him, the next morning, that she was going to see her dad. They were having coffee together in Costa, and Matt's reaction took her by surprise.

"But you can't go," he announced, a dull flush spreading up his neck.

Normally, they slid in and out of each other's lives, few questions asked. Her apartment was on the top floor of a run-down Victorian house in the outskirts of the city. She spent almost all of her spare time painting there, while Matt rented a smart penthouse suite downtown. They both loved their own personal space, and despite having been engaged for several months, they had never really discussed taking the next step in their relationship. It was only now that she realized perhaps they just didn't want to. It never occurred to her that he might object to her taking a trip.

"What do you mean, I can't?" she retaliated. "It's not until next weekend, and we don't have any plans. I really believe it's time I visited my dad. You can come with me, if you like."

He rolled his eyes, the flush receding. "You know I hate the country."

That put her on the defensive. "Well, I don't, and I've been irresponsible for far too long."

Matt took hold of her hand across the table, a pleading expression in his eyes. "I really need to close this deal, and I've arranged to meet Jack Noble again next Saturday night. A pretty face just might push him in the right direction."

"So basically," she responded, feeling a

prickle of irritation. "You don't want me there for me, you just want me to flirt with your client. And why can't you meet him sooner?"

"He's out of town until then. Why can't you go see your dad another time?"

Ellie drained her coffee cup and set it firmly on the table. "Because I've already told him I'm going on the weekend."

"It's not as if he's going to be bothered if you change your plans, though, is he? You haven't seen him in ages, and the last time you tried to visit he conveniently decided to go out. Surely that tells you something."

"Well, maybe this time I won't take no for an answer," Ellie said, pushing her mug away and standing up. "I'm sorry, Matt, but I really do want to go. I need to. I know this deal is important to you, but I'm not changing my plans just to be your arm candy. And besides, you've had a deal going down at least a couple of times a week ever since I met you. What's so special about this one?"

"Well…" He looked disconcerted. "Nothing, really, just another piece of property I bought from a bankruptcy sale. I've stretched myself a bit, though, so I need a quick turn-over."

Ellie sighed, pulling on her jacket. "Then why don't you try and find someone else to take it off your hands? I have to go. I'll call you later."

His deep voice followed her. "Don't bother, I'm going out tonight."

"Please yourself," she responded, to the amusement of the couple at the next table.

She hadn't expected to feel so unaffected by their disagreement. Perhaps their relationship had run its course. It was time, she realized, to stop and take stock, to catch up with the past she had spent so long trying to forget. And then she would decide where she was with Matt.

WHEN THE GARAGE called the next day to tell her that her car was ready to collect, Ellie didn't bother Matt, and took a bus to Tarnside instead. On the way home, she stopped in at Cravendale to check on the fox cub. Paula welcomed her, exclaiming over the little creature's recovery and promising to let Ellie know when she was about to let it go. "It's so rewarding," Paula said with a radiant smile. "When they run free again…you should come and watch."

Ellie pulled out her camera and took a few shots of the cub before she left, feeling a niggle of inspiration. Suddenly she knew what she wanted to paint next…her own interpretation of freedom.

For the next couple of days, she threw herself into her painting, embracing the focus she always had when she started a new project. It was only in the dead of night, when sleep proved elusive, that thoughts of Matt, Andy, her dad and the longing for times gone by came back to mess with her head.

AT THE END of her second day of painting, Ellie stood back to take in her work so far. Surprised to see that the light was fading she glanced at her watch. Could it really be eight already? She put down her brush and stretched out her arms, her body aching. The face of the rescued fox stared back at her, its yellow eyes filled with fear and ferocity. The rest of the painting faded out into a blur of color, drawing the observer's eye to what really mattered; the raw emotion of the piece, and the clear but distant glimpse of the freedom the wild creature craved. Smiling to herself, Ellie stood, contemplating her afternoon's work with a critical eye. She'd done enough, she decided. She didn't want to overwork it and she liked its slightly unfinished look.

With another quick glance at the painting she headed for the kitchen, her mind going back to the little fox and its plight. That morning, Paula had called to tell her that tomorrow was the day. She was so looking forward to watching its release. It would be like going full circle.

She hadn't heard from Matt, and she hadn't gotten in touch with him, either. Was she being selfish? Should she have changed her plans as he wanted her to? She flicked the switch on the kettle and waited for the water to boil. To be fair, Matt was right that her dad had called to dissuade her from coming the last time she tried to visit him. It felt right this time, though, and she didn't care what her dad said. Anyway, it didn't sound as if Matt's client was worth pursuing, so perhaps she'd done him a favor.

Picking up her phone, she dialed his number, listening to his deep tones on the voice mail. "Hi…just me," she said,

He called her back ten minutes later and they arranged to meet for a drink at the bar where they first met, Applejacks, but conversation was stilted, like two strangers on a first date.

He talked about his latest deal and she told him she'd started a new painting, but she sensed a shift in their relationship, a holding back that wasn't all her fault. And it couldn't just be because of their disagreement about her trip— Matt's client had dropped the deal. Fortunately, though, he already had someone else interested. Someone who hopefully didn't need any input from her.

At the end of the evening, she announced that she would get a cab back to her apartment, and he didn't protest. On the shiny, rain-washed pavement, he held her close in a hard, impersonal embrace, touching her lips briefly with his.

"Perhaps it's good that you're going home for a visit," he said. "I think we both need a break."

Ellie felt a surge of panic, her safe little

world rocking on its axis. "What…you mean split up?"

He shook his head. "Yes, I guess, but not forever, or at least not necessarily, but we both need to think about where this is going…because it feels to me as if we're going in different directions."

"I feel that, too," she admitted, knowing it was true.

THE NEXT MORNING dawned bright and clear. Ellie lay in her bed watching the sun rise above the tall houses across the street, experiencing a burst of longing for the wild hills of home. She recalled her brief conversation with Matt last night, but her sadness was fleeting. Was this the final blow to the safe haven she had secured for herself? It felt scary and strange, yet she knew he was right; they did seem to be pulling in different directions.

She turned her attention back to the present, pushing all thoughts of Matt out of her head. Today, she was going to watch the fox cub run free and she couldn't wait. Had she done its expression justice in her painting, or would she have to repaint the whole thing?

She should have waited to start on it until after she'd seen its release for herself, but inspiration didn't come to order. With one last satisfied glance at her handiwork, she reached for her car keys.

ELLIE FELT A song in her heart as she reached Cravendale, spotting Paula waiting impatiently in the yard. Paula urged her eagerly toward the fox's enclosure.

"I didn't want to start without you," she said excitedly as they entered the low stone building. "We're all ready to go, but we waited to catch the cub and put it into a travelling cage because we thought you'd like to see the whole thing."

We?

"That must be difficult to do."

Paula smiled. "Fortunately, we've got expert help."

"I thought you were the expert." The deep, familiar voice that came from the shadows made Ellie's pulse speed up. She stopped, her hand raised to the base of her throat.

"I didn't know you were going to be here." Her voice sounded strange in her ears, clipped and harsh, belying her breathlessness.

Andy laughed, stepping into view, his warm brown eyes full of merriment and holding hers with a quizzical expression. "Don't sound *too* pleased."

She blushed, glad of the semidarkness. "I am. I mean…I don't really care either way."

"Come on, then, Andy," Paula pressed him. "The poor little thing is terrified."

Andy deftly caught the fox, his hands firm but gentle as he lifted it into the small cage. Then they all loaded into Andy's 4X4 and set off.

Ellie sat in the back, listening to Andy and Paula chatter about the animals at Cravendale. His dark blond hair, as unruly as ever, shone in the morning sunshine. One broad, tanned hand was firm on the wheel and the other rested on the back of Paula's seat, right in front of Ellie. Resisting the temptation to reach out and place her hand over his, as she used to do so naturally, Ellie peered out the window.

"This is it," she cried, glad to be finally doing something positive that might take her mind away from the past and how things used to be. "This is where he got hit."

"I was there, remember?" Andy smiled, glancing back at her.

"I know this place," Paula said. "There's a den in the copse over there. We'll set him free under the cover of the trees."

THEY SET THE cage down under a bush and waited a while to let the cub absorb its surroundings. The three of them stood silently together, almost out of sight. Ellie listened to the rustling of the wind in the trees, entranced as Paula stepped forward quietly to unlatch the cage door. The little fox cowered, sniffing the air, yellow eyes fearful as he crept gingerly toward the opening. And then he made his dash for freedom and tears were flowing down Ellie's face. When Andy's arm crept around her shoulders, it felt so right.

"Amazing, isn't it," he murmured as the fox took one look back before disappearing into the undergrowth.

The spell was broken. Ellie stepped away from him, alarm bells ringing in her head. What was she thinking?

Paula glanced back at them, her lovely eyes alight with passion.

"Run free, little fox," she cried.

Andy held out his hand to her and when she took it, Ellie felt something wither deep inside.

"Right," Ellie said curtly. "That was really something, but unfortunately I have to get home pretty soon. Thanks so much for inviting me, though."

Dropping Andy's hand, Paula gave her a quick hug. "You were the one who rescued him."

"And I was the one whose fiancé knocked him down in the first place," Ellie said.

Paula shrugged. "As I already said, accidents happen. At least you did the right thing."

Ellie glanced at Andy, holding his gaze for a moment.

"We all do things we regret," he said quietly.

"Do we?" she asked. "So what are your regrets?"

He stepped forward, still holding her eyes in his. "I—" he began.

"Come on, then," urged Paula, heading for Andy's truck. "I thought you were in a rush, Ellie."

"I am," Ellie responded, turning to follow

her, vaguely disappointed that she hadn't gotten to hear Andy out. Then again, did she really want to know his regrets?

CHAPTER FOUR

ELLIE STARED CRITICALLY at her painting, comparing it to her experience of seeing the cub being set free. Had she caught the fox's expression, fear and ferocity firmly linked?

She felt Andy's arm around her again, connecting them in the emotional moment when the wild creature finally ran free. He'd followed her when she'd said her goodbyes, leaning in through her car window to ask for her number. "For old times' sake," he'd said with a smile.

"Our old times are long gone, Andy," she'd told him, clamping down a rush of emotion as all the painful memories kicked in again. Then she'd turned the key in the ignition and the engine roared into life, defusing the situation. "See you," she'd called, forcing a light-hearted tone and pulling away. She'd seen him in her mirror, shading his eyes to watch her drive off, then she rounded a corner and he was out of sight.

There was no doubt in her mind that what she'd told Andy was true. Their old times *were* long gone, and he was well in the past. So why, she asked herself, did she feel this unexpected longing for everything they used to have? Nostalgia, she supposed. Nothing more.

Ellie turned away from the painting, trying to shake her confusion. Today she was facing up to another part of her past by going to see her dad. That was was what she needed to focus on now, rekindling the father-daughter relationship that tragedy had torn apart.

Yet as she drove out of the city a few hours later, Ellie found her mind wandering back to Andy. Busy roads and concrete gave way to the gentle greens of wide-open countryside, and she couldn't stop the flood of memories. She and Andy had been together almost all of their teenage years, an inseparable couple, loving the same things, loving each other. Of course she had regret for what they'd lost. Perhaps she *should* have kept in touch with him, for old times' sake. But she couldn't let go of what he'd done to her, and he'd probably done the same to others since. No matter how well he came across, Andy Montgomery was shallow and selfish. What was in the past should stay in the past.

Hardening her heart, she turned her thoughts to her dad and the stud. Excitement at seeing home and all the horses and animals there washed over her. No matter how unsociable and unwelcoming her dad proved to be, she wouldn't let him get to her. It was time to build bridges, and nothing was going to stop her.

Another hour passed by, and familiar landmarks dotted the landscape—lakes sparkling in the midday sun, looming hills and clear, endless skies. When the road narrowed to a single, fenceless track and she had to stop for an amber-eyed, wild-looking Fell sheep, Ellie knew that she was home.

She drove through the quaint stone village of Little Dale, past Low Fell Veterinary Clinic and the busy market, then up the steep fell side again, dropping down to follow the road that meandered around the lake. Butterflies fluttered madly in her chest. What if her dad didn't want to see her? What if he turned her away? Three years ago, when she'd visited at Christmas, the atmosphere had been so uncomfortable that she hadn't stayed for very long, and she'd only been back twice since. Well, things were different now, she told herself. *She* was different. If her dad was unwelcoming, then she'd just ignore it. This was still her home, after all, and her dad had no other family to share it with.

Still, as Ellie turned down the lane that led to Hope Farm, she began to doubt her own confidence. The old sign had been repainted, but not replaced. Her mother had chosen that sign, and she was glad her father had seen fit to keep it. The rest of the place looked as if it had been tidied up, too, she noted with surprise as she pulled into the yard. She had expected it to be just as neglected as it had been the last time she came home.

Parking her car next to her dad's cream horsebox, she sat for a moment, suddenly overcome by memories. Her first pony, Midge, a brown-and-white Shetland, had been kept in the stable across from her. She couldn't even count the times he'd dumped her unceremoniously on the ground. "You're fine, Ellie," her mum had always told her, insisting that she get straight back on. Eventually, Midge had been retired and was replaced by a pretty gray Welsh mare called Starlight, but Ellie had always missed her old friend and visited him daily in the meadow he shared with her dad's retired hunter, Jock. They were both long gone now, though. As a teenager, Ellie had liked to think that they were with her mum in Heaven. Did she still believe that? she asked herself. Tears welled behind her eyelids, heavy and hot. She brushed them aside. The last thing she wanted was for her dad to find her sitting in the car crying. She had come home to try and bring some joy back into both their lives… some closure. Where was he, anyway?

Ellie climbed out of the car, taking her bag from the backseat, and headed for the house. A mud-splattered truck was parked in the middle of the yard. Her dad's, she presumed, so he must be home.

She stood outside the kitchen door. Should she knock, or just walk in? Deciding on the latter, she pushed open the door and peered inside. Her father was asleep in his favorite chair, slumped forward slightly, a magazine slowly slipping off his knee. He looked so small and old, she realized with a jolt, so vulnerable.

"Dad," she called quietly, unsure of whether or not to disturb him.

He stirred with a slight snorting sound, opening his eyes as the magazine fell to the ground. Ellie smiled to herself as she read the title. *Horse and Hound.* Of course it was.

"Ellie?" he gasped, pulling himself awkwardly upright and staring at her as if he could hardly believe his eyes.

"One and the same," she said. "It's good to see you, Dad."

"Better put the kettle on, then, lass," he suggested. Whatever he might say later, she knew he was pleased to have her home.

"I thought it was time I checked up on you," she told him as she made herself busy brewing a pot of tea. It was like going back in time a hundred years in her father's house. Perhaps she'd buy him an electric kettle before she left. Maybe even a toaster.

"Biscuits are in the barrel," he said as she handed him a steaming mug.

She picked it up from its prominent position on the counter and sat down at the table.

"Same one, I see."

"Not much changes around here," he grunted. "Except you, of course."

Ellie shrugged. "Circumstances changed us both, Dad, but I think it's time to finally move on."

He dunked a biscuit in his tea, considering her remark before looking up with a half smile. "So that's what you think, eh… Still painting those pictures of yours?"

She nodded eagerly. "I've been given a bit of space in an exhibition soon. It's not much, I know, but at least it's a start. And what about you, how's the new stallion you told me about, and Blue?"

"Doing good."

"Had some nice foals this year?"

His eyes, still as bright a blue as hers, lit up his weathered face.

"The best. And Jake Munro has put his top jumping mare, Carlotta, to Dennis. Their foal should really be something special. You'll have to come and see the horses when we've finished our tea."

They fell then into a surprisingly comfortable silence and Ellie felt warm inside. She'd been right. It was time to make peace with the past and move on. Her dad knew it, too; she was sure of it.

When her tea was done, Ellie jumped up. "Let's go check out this Dennis of yours. How's he bred, anyway?"

Bob Nelson followed more slowly, easing out of the chair and pulling on his jacket.

"Irish Thoroughbred," he said. "With a lineage as long as your arm."

WHEN THEY REACHED the stable, they saw Blue first. His head was over the half door, as if he'd been expecting them.

As her dad ran his hand down the elegant horse's face, the stallion nickered, lowering his head for his master's caress.

Ellie thought of the morning Blue was born. Her mum had been so excited.

"Wake up, Ellie," she'd called, bursting into her bedroom. "Come and see our new sire! He's going to be the making of Hope Farm."

"Some sire, that." Ellie had smiled as she and her parents watched the newborn foal wobble around in the straw on legs that seemed way too long for its body. Even then, though, in the very first hour of his life, Blue had had a proud, almost regal look to him; the look of eagles, her mother had called it. And he still had it now. Ellie reached up to stroke the big horse's silken coat, as well. He had been iron gray when she last saw him, and the years had turned him almost white now, but he still had that same pride and class he'd always had.

"He's done your mum proud," murmured her dad. "Done us all proud. One of his offspring is shortlisted for the British Horse Trials team, you know, and another two have been sold to America."

"So Dennis has a lot to live up to, I guess."

"Not really. He'd already proven himself competing in show jumping when I bought him. Cost me an arm and a leg. That's why Jake Munro was so keen to use him."

"Jake Munro," Ellie repeated. "Do I know him?"

"You must. He's quite a bit older than you, but he was brought up around here, at Sky View. He went away to work on a show-jumping yard in the South not long after he left school. Then he came back a few years later, after his wife left him and their twins, to set up a yard at home."

"I know who you mean," Ellie said. "I heard about that. He was married to Tamara, the singer. Wasn't there some kind of tragedy?"

Her dad shook his head sadly. "Terrible business. His mother and one of the children were killed in a car crash."

A heavy weight settled on Ellie's heart. "That must have been awful."

"He was in a very bad place for a while, I believe."

"Like you, then, Dad." She needed to say it.

For the first time in years, Bob Nelson looked his daughter in the eyes without withdrawing his gaze. His face darkened, and for one horrible moment she thought she'd overstepped the mark. Well, if he told her to leave, she'd just refuse.

"I have to go and let the pup out," he said, turning away. "He's been locked in all morning."

She followed slowly as he walked across to the barn and opened the door. The black whirlwind that hurled itself on them took her totally by surprise.

"How long have you had him?" she cried, crouching down to welcome the half-grown sheepdog that covered her in sloppy kisses.

"Quite a while now. He was part of the deal for Jake Munro's mare's stud fee."

"What's his name?"

"I call him Shadow. Jake's fiancée, Cass, has his sister, Puddle."

At the sound of his name, Shadow raced over to greet his master, tearing around him in crazy circles before waiting eagerly to be petted.

Bob rubbed the backs of the dog's ears. Ellie hadn't seen the same softness in his eyes for years.

"I've got a few sheep," he told her, as if compelled to justify his acquisition. "I thought it might be useful to have a dog. I'm going to train him."

"And he'll be good company for you," Ellie added.

"That, too," he admitted. "To be honest, I haven't felt like having company for a very long time."

Ellie seized her opening. "I know exactly how you feel, Dad. But maybe it's time to look back and move on. That's what I'm trying to do, at last. That's why I'm here. And your friend, Jake, seems to have managed to come to terms with his past."

"I guess meeting him is what got me thinking. He's been through some bad times, too, but now he's got his training and breeding business up and running, and he's getting married again. He's even gone into partnership with his dad, converting some barns."

"Perhaps I should stay around for a while," Ellie suggested on impulse. "Help you get things in the house straight again."

Her idea met a blank wall of silence.

"Dog needs some exercise," her dad eventually muttered, turning abruptly away.

Ellie's heart fell as she watched his slightly stooped figure walk off, closely followed by the dog. Then he paused, looking back.

"Come and see my new ewes if you like," he said. "They're in the fell meadow."

As they headed, side by side, toward the imposing mass of the Lakeland Hills, the pup raced ahead, glancing back every now and then to make sure his master was following. Ellie studied his black face with its white stripe between two of the friendliest brown eyes she had ever seen. He appeared to be smiling, Ellie thought, her head already whirling with ideas for a new painting.

The black-headed ewes were as nervous as wild deer, rushing to the corner of the paddock when they saw the dog. Shadow slunk down, belly on the ground, his eyes firmly fixed on the sheep.

Now that would make a great painting— the keen expression on the young dog's face and the startled eyes of the cautious sheep.

"You've started training him already, I see," she exclaimed.

Her dad shook his head. "No, that's just natural. It seems to be bred into him to know how quiet you have to be with these Fell sheep. They're as wild as the hills. I've had to put wire all around the tops of the walls to keep them in."

With a low whistle to Shadow, he turned back toward the stable yard, beckoning her.

"You haven't met Dennis yet."

CHAPTER FIVE

GRAND DESIGN WAS probably the most beautiful horse Ellie had ever seen. Not as noble as Blue, who would always hold a very special place in her heart, but classically perfect in his conformation. His gleaming, rich bay coat rippled beneath her fingers as she stroked his arched neck. She reached up to trace the outline of the large white star in the middle of his broad forehead. He tossed his head, moving to nip her arm, and she drew back.

"You've been spoiled by Blue, I'm afraid," her dad said, smiling. "Not many stallions are as friendly as him. Dennis is a different ball game altogether. He's pure Thoroughbred, for a start, and they're often a bit feisty. You have to treat him with respect—if you don't want to get bitten, that is. Fortunately, though, he's very gentle with his mares."

Ellie took hold of the stallion's nose as she

rubbed the backs of his ears, determined not to be daunted by his behavior.

"You know, I've already had two brilliant ideas for paintings since I've been home," she said reflectively. "Shadow with the sheep, and the arrogant expression on Dennis's face just now. I think maybe I could get lots of new ideas around here,"

"Best get some sketches done, then. Is that how it works?"

She shrugged. "Sometimes. Or I just paint from memory. I thought I might do a painting of Blue for you, too. Not in my usual style, but more of a classic painting. I might take some pictures of him before I go, so that I can really get his likeness."

"Your mother would have liked that," he said.

Were those tears in his eyes? Ellie had never seen her dad cry, not even at the funeral. Anger had driven him then. Now, though, he seemed different—softer and more approachable. Perhaps he saw in her something of her mother. She liked that idea.

"So you don't mind if I stay over?" she asked tentatively.

"Plenty of room," he muttered. "Bedding will want airing, though."

Ellie felt a warm wave of happiness wash over her. Her timing had been right; she was home at last.

AFTER A FEW HOURS of cleaning up the house, Ellie felt totally drained, having relived a million memories both happy and sad. Her dad had kept himself busy in the yard all afternoon. He came back into the house around supper time, preceded by Shadow, who burst into the kitchen and rolled onto his back for her to scratch his belly, legs raised ecstatically.

"Daft as a brush," declared her dad.

"Can we take those pictures of Dennis and Blue after supper?" she asked. "It's such a lovey evening, and I'd like to start on them as soon as I get back."

"You're going in the morning, then?"

Was that disappointment she could hear in his voice?

"I could stay until after lunch, I guess."

"Please yourself," he said.

Ellie felt a glow of happiness. Her dad could try to pretend he didn't care, but his disappointment at her leaving the next day was obvious.

"I'll be back soon, though," she told him. "If you'll have me."

His silence spoke volumes.

As Ellie started her car the next afternoon, to go back to her city life, she felt an acute sense of loss. She had been at Hope Farm for just one night, but already it felt like home again. Her dad was over by Blue's stable, pretending not to care, but last night they had talked about her mum, finally, and about the stud and Bob's hopes for the future. The two of them both had a long way to go, she was well aware of that, but at least they were getting back on track.

On impulse, Ellie switched off the engine and ran across the yard to give her dad a hug. He stood stock-still, awkwardly accepting her embrace.

"You'll be back before too long, lass?"

"Yes…" The flicker of an idea formed inside her head. "I'll be back before you know it, and I'll stay for a few days, if you like." She didn't miss the indecision on his face, but she knew how to convince him. "I'll finish the painting of Blue first and bring it with me."

He nodded, returning her smile.

"I'll look forward to seeing that," he said. Ellie got back in her car and set off for Manchester. Her phone rang just as she hit the highway. She glanced at it and declined the call. Now wasn't the right time to talk to Matt; she had way too much going on inside her head.

Her phone rang again as she opened the door to her apartment, and she heard a ping telling her she had a new message. Dumping her bags onto the floor, she listened to what he had to say.

"Hi, Ellie, are you back yet? We need to talk…about us. Call me when you get this."

She stared at the phone. What was there to say? Plenty, she realized. They needed to figure out where their relationship was going, for a start—if anywhere. Perhaps it was just a convenient arrangement for both of them, nothing more meaningful.

Ellie had driven back in a euphoric cloud, a sense of well-being in her veins, but now she felt strangely empty and a little lost.

Everything she'd thought she wanted, her

relationship with Matt, her job, her life in the city, seemed somehow less appealing. A vague longing lodged itself in her chest. A longing for what, though? she asked herself. What *did* she want? The longing to paint remained, to lose herself in her work, but what about Matt... What about love?

An image of Andy slipped past her barriers, and her chest tightened. He had seemed so genuine when he looked in through her car window at Cravendale, begging for her to stay in touch. His scent still lingered in her nostrils, as if he was here in the room with her, and the outlines of his face were so firmly etched in her brain that she could paint his likeness with her eyes closed. Was that what she should do? Would painting his image expel him from her psyche and heal those old wounds?

No, she decided, for then he would be forever staring at her...unless she just put the painting away in a cupboard somewhere. But what would be the point of that?

Determinedly pushing Andy to the back of her mind, she picked up her phone and dialed Matt.

"We need to talk," he repeated when he

picked up. His voice sounded distant and serious. "Meet me tonight, at Applejacks. I'll pick you up, if you like."

"No, it's fine. I'll see you there about seven. Is everything all right, Matt?"

For a moment she thought he'd hung up, but then his deep voice cut through the silence. "You tell me. I'll see you later."

THE SUN WAS still shining when Ellie set off to walk to Applejacks, and as she strode purposefully along the sidewalk she couldn't help thinking about the first time she met Matt there. It felt now as if they were two different people, and it hadn't even been all that long ago. Perhaps they should have just gone for a walk down by the river instead, stayed out in the evening sun. It seemed a shame to miss it. Then again, Matt didn't really do walks.

She saw him right away, sitting in a secluded corner and staring into his lager. He glanced around and caught her gaze, then stood up to greet her. He was so handsome and striking, she thought, with his sleek dark hair, designer clothes and clear, silvery gray eyes. So why wasn't her heart racing as it used to?

"Did you sort out your deal?" she asked, sitting down.

He shrugged, handing her a glass of white wine. "Almost. Have a good time in the country?"

Her eyes lit up. "It was great to see my dad. We actually *talked* for the first time in years. I'm going back soon, to stay for a few days this time. He keeps the yard spotless, but the house is a mess. How've you been, anyway?"

"So-so..."

"You said you wanted to talk." She took a sip of her wine before twirling the glass by its stem, watching the clear liquid swirl around and around.

Matt reached out to still her fingers, covering her hand with his.

"We're both grown adults, Ellie, and we need to talk because as far as I can see, we're going nowhere."

She looked up at him, meeting disappointment in his eyes.

"Do you love me, Matt?" she asked on impulse.

His hand dropped away.

"Do you love *me* is perhaps more to the point."

"I thought I did…"

"Until when, Ellie? What changed?"

She sighed heavily. "I don't know. It's just—"

"That we both seem to want different things," he finished for her.

"And what do you want of *me*?" she asked.

His voice was full of passion. "I want you to be the same person I thought I met," he said. "The person I got engaged to."

"But I am that same person."

"No, you're not. You were fun loving and up for anything when I met you." He drained his glass. "Now all you seem to want to do is paint…and go off for days in the country to get new material. When is the last time we went to a club, for instance? We used to go out all the time. And now you're talking about going back home to sort your dad's farm out. You never bothered before, so why now?"

"Maybe I've just grown up, Matt. Maybe I've realized there's more to life than clubbing."

He reached forward, taking hold of her

chin with his thumb and forefinger. His touch was gentle. "The answer to your question is yes. I suppose I'll always love you, Ellie, in a way, but it's not enough anymore. We're not on the same page."

"And I still really care about you, but I feel that way, too," she admitted.

He smiled, and Ellie thought she saw relief in his expression.

"Then I think we should have a break for a while, a total break, so that we can both decide where we are. You can go and do your country thing and I'll meet up with some of my old friends again...catch up on what I've been missing."

In a sudden flutter of panic, Ellie reached out to take hold of his hand, clutching it tightly in both of hers.

"Are you trying to tell me that we're over?"

"I suppose I am... Is that a problem?"

Ellie shook her head slowly, staring at the man she had once intended to spend the rest of her life with. The panic faded and she withdrew her hands. "You may as well have this back then," she said quietly, sliding off her diamond ring.

"No!" His objection was immediate, from

the heart. "I never said I wanted the ring back."

"What do you want then, Matt?"

"I told you... A proper break."

"We're over, Matt. I think we both know that."

Taking the ring, he pressed it against her palm, closing his fingers around her hand.

"Don't wear it, then. Just keep it for a while, say a couple of weeks or so. And then we'll meet up again. If you've got this country thing out of your system..."

"Country thing!" Her voice was cold, her hands shaking. "I was born in the country, Matt."

"Yes, and you hated it. That's why you moved to the city."

"No, I never hated the country. I just couldn't stand the memories it held for me."

"Exactly," he declared. "And now you've changed. I loved the crazy girl I met, you see, but it feels as if she's gone."

"I'm still me, Matt. Aren't you supposed to love me for myself?"

"And I'm still me. I've never made a secret of who I am."

"So you're saying that I have?"

Matt's jaw tightened. "No," he responded. "Of course not—well, not intentionally, anyway."

Ellie stood up, reaching for her bag and slinging it over her shoulder.

"I guess it's goodbye, then."

An acute sense of loss dragged through her chest as she kissed him on the cheek. He grabbed her arm, pulling her down to press his lips fiercely against hers.

"For now," he murmured, releasing her. "Ring me when you're ready."

As she walked out of the bar, into the golden light of the late evening sun, Ellie's sense of loss was replaced with a glimmer of excitement. She would never be ready to get back with Matt, she knew that now. There was so much to think about, so many memories still to relive. So many pictures to paint…beginning with Blue's.

CHAPTER SIX

ELLIE NOSED HER car along the street, looking for a parking place. An angry driver honked his horn and she threw him a smile, mouthing sorry as she carefully maneuvered into a tiny space, holding up the traffic.

For over a week, apart from the nights when she worked at Dominoes, Ellie had spent most of her time painting, totally inspired by her new ideas and material. Her image of Into the Blue—no horse with the majesty he displayed in her painting could ever be thought of as *just* Blue—was probably the most satisfying work she had ever completed. He stared out from the canvas with real expression in his eyes, exuding presence. She couldn't wait to show it to her dad.

Mel was waiting impatiently when Ellie staggered through the huge front door of the gallery, clutching two paintings.

"I've got an appointment at three," Mel said, looking pointedly at her watch.

Ellie placed the paintings carefully against the wall.

"Sorry, the traffic was awful and I couldn't find a parking place close enough to carry them all in at once. I'll go back for the other one in a minute."

"Well, let me see the ones you've brought."

Mel Morton was revered as an art critic and gallery owner, and Ellie was well aware that being given some space in one of her exhibitions, however small, was a huge honor as well as a chance to get her work seen. She believed that the two paintings she'd just brought in, the fox cub on its day of freedom and the one of her dad's pup, Shadow, working the sheep, were probably the best she had ever done, along with her portrait of Into the Blue.

As the tall, elegant, middle-aged woman lifted them onto the display table, standing back to survey them with a critical eye, Ellie's nerves jangled.

For several minutes the two women stood side by side in silence, absorbing the emotion displayed before them: the young fox's look of fury combined with vulnerability, the dog's keen expression and the apprehension of the sheep.

"I'd like to exhibit them if I can," said Ellie. "But they're not for sale right now."

"They'd make a good price," remarked Mel. "But maybe it would be better not to sell yet—drive up the value. The other paintings you've shown me aren't bad, but they aren't in the same league as these two. Did you say there was a third?"

Ellie nodded, trying to contain her excitement. "I'll go and get it."

When she arrived back at the gallery with her third painting, Mel was still absorbed by the two already on display.

"It's the emotion," she exclaimed. "It draws you in. You can feel the fox's fear behind his snarl and the intelligence on the sheepdog's face is something else."

Ellie hesitated in the act of removing the cover from the painting of Into the Blue. "It's not quite as contemporary a style as these two…more traditional."

"Well, you don't need to apologize for that," Mel said. "Come on, let me see."

Into the Blue looked magnificent, thought

Ellie, staring out across the countryside like a king surveying his kingdom. It was hard to believe that *she* had actually painted it.

"It's called *The Look of Eagles*," she said, trying to swallow the lump that had formed in her throat. Her mum would have loved to see this painting.

Mel nodded. "It's magnificent. And the other two, what have you named them?"

"*Freedom*, that's the one of the fox, and *Working the Wild Flock*."

Mel took a step back, tearing her eyes from the painting to glance at Ellie, eyebrows raised in anticipation. "Please tell me this one's for sale."

Ellie shook her head. "Sorry, I painted it for my dad. I'm on my way home right now, to show it to him. I'll bring it back for the exhibition, though, if you want it."

Mel held her chin thoughtfully with her thumb and forefinger. "I'd be more than happy to exhibit these three."

A warm glow spread right up into the roots of Ellie's hair. "Thanks," she said. "It's the first time I've exhibited, apart from art school, and I'm really excited about it."

"My exhibitions are always exciting," Mel remarked. "Now I really must go."

It was only much later, as Ellie drove her small car out of the city, that she realized Matt hadn't figured in her happiness. Sadness lodged itself in her heart as she said goodbye to the safety net that had protected her for so long. On impulse, she pulled her phone from her pocket, dialing Dominoes with trembling fingers.

Her boss Pedro answered, his thick, familiar accent filling her head with doubt. "Hello? Who is this?"

"It's Ellie. I'm really sorry, Pedro, but I'm going away for longer than I thought—a week at least. I need to cancel my shifts."

"Are you serious?" She could almost see him raising his hands in the air.

"I'm sorry it's such short notice, but I'm sure Mary will fill in. She's always looking for more work"

"You can call me when you get back, if you like." His tone was curt and angry. "But I cannot promise I'll have work for you."

Ellie hesitated, panicking slightly at the thought of having no job. Well, there was nothing she could do about it. "That's okay, Pedro. I'm sorry for letting you down."

When the phone clicked off, she felt as if she had been set free.

BOB NELSON WAS in the barn when he heard a car pull up outside. His old heart lightened when he heard Ellie's bright tones.

"Hey, Shadow, it's me. Where's your master?"

Peering out of the barn door, Bob watched for a moment as she crouched down to scratch the pup's ears, wrapping her fingers around the ruff of his neck and allowing him to lick her cheek ecstatically. Her every gesture reminded him of Sally, he realized, wondering why he had shut himself off for so long. Closing the lid on his emotions, he stepped out into the sunshine. Ellie would probably only go running back to that boyfriend of hers when she got bored with country life again.

ELLIE GAVE SHADOW a final pat and stood up when she saw her dad approaching.

"Hello again, Dad."

He responded in a gruff, slightly awkward tone. "You came back, then. It looks like someone's pleased to see you, anyway."

"And you aren't?"

He shrugged, heading for the house. "I'll be a whole lot happier when you've made us a cup of tea."

It occurred to Ellie that slotting back into life here at Hope Farm might not be as easy as she'd anticipated. Maybe she'd been a bit hasty in canceling work for a whole week, especially since she didn't know if she had a job to go back to. She watched her dad walk off across the yard with the dog at his heels. Whether he realized it or not, she knew that he needed her here, so she'd just have to ignore his grumpiness and mood swings.

He paused, turning toward her, and she noticed with a heavy lurch just how much he'd aged. He seemed so much smaller than he had when she was young, and his thick dark hair had turned gray, thinning on the top. She had always thought of him as a powerful character, but now he seemed vulnerable, a mere shadow of the man she remembered.

"I've got something for you," she called. "You go and put the kettle on and I'll bring it into the house."

When Ellie appeared in the kitchen doorway, carrying the painting in her arms, her father couldn't help revealing a prickle of interest. His blue eyes brightened and his face cracked into a smile.

"Is that Blue?" he asked. "Have you done it already?"

Ellie placed the painting on the kitchen table, propping it against the wall, but she hesitated before removing the sheet that covered it.

"Come on, then," her dad said impatiently. "It can't be all that bad, surely."

As she pulled away the cover to reveal Into the Blue in all his glory, Ellie concentrated her attention on her dad's face. He had never been one to show much emotion, even when she was a child. Now, though, as he feasted his eyes on the stallion, his whole face glowed.

"I told you I'd bring it back with me," she said.

He turned to her, unshed tears glistening in his eyes. "You're genius, lass. Your mother would have loved it."

"I said I'd take it to the gallery for my exhibition next month, but I'd only be borrowing it. It's yours, Dad…yours and Mum's."

AFTER STUDYING THE painting without comment for several minutes, Bob Nelson stood and strode out into the yard again. Pride for his only child filled his whole being. To think his little Ellie could paint like that…

His heart beat heavy in his chest as memories barraged his emotions. The gray stallion watched his approach from over the stable door.

"She's done you proud, lad," he murmured, reaching up to rub one hand down the big horse's face.

He recalled that wondrous day when the future of Hope Farm staggered around this very stable on wobbly legs.

"Who'd have thought it, Sally," he said. "He's done us proud, too, just like you said he would."

When Ellie's voice floated out across the yard, the memories faded. That was all a long time ago. It was the future he had to think of now, a future that, hopefully, held his only daughter.

"Tea's brewed dad," she called. "And I've made you a sandwich."

ELLIE AND HER dad sat in something approaching companionable silence, sipping tea and chewing on cheese sandwiches. She noticed her dad kept glancing across at the painting.

"Do you have lots of others as good as this?" he asked. "Maybe I should be coming to your exhibition."

"No, I don't have lots like this, and I'm only exhibiting three paintings, but at least it's a start. I'd be happy for you to come see them, but it's a long way to go just for that."

Bob nodded. "I guess you're right. Does it have a title, the painting?"

She chewed her lip, unsure how the title would affect her dad. "Do you remember what Mum said when Blue was born?"

He narrowed his eyes as he relived the moment. "She said he had the look of eagles."

"And that's it. That's what I've called it. *The Look of Eagles.*"

Silence fell between them as they studied the painting.

"Do you mind if I stay a bit longer this

time, Dad?" Ellie asked. "A week or so, maybe?"

She held her breath, but he looked like he was considering the idea.

"Well, it is your home, too…"

The sound of a vehicle outside cut him off. Footsteps crunched on the gravel, and as her dad stood, a face appeared in the kitchen doorway. Ellie noticed huge brown eyes first, and silky dark hair framing fine, perfectly drawn features.

"Sorry, Bob," the young woman said with a bright smile. "I didn't know you had company. Donald asked me to drop by and check on the three-year-old for him, but I can come back later…"

He raised his hand. "No, no. It's fine. Come in and meet my daughter."

"Daughter?" She pushed her hair behind her ears. "I didn't know you had a daughter."

"She's been away for a while," he explained. "But she's back now. Ellie, meet Cass Truman…soon to be Cass Munro."

Ellie stepped forward to shake the young woman's hand. "Congratulations," she said. "My dad's been telling me about Jake Munro and his horses. I suppose that's the Munro you're marrying?"

"Sure is." Cass smiled. "In two weeks, to be precise. It's nice to meet you, Ellie. I'm glad your dad finally has someone to take proper care of him. Not that he—"

She stopped midsentence, staring at the painting on the table.

"Wow," Cass said. "That is awesome. Where did you get it?"

"Ellie painted it," Bob said proudly. "She's an artist."

"It's the most beautiful picture I've ever seen!" Cass's face was alight with excitement. "Do you take commissions? I've been trying to think of a really good wedding present for Jake, and a painting like this of Carlotta would blow him away. I'd pay whatever you're asking."

"I'd be more than happy to," Ellie said, thrilled by the prospect of being accepted into this tight-knit community in such a way. Perhaps it would bring more commissions her way. "But you don't need to pay me," she insisted. "It can be our wedding present to you both, can't it, Dad?"

Bob grinned. "It's a grand idea…"

"Then you must come to the wedding, too," Cass said. "Your dad accepted his invitation a month ago."

"Thanks, Cass, I'd love to come!" Ellie's mind was already brimming with ideas for the new painting. "Just let me know when Jake is out so I can visit Carlotta, take a few photos and do some sketches. I'll need to get started right away."

"Great. I'll just go check out the three-year-old and then we can have another chat," Cass suggested.

"Of course, you're a vet," Ellie said. "I have to say…"

"I know, I don't look like one at all." Cass laughed. "How many times have I heard that since I came to the Lake District?"

"But I reckon she's won most of us over by now," Bob said. "Anyway, the three-year-old's abscess seems a whole lot better today."

"Good." Cass headed for the door. "I've still got some visits to do this afternoon. There's a pony with what sounds like a strained tendon at Ambleside and Ben Myers has some calves with scours, so I need to get to work."

"I'll come and help you with her," Bob

said, reaching for his jacket. "She's a feisty little thing."

As her dad and the vet walked toward the stable together, deep in discussion, Ellie felt a huge smile swell inside her. She had a commission, a real commission, and she was going to a wedding. She had been so right in her decision to come back and see her dad.

"What do you think, Mum?" she murmured. "Are you pleased that I'm home?"

The tall tree in the yard rustled as a sudden wind sprang up. Bob and Cass heard it too, turning back in surprise

"I guess you are." Ellie smiled.

CHAPTER SEVEN

OVER THE NEXT couple of days, life at Hope Farm settled into a kind of normality. Ellie began to feel as if she'd never left the rambling, cozy farmhouse, and the city seemed a million miles away. She rekindled her old skills, helping her dad with the mucking out and grooming, familiarizing herself once again with the aroma of horses, enjoying their quiet companionship.

On the morning of her third day, while she and her dad were having breakfast after doing all the yard chores, she announced that she was going into Little Dale to get some groceries.

"We're fine," Bob insisted. "There's meat in the freezer and plenty of veg for lunch… if you're making it, that is."

Ellie laughed. "Don't worry, Dad, I'll make it. Someone certainly needs to—you look like you're wasting away."

She realized she'd overstepped when her dad's face darkened. He'd been in such good humor since she'd come home that she'd forgotten how prickly he could be. Pushing back his chair, he stood abruptly.

"I've managed on my own for the last six years," he snapped. "And I can certainly manage without you now. In fact, why don't you just go back to the city and give me and the horses our peace back?"

She shook her head firmly. "You don't mean that, Dad, you know you don't. Look, we talked about this the last time I came home, and I'm sorry for abandoning you for so long, but things are different now... we're both different. It's time to undo all our wrongs, and I'm going to give you a hand around here, whether you like it or not."

He sank down into his chair again with a heavy sigh. "Maybe you're right. I'm not as young as I used to be, and the stud's going to be busy in spring..."

He looked at her long and hard, revealing an emotion she hadn't seen before.

"You will still be around in spring?" he asked.

Ellie squeezed his shoulder, surprised

by the sharpness of his bones beneath his sweater.

"I'm back for you now, Dad, I promise, and I'm going to keep on coming back. You need someone to take care of you, and I intend to do just that."

"What about that fiancé of yours, though? I see you're not wearing your ring."

"I still have it," she told him, with a sudden lurch of guilt as she realized she hadn't even thought about Matt since she left the city. "We're not together right now, though." She stood up, reaching across the table to start collecting the dishes. "And now I'm off into Little Dale as soon as I've tidied up here, to get some groceries. I'll see you at lunch."

AN HOUR LATER, Ellie was wandering through the village she used to know so well, recognizing landmarks that had been a huge part of her life when she was growing up. She passed the candy shop where her mum used to take her after school on Fridays, the pretty gray stone church and the village green. Memories hit her like a tidal wave when she saw her old high school. There was the tree where she and Andy would meet between classes. A vision of his smile flashed into her mind, too wide for his face, and that lock of blond hair that always flopped forward into his eyes…still flopped forward now. When he'd been working on the fox cub, she'd almost put out her hand to push it back. A warm glow flowed through her veins. Just for a minute, she allowed herself to remember how things had been back then: his lips on hers, their sweet, all-consuming, innocent love. She stopped in her tracks. What was she thinking? That had all been childish pretense. She'd been in love with love, not Andy Montgomery, and luckily she'd found out what he was really like before it was too late. Returning to her car, shopping bags firmly clutched in both hands, she focused on the future. Excitement prickled. She had Jake Munro's mare to paint, a wedding to go to and, of course, her exhibition. What more could she want?

THE HOUSE PHONE rang just as Ellie and her dad were finishing lunch. She answered it automatically. "Hello, Hope Farm, can I help you?"

It was Cass Truman. "Jake and his dad have gone off this afternoon," she said. "And they won't be back for two or three hours at least. I thought it might be a good opportunity for you to do those sketches and photos, if it's convenient."

Ellie's response was instant. "Yes, of course it's convenient. I need to get started if I'm going to finish the painting before the wedding. I'll meet you there at one."

Hanging up the phone, she glanced at her dad. "Do you want to come with me? You can show me where Sky View is."

Bob nodded. "I'd like to see how the mare's looking. Her foal's due in early March, and I reckon it's going to be something really special. Anyway..."

"Anyway what?"

"I'd like to see how it works, this painting talent of yours."

Ellie laughed and began clearing up their plates.

Half an hour later, they were in her car, following a narrow lane that led way up the steep fell slopes before dipping down into an almost hidden valley where the shiny gray roofs of the old stone buildings, damp with a recent shower of rain, were nestled comfortably together.

"This is it," her dad said when the sign for Sky View came into sight.

Ellie pulled up on a gravel area, cutting the engine and opening her car door just as Cass appeared. A young black, white and tan sheepdog clung to her heels like glue, wagging its plumed tail slowly as it watched the new arrivals climb out of the car. Bob held out his hand and the dog approached cautiously, tail waving so hard that its whole body wriggled.

"This is Shadow's sister," he said as Ellie stooped to scratch the dog's ears.

"She's called Puddle," Cass added. "Their mum, Bess, is off with Jake. She never leaves his side if she can help it."

"Puddle seems pretty fond of you, too," Ellie remarked.

"She's my best friend. You can't beat these Welsh collies for love and loyalty. Anyway, come with me and I'll introduce you to our subject."

"Do you live here at Sky View, too?" Ellie asked as they followed her across the yard.

Cass shook her head. "No, not here at the stables—although I'll move into the house in two weeks, of course. Right now, I rent a cottage from Bill, Jake's dad. It's just a bit farther up the lane."

"I haven't been here for a while," Bob said, looking around the yard with interest. "Bill and Jake haven't wasted any time with the building project, I see."

Cass followed his gaze to where painters were working on the windows of a tastefully converted barn. "That one's nearly finished, but there's another one to do still. They're going to be holiday rentals. My cottage will be, too, when I've officially moved into the farmhouse. Anyway…" She gestured toward a stable just ahead. "Here's our subject."

The silvery-gray mare was stunning, thought Ellie. Her huge, dark eyes were bright with interest to see her visitors.

"I've been grooming her for over an hour," Cass told them, reaching for a head collar. "I wanted her to look amazing. I'll bring her out into the yard, and then you can decide how you want to shoot her."

"What about with you, since it's a wedding present," Ellie suggested. "Jake can have his two favorite females captured together for eternity. What do you think?"

Cass paused.

"Well, it wasn't quite what I imagined…"

"We could take her into the meadow over

there, if you want a background. It has a fantastic view."

"I know, but…"

"I'm sorry," Ellie said, seeing Cass's indecision. "I'm getting carried away. Why don't you just tell me what you have in mind?"

Cass shrugged. "Well, that's just it. I'm not really sure. I want the painting to be all about Carlotta, though, with no distractions."

"I have some photographs of my more contemporary paintings you could look at, if you'd like. The painting of Blue shows him in his own surroundings because I knew what Dad would like, but—"

"Oh, so I'm old-fashioned now, am I?" Bob interrupted.

Seeing the smile behind his disgruntled expression, Ellie laughed. "There's nothing wrong with being old-fashioned, and you know what I mean. Besides, I thought you liked the painting."

"I love it," he said. "Look, why don't you do what you have to do before Jake gets back, and then Cass can call in at Hope Farm to see the photographs of your other paintings before she takes a decision? I'd like to see them, too."

"Good idea," Ellie agreed

When Cass led Carlotta out into the yard, Ellie gasped. Everything about the mare shrieked class, from her fine-boned, delicate-looking limbs to her beautiful, elegant head.

"Wow," she exclaimed. "She looks like royalty. I know how she needs to be painted now—standing center stage, relaxed but proud and totally aware of her own importance." Her voice rose with excitement. "And then I could paint her again with her newborn foal, all soft and motherly."

"Like two sides of a coin," Cass said. "That's brilliant. But I will definitely be paying you for the second painting."

"Seems to me you should be doing your sketches and photos instead of all this dreaming. It won't be a surprise if Jake catches you," Bob said.

Ellie agreed. "Let's just take her over there, by the tree."

An hour later, armed with half a dozen charcoal sketches and a ton of photos, Ellie said goodbye to gracious Carlotta.

"Stop in when you're passing by, and we'll have a chat about exactly what you want," Ellie told Cass.

Cass smiled, shaking her hand vigorously. "I can't wait. And thanks for doing this. It's going to be so special."

"And you'll already have a birthday present for Jake next year," Bob added.

"Actually, that's perfect, too," Cass said. "The foal is due in early March, and Jake's birthday's in June. Will that be enough time, though?"

"I'll make sure it is," Ellie promised.

AS THEY DROVE homeward in companionable silence through the dramatically beautiful countryside, Ellie couldn't stop thinking of her painting of Carlotta.

"It's a shame that the mare's foal isn't by Blue." Her dad sighed, jerking her out of her reverie.

"Exactly what I thought," she agreed. "Why did Jake choose Dennis?"

"Performance. He's a proven show jumper, and that's what Jake wanted. He said he might put her to Blue next year, though."

"Great, another commission for me!" Ellie said.

"He'll have a whole gallery before you're

done." Her dad chortled. "And speaking of galleries, when's your exhibition?"

"In a couple of weeks. It starts on the Monday after the wedding, but showing a few paintings at a gallery can hardly be called *my* exhibition. I'll probably be one of at least a dozen others."

"So you'll be going back to the city before that, I guess."

Ellie glanced at her father, noting the lines in his face. He seemed tired. "You know, Dad, I really don't feel like going back there ever again. I will have to take the paintings in to the gallery, though, and I need to check on my apartment…and buy a dress for Cass and Jake's wedding, obviously."

"Will you see your fiancé while you're there or is it really all over?"

"I think so," she said. "We're going to meet up in a month, though, just to see how we both feel."

"Surely you already know how you feel."

Ellie frowned, clutching the steering wheel tightly. Did she know how she felt? "Yes," she said, suddenly sure. "I think I do."

"I always thought that you'd end up with the other boy, the one who used to come around all the time when you were at school. He's a vet now, you know, at Low Fell."

"Yes…" Ellie's voice sounded a long way off in her ears. "I heard. I didn't think you even noticed him back then. Anyway, we fizzled out. The usual thing, too young to be serious…"

"Your mother said he broke your heart."

Ellie's breath caught and she fought to contain her emotions as the memories that lurked so close to the surface kicked in. Andy's lips closing over hers as he whispered "I love you."

"It was just a teenage fling," she said, determined to believe it. "I was way too young to get my heart broken."

Her dad nodded. "That's good. He's a very good vet, but they say that he has an eye for the ladies."

"Now that's an old-fashioned way to put it," Ellie said. "I think you may be right, though."

"Well, I am an old-fashioned guy." Her dad laughed.

As soon as they got back to Hope Farm, Ellie took out her sketch pad. Carlotta's lines and proud expression were already forming into a picture in her imagination. She flipped through the pad, stopping at a brief sketch she'd done on the morning they set the fox free.

Her heart skipped a beat as she took in Andy's face, soft and caring, lowered over the terrified creature whose life was at his disposal. One thing was for sure: whatever she thought about Andy, it was obvious that he loved all animals with a passion. Wrapping her arms around herself, for an indulgent moment she allowed the memories to trickle in. The trickle turned into a flood. She'd loved him so much. No...it couldn't have been love. Just teenage hormones running riot.

Unpacking her paints and canvases from their protective wrapping, she turned her attention to Carlotta's portrait, knowing that as soon as she began working on it, everything else would go straight out of her mind. Is that what her passion for drawing and painting was? she wondered. An escape from reality? Picking up a piece of charcoal, she made a sweeping stroke across the page and there, almost magically, were the lines of the beautiful gray mare, neck proudly arched.

Andy Montgomery, she decided, was firmly locked in the past and always would be.

CASS CAME TO Hope Farm the following afternoon.

"I've decided," she announced as she burst in through the door.

Ellie smiled, running her hand through her cap of blond curls.

"Go on, then."

"I thought about what you said, you know, yesterday…about Carlotta being like royalty. You said she should be center stage, relaxed but proud and aware of her own importance."

"Exactly," agreed Ellie.

"Well, that's definitely how I'd like to see her painted, you know, to show off her personality."

Ellie nodded. "And that's exactly what my new style is about. Some of my paintings don't even show the subject's whole form; they just focus on the expression. Here…"

She reached for her iPad, flicking into pictures. "Look at these two paintings I've just done. I call them *Freedom* and *Working the Wild Flock*."

For a moment Cass just stared at the images on the screen. "They're brilliant," she said. "And different to anything else I've seen. There's just so much emotion."

"I thought Carlotta's should be more of a full picture without the blurry outlines, to show all of her."

"No scenery, though."

The two young women looked at each other as if sharing a secret.

"No scenery," agreed Ellie. "I'll start it today."

CHAPTER EIGHT

THE IMPOSING FRONT DOOR of The Morton Art Gallery was locked. Ellie propped her painting on the old stone step as she knocked one last time. She'd arranged to be here at three and it was quarter past.

The sound of stiletto heels on concrete tip-tapped into her consciousness just as Mel Morton's resounding tones cut through the hum of traffic. "Sorry I'm late. Traffic was awful. Oh, good, I see you've brought your new painting. The other two have been hung already. Come and see."

She turned her key in the lock and the huge door swung open, revealing the stately interior of the spacious building. The door thudded softly shut behind them, and peacefulness descended.

"It's amazing in here," Ellie said. "Like another world. It feels as if the city is miles away."

"It cost a lot of money to create this atmosphere. I'm glad you appreciate it. Now grab your painting and let me show you where it's going."

Ellie only had three paintings in the show, but Mel had certainly given her work prominence. Ellie stared in amazement at her own paintings beautifully displayed on the far wall of a large, chic room. She was speechless. Her heart thudded overtime and her body quivered.

"These really are my paintings," she eventually managed, wringing her hands together. "In a real exhibition."

Mel smiled. "Well, you've a long way to go, and I have to warn you that something different often takes a while to get off the ground unless you're already well-known. But your paintings do have a reality and freshness about them. I like that." She pointed to an empty space on the wall. "The third painting is going there. Roger will be here in a minute to hang it."

As if on cue, an elderly man with snowy white hair arrived carrying a stepladder. Ellie gently unwrapped the painting of Into the

Blue and felt a thrill go through her as he hung it on the white wall.

"There," Mel said. "Now stand back and look at them critically."

As Ellie stood beside the gallery owner, staring at her own paintings, she thought she'd never been so proud. It might be a small start from Mel Morton's perspective, but to her, it was everything. There was the beautiful stallion her mother had loved so much, and just below it were the other two paintings that drew on her emotions—the wild fox cub and her dad's dog working the sheep.

Her fists clenched, and she glanced at Mel. "Do you think anyone will try to buy them?"

"I thought they weren't for sale."

"They aren't, but maybe I'll get some commissions."

"I hope you do," Mel said. "But remember, it's a tough game. You need a recognizable style and subject matter. Artists can make good money on commissions, but that often comes at the price of their own reputation and recognition. Honestly, I think you should focus on this kind of thing—real situations involving animals, showing all the emotion you've portrayed here."

"That's easier said than done." Ellie sighed. "The inspiration isn't easy to come by. I think I might get work doing animal likenesses—you know, dogs and horses, for presents, mainly. But that's not what I want."

"What do you want?" Mel stared at her with such intensity that Ellie felt her whole career hanging on the answer.

"I want to paint real pieces, emotional pieces that everyone wants—paintings of importance that will be remembered forever."

Mel smiled. "Right answer. Let nothing stand in your way, then, Ellie. Be ruthless in your quest for inspiration. But listen, I was supposed to be somewhere fifteen minutes ago. I'll see you on Monday."

"See you on Monday," Ellie echoed. It occurred to her that Mel Morton would definitely have been ruthless in her quest for success. But ruthless was a word that didn't really sit right in Ellie Nelson's conscience.

Putting their conversation on the back burner for now, she decided to go look for a wedding outfit.

AFTER AN HOUR of trailing around clothing stores downtown, Ellie headed eagerly for a

Costa coffee shop, sinking into the first available chair to sip her cappuccino and take a quick peek into her bag to admire the outfit she'd chosen.

Wanting to appear elegant, she'd decided on a black-and-white suit, until she'd spotted a simple, classy, vibrant blue figure-hugging dress that perfectly matched her eyes. The salesperson didn't need to tell her it suited her; she could see it for herself. The high heels in the same shade of blue had been an extravagance, but she hadn't been able to resist them. And after all, she told herself, she could wear the outfit for both the wedding and the exhibition next week.

She felt a shiver of anticipation as she clasped her thick white cup with both hands, watching the busy world go by outside. Her mind wandered to her paintings and her conversation with Mel Morton. Reliving her childhood and all the memories that rested in Little Dale and getting to know her dad again had made her very sure of where she wanted her life to go now. And it wasn't all about the painting opportunities, though that was part of it. She was figuring out who she really was. Last night, her apartment had felt alien to her, despite the fact that her brushes, paints and canvases were everywhere. City life had no place in her future anymore; she knew that now. It was time to move on.

She had the wedding to look forward to, the exhibition on Monday and the painting for Cass Truman to finish, as well as all the inspirational moments she was determined to find. No time for regrets. Tonight she'd sort out her apartment and pack everything into her car ready for the journey home tomorrow. She'd already paid a month's rent up front so she didn't need to worry about it for a while and at the end of the month... At the end of the month, who knew? It was now that mattered.

DRIVING BACK TO Little Dale next morning filled with euphoria, Ellie decided to take the route that passed by Cravendale Animal Sanctuary. It was out of her way but she wasn't in a rush, and her experiences there were what had rekindled her love for animals and the countryside. Remembering the day she saved the fox cub brought Andy sharply to mind. Were he and Paula an item? she wondered. They seemed so well suited. An image of them together brought a strange pang and memories flooded in, of *herself* and Andy: the school dance; holding hands as they walked along the sun-baked path beside the lake the year she turned sixteen; the feel of his lips on hers the first time they kissed…the way her heart split in two when he told her it was over.

"Ellie Nelson," she said out loud. "Get out of memory lane right now."

The sign for Cravendale Animal Sanctuary loomed through the trees on the side of the road, and she pulled up for a moment to look at it. The colors had faded and the wording was crude, to say the least. Perhaps she should offer to repaint it for them, make it a real artwork as well as a sign. Excited by the idea, she drove through the gates and parked near the low stone building. Everything was quiet and still, and Ellie felt disappointment creep in. Perhaps Paula wasn't here.

Ellie was still sitting in her car, wondering whether to take a look around or leave, when Paula drove up. She parked beside Ellie and clambered out into the sunshine clutching a small cage.

"Squirrel," she announced. "Gray, of

course, but it's not his fault. Hello again, by the way."

Ellie's heartbeat quickened. "Did you just pick it up?"

Paula nodded. "Yes, someone brought it in to the local vets'. Found it in the side of the lane."

"Like my fox cub."

"Lunatic drivers... Anyway, it has a broken leg but they said it should heal okay."

"I thought Andy took care of the animals here," Ellie said with a puzzled frown.

"He still comes in as much as he can, but he has his regular job, too. He's been helping me with some fund-raisers, as well. When he first got involved here he was just a locum at the local vet center, so he had a lot more free time. If he's not around, I still use the vet center in Tarnside."

"Of course, I don't know what I was thinking—he's working in Little Dale. But where does that leave you? I mean...the *two* of you?"

Curiosity clouded Paula's honey-colored eyes. Then her face crumpled into laughter. "Me and Andy? That's crazy." Tears streamed down her face. "I think my husband might have something to say if there was a 'me and Andy.'"

A hot flush crept up Ellie's neck, turning her cheeks an embarrassing shade of red. "Sorry, I suppose I jumped to conclusions. You just seemed like such an…item."

"Don't worry about it. If I wasn't already happily married, it might be a different story. Andy's a nice guy."

Desperate to move past the awkward moment, Ellie changed the subject. "I wanted to offer to paint your sign again."

"What a lovely idea!" she said. "I'll get this little chap settled, and we can talk about it over a coffee. I have some home-baked chocolate muffins, too—my husband's a chef." She patted her stomach. "Hence my generous proportions."

As Paula took the squirrel into the clinic, Ellie felt a warm sense of relief. So Paula was happily married and definitely not in a relationship with Andy. Not that it mattered to her, of course.

CHAPTER NINE

THE AFTERNOON SUN was sinking down below the hills as Ellie drove into the yard at Hope Farm. She could see her dad over by the stallion boxes, talking to a large man sporting a trilby hat. She caught her dad's eye and waved, and he beckoned her over, walking forward to meet her while the other man remained by Blue's door.

"You came back then, lass," he murmured.

She nodded. "I said I would, didn't I?"

"You never told me you had such an attractive daughter, Bob," his companion announced as they approached. He held out his broad hand to Ellie and she took it, feeling the rough calluses of a working man against her palm.

"Oscar Goulding," he announced. "I'm here to try and buy your father's gray stallion...or use him, at least."

"I think it will be use him, then." Ellie smiled. "Dad would rather die than sell Blue."

Oscar held her gaze. "Everything has its price."

She retrieved her hand. "That's very cynical."

"I've had cause to be cynical," he told her, turning back to her dad. "Now, let me get you the details of my mare. I was thinking of bringing her to stud in, say...early April?"

As the two men ambled off toward Oscar's car, Ellie gazed at her surroundings with a renewed sense of wonder. How could she have missed all of this for so long? Her dad needed help, she could see that. If she did his paperwork for him, he'd have more time for what really mattered, like taking care of the horses and the farm and dealing with clients. She could combine painting, office duties and yard work, making herself useful around here on a more permanent basis. She could always get a part-time job to keep her going until her paintings started to sell. Her dad had totally changed his attitude toward her since she'd come home, so perhaps he'd finally realized he couldn't do everything on his own anymore. And if he hadn't, she'd just have to persuade him.

It wasn't until after supper that Ellie plucked up the courage to run her idea past her dad.

She was washing pots at the kitchen sink, making a mental note to convince him to buy a dishwasher, while he sat at the table going through some paperwork.

"Need any help with that, Dad?" she asked.

He looked up in surprise and she seized the moment.

"In fact, if you think about it, there are quite a lot of things around here I could help you with."

Sliding the papers he was studying back into a blue file marked "Stud Mares 2015," he remained silent for a moment, a thoughtful expression on his face.

"Like what?"

She dried her hands on a towel, splaying her palms

"For a start, I could make your life a bit easier by helping you with the yard work. And I could help do your books, you know, keep records of visiting mares and help with your accounts, that kind of thing—as well as looking after the house, cooking…and I'd still be able to do my painting."

"How *is* the picture coming along, by the way?" he asked, as if deliberately changing the subject. "The wedding is only a couple of days away, you know."

She was disappointed by his lack of enthusiasm for her suggestions. "It's done. Or at least it will be by tonight. There's hardly enough time for it to dry as it is."

He nodded, picking up his file again, and an awkward silence fell between them. Words whirled around in Ellie's head, but she held them back. She'd made her offer and now she just had to wait for him to think it through. She turned back to the sink reluctantly.

A full five minutes passed, and Ellie finished the dishes, hanging her tea towel on the stove.

"I'd better get on with this painting," she said.

Her dad ran a hand through his thinning hair, looking at her pensively. "Are you planning on staying around here for long?"

She shrugged. "Indefinitely, I suppose…if you'll have me. There's nothing in the city to hold me anymore, and I realize now just how much I've missed this place, this way of life. Look, Dad…" Tears sprang to her eyes and she blinked, brushing them away with her fingers. "I really do think I can fit in here. It's time to move on, for both of us to think of the future. We could help each other."

"So you really want a proper job here, at Hope Farm?"

"Yes." Her mouth went dry and she ran the tip of her tongue across her lips.

The glimmer of a smile creased his lined face.

"It's hard work."

"I recognize that, Dad. All I need is a few hours a day to paint and do some research. The rest of the time I'll work as hard as you like."

"It'll have to be done right."

"I expected nothing else."

He held out his hand. "Working partnership, then. You'd own nothing, mind, but you'd have a stake in the profits."

Ellie took his hand, shaking it up and down ecstatically. "I won't let you down. In fact, it'll make your life so much easier. You'll have more time to impress people like Oscar

Goulding. Is he bringing his mare, by the way?"

"End of March, and you may as well start by sending him confirmation. After your exhibition, we'll make an appointment with William Richmond, my accountant, to make it official…if you haven't changed your mind by then."

"I won't be changing my mind," she assured him. "It's what I really want. I'm determined to make it work."

"Make sure you do, then. Now go finish that painting. Cass is coming tomorrow to do a flu injection and she'll want to pick it up."

DESPITE A LATE night perfecting her painting, Ellie woke up at five-thirty the next morning, eyes groggy. A vague fluttering sensation took away her breath. Something had happened, something special. Sleep cleared itself from her head and as clarity dawned, the fluttering increased. She had changed her whole life, that's what, and she didn't have a single doubt about it.

Jumping eagerly out of bed, she pulled on her jeans, grabbed a bright T-shirt and splashed water on her face before racing downstairs. The painting stopped her in her tracks as she burst into the kitchen. Her dad must have brought it out from the office last night. He'd propped it against the wall on the counter, ready for Cass to collect.

She stared at it critically. It was always the same when she finished a painting. While working on it, she was transported to another place. Seeing it again next day was like looking at it for the first time.

The mare's beautiful, gentle face stared out from the canvas, huge dark eyes holding her entranced. They seemed to express something much deeper than paint on canvas. Touching her hand to her heart, Ellie felt the mare's emotion. That was another thing she strived for in her paintings—a kind of truth that stemmed from her own emotion, her own bond with her subject.

"It's beautiful," her dad said from behind her. "A masterpiece. Have you always been able to paint like this? Why did I never notice it when you were growing up?"

"I haven't," Ellie admitted. "I mean, I've always loved to paint but this emotional thing is new. I've really only found it since I decided to come home. I feel this…connection with the creatures I'm painting. It's as if I can feel what they're feeling."

"Well, Jake Munro is going to be blown away."

CASS ARRIVED AT NINE, just after they'd finished doing the horses. To Ellie's embarrassment, her dad made a big show of unveiling the painting.

"Careful," she cried as he went to pull off the cover. "The paint isn't even dry yet."

When he finally revealed it, Cass just stood and stared, hand raised to her mouth as she smothered a gasp of amazement.

"It's…" She turned to look at Ellie, tears flooding her dark eyes. "It's Carlotta."

Ellie smiled. "She *is* the one you wanted me to paint."

"No, I mean, it really is Carlotta, *her* expression. More than her expression. It's as if she's revealing all her feelings. They have such a bond, Jake and Carlotta. She helped him through a pretty bad time."

Ellie nodded. "I know. It's none of my business, but I have heard something about it. I believe you helped him, too."

Cass's eyes lit up. "I just fell in love with him," she said.

Cass's simple statement was a revelation to Ellie. She had never felt like that about Matt, she realized now. Their relationship had been based on mutual attraction and convenience...

But you did about Andy.

A sudden shaft of a bittersweet pain took Ellie's breath away. They *had* felt like that once, hadn't they? So what had gone wrong? Had he just been too young to accept the enormity of their love, or was he the kind of person who would always be fickle?

Perhaps she'd been too hasty in her judgment of him...too unforgiving. Noting a puzzled expression on Cass's face, she forced a bright smile.

"I'm glad you like it."

"Like it!" Cass exclaimed, giving her a hug. "It's a masterpiece!"

Her dad smiled. "That's what I said."

CHAPTER TEN

ELLIE STARED INTO the tall mirror that graced the wall of her childhood bedroom. It felt strange, sometimes, being here again. She half expected her mum's face to appear around the door, warning her that she'd be late for school if she didn't hurry. Ellie could finally think about her mother with a smile, though. Here at Hope Farm, she felt her mum's presence all around and reveled in the memories she had once tried to keep hidden.

She and her dad had been up early that morning to get the horses and yard work done before they set off for Jake and Cass's wedding. Anticipation spiraled inside her. It had been a long time since she'd had the opportunity to dress up for a whole day out, especially for such a happy occasion. Cass Truman was obviously head over heels in love, and although Ellie hadn't met Jake yet, her dad assured her that he was just as smitten. There was a little boy, too, Jake's seven-year-old son, Robbie. He was going to be a ring bearer and Cass already adored him, so they'd be a family right from the start.

Ellie took her new blue dress from the wardrobe and hung it on the door, even more pleased with it now than when she'd first seen it in the store. She touched the soft, bright material with a sigh, removing the blue suede shoes from their box. Would she manage to wear them all day? she wondered, glancing at the height of the heels with a knot in her stomach before turning back to the mirror. Her short blond curls, damp from the shower, had turned into corkscrews that she hoped would settle down into their usual, undisciplined style. She used to spend ages with a hair dryer and mousse, but now she allowed her hair to dry naturally. It suited her, she thought, the cap of bubbling curls that framed her face, making her blue eyes stand out. No wonder Andy hadn't recognized her immediately, though. When they were dating, her hair had been almost to her waist. Turning her head this way and that, she decided she was glad she looked different now. She was no longer that heartbroken teenager; she was a woman who had faced pain and loss and had come out the other side with a successful career and big hopes for the future. Finally, she knew what she wanted from life.

As if to strengthen that newfound confidence, she chose a bright red lipstick, brushed bronzing powder across her face and accentuated her eyes with a kohl pencil before standing back to survey the result. "If he could see me now," she murmured, imagining Andy's wide grin.

Her dad's voice floated up the stairs.

"Are you ready, lass?"

Ellie blinked. She really needed to stop thinking about someone she was totally over and would hopefully never meet again.

"Five minutes," she called, reaching for her dress and slipping it over her head. Some simple, delicate crystal jewelry and the amazing shoes finished off her outfit, then she picked up her bag and made her way downstairs, feeling gloriously elegant for what felt like the first time in her life.

"You look grand, lass," her dad said, and she smiled, noting his smart new shirt and tie.

"You look pretty grand yourself," she said.

THE VILLAGE CHURCH looked pretty in the sun-shine, its bells ringing out in the clear, fragrant air. Ellie linked her arm through her father's, and they walked through the huge old doors into the somber calm of the ancient building. With a sense of awe, she felt the presence of those who had gathered here for so many years gone by.

Flowers graced the ends of every pew, and two beautiful arrangements stood on either side of the step where the young couple would stand. Their heavy, intoxicating scent brought a sudden rush of memories and tears sprang to Ellie's eyes as she remembered another day, a day when the flowers had been not for a beginning but for a sad and painful end.

"Are you watching, Mum?" she whispered.

Her father squeezed her arm. "Of course she is. I often come here and talk to her, you know. She'd want you to be happy today, though. Not sad."

Ellie smiled. "And I am happy, happier than I've been in a very long time."

As they slid into a pew halfway down the aisle, she saw the two men at the front of the church who must be Jake Munro and his best man, Donald Darwen—Jake's vet and best friend, according to her dad. The vet, middle-aged, sandy-haired and average height, was overshadowed by Jake's tall, broad figure, until he turned around and caught her father's eye. He lifted his hand in greeting and the smile that lit up his pale face revealed the kindness in his heart.

"He looks nice," Ellie said.

"Heart of gold," her dad responded.

Jake Munro also acknowledged them, but his ruggedly handsome face appeared set and drawn.

"And *he* looks terrified," Ellie added.

Her dad nodded. "I'm not surprised. He hates the limelight. He'll be fine as soon as Cass comes in, though. I've never seen a couple more in love."

That's what *she* wanted, Ellie realized, a love that shone so brightly it couldn't be mistaken for anything else. No second bests and no making do with less.

THE WEDDING MARCH'S resounding tones burst out into the peace of the church and everyone stood, peering discreetly around for a glimpse of the bride. She appeared almost silently, gliding down the aisle clutching her father's arm. Her shimmering white dress, close fitting and beautifully decorated with embroidered flowers, trailed behind her. A little boy followed proudly, holding out a satin cushion. Cass glanced back at him and Ellie held back her tears as she saw the expression on the young woman's face. The boy—Robbie, she assumed—gave Cass a little smile and she smiled back, her whole face glowing with love. And then Jake and Cass's eyes met and Ellie's tears spilled over.

Her dad handed her a tissue and she gulped. What was happening to her? Where had all this newfound emotion come from?

The rest of the ceremony passed in a haze. Ellie sang each hymn with real feeling and listened to each magical word of the service, even more convinced that she would never settle for second best.

"I now pronounce you man and wife," the vicar declared, and suddenly Cass was in her new husband's arms. Then she reached back for Robbie, drawing the little boy close to include him in their embrace.

Ellie reached for her tissue again, glowing

inside and feeling very privileged to have witnessed such joy.

When they followed the happy couple outside into the sunshine, the churchyard was abuzz with guests congratulating them with a kiss for Cass and a firm handshake for Jake and Robbie, who stood up proudly beside his dad. Chattering voices and laughter filled the air. Bob Nelson was in his element, introducing his daughter to everyone, many of whom she vaguely remembered.

A blonde woman came toward them, holding the hands of two small, cherubic children. Her pleasant face was pink and flustered.

"Jenny," Bob said. "Have you met my daughter? She's an artist, you know. Ellie, this is Jenny Darwen, the long-suffering wife of Donald, the best man."

Ellie smiled. "You seem to have your hands full."

"Lovely to meet you," Jenny said. "And yes, I do have my hands pretty full. They're good kids, but they're so excited today that I don't know what to do with them."

"I'm sure they'll settle down when they get to the reception," Ellie offered.

Jenny rolled her eyes. "I hope so, or I'll

have to take them outside." Suddenly, giggling merrily, the little girl made a bid for freedom. "Evie! Come back here right now," Jenny called.

Evie just ran faster. Jenny flashed Ellie and her dad an apologetic smile and dashed off after her daughter.

"Sorry," Jenny said, looking back. "Would you mind keeping an eye on Ollie for me?"

The little boy stood beside Ellie, his bottom lip quivering.

"Hello," she said, crouching down to his height. "What's your name?"

He stared at her solemnly, big brown eyes assessing her, then he smiled. "I'm Ollie," he said. "Where's my mum?"

"Your mum's coming back right now. Look, there she is."

Jenny was waving at Ollie with one hand while clutching Evie's arm with the other.

"Thanks," she said breathlessly. "You'll have to come around for coffee one day so that we can really get to know each other. How does Thursday morning sound?"

Ellie began to respond, but Jenny was gazing straight past her, waving excitedly to someone in the crowd.

"The new vet at Low Fell is over there," she explained. "I really must introduce you. He's crazy about helping wild animals, but Don's always complaining that treating them isn't very lucrative. Not that he really minds—he just loves winding people up."

"Hello, Ells," came a voice from behind her.

Ellie froze. She should have guessed that he might be here.

"Oh, you already know each other," Jenny said in surprise.

Ellie stood slowly, one hand still resting on Ollie's small shoulder as she turned to face Andy Montgomery.

He stared at her, a long, deliberate stare, taking in her bright blue dress and suede shoes.

"From high school," she said, setting her jaw while trying to quiet the pounding in her chest. How was it possible for him to still have this effect on her? Old habits, she supposed.

"You see, Ellie? I told you he was working at the vets'," her dad said. Then he turned to Jenny. "They used to date when they were still in school."

"Only briefly," Ellie said.

"That's not the way I remember it." Andy grinned, holding her gaze.

Jenny raised her eyebrows. "Well, there's a surprise."

Ellie shrugged. "Not really. Andy lived around here then, and we went out a few times. No big deal."

Andy pushed back his floppy blond bangs, disappointment clouding his eyes. For one crazy moment, Ellie felt a prickle of guilt. No matter what she thought of him now, she and Andy had once been in love.

"Well, to be honest, it was a big deal at the time," she said reluctantly. "But you know what these teenage romances are like."

"Mine was with Don." Jenny smiled. "And it ended up the biggest 'deal' of my life. Come to think of it, I'd better go and find him. We need to get to the reception soon. They're doing most of the photographs at the hotel because they have such beautiful gardens."

She hurried off, a child in each hand, leaving Bob, Ellie and Andy standing together awkwardly. Or was it just she who felt awkward? Ellie wondered as her dad and Andy chatted happily.

"You never told me where the fox painting idea came from," her dad said. "Perhaps you can get more ideas from Andy here. Wild animals make good subjects."

Ellie sighed. "That's true, but I don't think Andy will want me tagging along."

"You're welcome anytime," Andy told her, stepping closer.

"Thanks," said Ellie. "Now come on, Dad, we need to get to the reception."

"See you there, then." Andy held her eyes for a moment. She looked away with a rush of anger. He had no right to come blundering back into the life again, just like the Labrador puppy she always used to compare him to. Then again, what did she care if an ex-boyfriend had turned up on her doorstep? She'd finally straightened her life out. Her romance with Andy was a very long time ago, and as far as she was concerned, she'd had a lucky escape.

"You'll have to take him up on that. It's a great opportunity," her dad said.

"Come on," she urged, pulling on his arm. "Or we won't get a parking space."

CHAPTER ELEVEN

To Ellie's relief, she and her dad weren't placed near Andy at the reception. He was seated with the other vets and staff from Low Fell, while they were at a large round table on the other side of the room. Her dad introduced her to the elderly farmer next to him.

"Have you met my daughter, Ray?" he asked. "Ellie, meet Raymond Johnston, breeder of Fell ponies and, in particular, one really nice three-year-old Fell-cross-Thoroughbred filly."

"Pleased to meet you." Ellie smiled. "Perhaps you should bring your filly to one of our stallions."

He nodded, looking thoughtful. "Can't say it hasn't crossed my mind…if the price was right, of course. I do admire the gray."

"Good choice," Ellie agreed. "I'm sure we can work something out."

"Or better still, how about selling me the

filly and then I can put her to Blue?" her dad suggested.

Ray Johnston stroked his chin. "Can't say that hasn't crossed my mind, either. I could do with cutting down on some stock before winter sets in. In fact, while we're on the subject, you don't know anyone who wants to buy some sheep, do you? Nice fit, young Fell sheep, they are. There's only me and the missus here to lamb them, now that our John's gone to work in town, and we're not as young as we used to be, are we, love?"

Appearing startled at being included in the conversation, Ray's wife nodded. "Not as young as we used to be," she echoed before going back to nibbling her bread roll.

When the two men moved on to talking about sheep, Ellie found her attention wandering. She looked around the beautifully decorated room, picking out faces from her childhood, children grown into men and women, some who looked almost the same and some who bore only the vaguest resemblance to who they once were. Billy Valentine, a boy who'd had a crush on her when she was thirteen, raised his hand and she smiled, waving back, remembering with a flash of nostalgia for how simple things had been back then. Or had they? Perhaps they were only simple in retrospect.

At the head table, the bride and groom, sitting with immediate family and close friends, were already raising their champagne glasses. To Ellie's surprise, however, Cass stood up first, instead of the best man. Donald got to his feet after her, tapping the stem of his glass with a spoon.

"Welcome, everyone, and thank you for coming," he said. "Before we start with the speeches, Mrs. Munro here has something to say."

Cass's face turned a delicate shade of pink and there was a wobble in her voice as she started to speak. Jake laced his fingers through hers, showing his support, and they exchanged a glance that brought a tear to the eyes of half the gathered guests.

"Before I hand you over to Donald, who will start the speeches, I would like to gift my new husband with his present from me. I wanted everyone to see it, so if you'll all look to the wall behind us…"

A hush fell over the guests as Donald made a show of drawing back a room divider. The breath caught in Ellie's throat as everyone gasped. There was Carlotta, staring out at them, Ellie's painting displayed for all to see.

"And the incredibly talented artist," Cass continued, motioning Ellie to stand up, "is Ellie Nelson, Bob's daughter, from Hope Farm. So if you have any commissions, let her know."

Ellie blushed, and her dad urged her to stand, too, but fortunately everyone's attention had turned to Jake, who was staring, speechless, at the image of his favorite horse. He raised his glass, wrapping his other arm around Cass's shoulders and drawing her close, pressing his lips to the top of her head.

"To the most beautiful painting ever, to my beautiful wife, to my amazing son and last but not least, to an amazing artist. Now let's get on with the speeches."

Out of the corner of her eye, Ellie saw Andy across the room, raising his glass to her in a private salute. For an endless moment, his warm brown eyes seemed to delve into her soul and she was a teenager in love again.

She tore her gaze away.

"Lovely painting, lass," Ray Johnston remarked, and his wife smiled eagerly in agreement as Bob refilled all their glasses.

"To my daughter," he proudly announced, and Ellie took a large gulp, starting to breathe again.

The rest of the speeches had everyone either crying or in hysterics, especially Donald Darwen's. His huge character seemed to take over the room. When Robbie stood up to say something, his courage and determination brought a hush over the gathered guests. He made a short speech that was obviously all his own work, about how happy he was to have Cass in their family. When he sat down, she reached over to give him a hug, tears rolling unchecked down her face.

"You'd never believe now what a lonely, traumatized little chap he was when his mum brought him back here last year," Bob said. "Cass told me all about him once when she came to the farm on a call. But everything seems to have out worked for him."

"Like us then, eh, Dad? Things are finally working out for us…aren't they?"

He raised his glass, chinking it against hers. "I certainly hope so, love."

With a sudden rush of nostalgia, Ellie realized what a huge step she'd taken in such a short time. She'd ditched both her fiancé and her lifestyle on a whim, given up five years of a life she'd fought hard to forge for herself. Had she been right? She was so sure of it now, but what about the future? Tomorrow, she was going back to stay in her flat for the last time, to attend the exhibition. It felt like a huge and final leap, but then again, this new life wasn't really new at all. She was coming back home, that's all, to where she really belonged.

ELLIE AND HER DAD had planned to leave the reception fairly early. Jed, a young man who worked part-time at Hope Farm, would drop by to feed the horses, but the chickens needed to be locked up and poor Shadow had been alone in the house all day. Bob offered to go home, do the chores and then come back for her.

"No," Ellie insisted. "I've really enjoyed the wedding, but I've got a long day tomorrow."

Bob nodded. "Of course, you're going to Manchester for the exhibition. Are you nervous about it?"

Was she nervous?

"Not really. I mean, it's hardly an exhibition, is it? I only have three paintings there, after all."

"It's a start, though, a chance to get your paintings seen. Everyone will fall in love with them, I'm sure."

Ellie clasped her hands tightly together. "Oh, I hope so."

"Well, don't you go getting too successful." Bob laughed. "Or you might end up wanting to go back to city life."

She shook her head emphatically. "No, that will never happen. Anyway, all my material is here. I'd have no inspiration in the city."

"Speaking of inspiration, you'll have to take Andy Montgomery up on his offer."

"We'll see," responded Ellie.

While it would be a great opportunity to get up close with wildlife, the idea of spending time with her ex made her feel weird. She was scared, too, she supposed. Scared of the feelings that still simmered uncontrollably whenever he was around. In her head she knew those feelings were just an echo of the past, but her heart didn't always feel so sure.

They decided to stay at the reception at least until the dancing started. It was led off by Jake and Cass, who twirled around the dance floor in a euphoric haze.

That's going to be me one day, Ellie decided. *No second bests and no making do.*

"I'll just go over to talk to Ray about his mare and then we'll get off, shall we?" suggested her dad. "Unless you want to stay a bit longer."

Ellie yawned, stretching out her arms.

"No, I'm ready when you are."

After her dad left, she sat watching the couples on the dance floor gyrating to a '60s classic.

"Would you care for a dance?"

She looked up with a start to see Andy's tall shape looming over her.

Her response was instant. "No...thanks. Not to this."

He smiled, moving away immediately, and her stomach lurched. How could fate have brought them both back here? She was just going to have to put their past in the past where it belonged, put aside all her crazy feelings and stop being so melodramatic about them. He was nothing to her now, and hadn't been for years. Nothing but a stupid teenage crush that had ended in hurt pride and left a load of painful memories.

The loud beat of the music faded. Ellie scanned the room for her dad, and suddenly there was Andy again, standing so close that she could feel the heat of him.

"I've changed the song just for you," he said. "So now will you dance with me?"

Mesmerized by the moment and unsure of what to say, Ellie stood automatically, allowing him to propel her onto the dance floor, which was clearing rapidly. When Tamara's soulful voice flooded the atmosphere with "Love Me True," she froze.

"This song," the DJ announced, "has been requested by Andy the vet on Robbie Munro's behalf. And don't worry, he says, he did run it past Jake and Cass first. It is also, he tells me, for some wonderful memories."

Ellie tried to turn and run. She was desperate to be anywhere but here in the semi-darkness with long-buried emotions churning inside her.

Andy took a firm hold of her elbow.

"Stop overreacting and just go with the flow," he insisted. "For old times' sake."

"Fine, but that's *all* this is," hissed Ellie, reluctantly allowing him to draw her into his arms.

"I wouldn't expect anything else," he told her, grinning.

To Ellie's relief, the dance floor soon filled up again, allowing them to blend in with all the other couples. She tried to focus on something else, to stave off the emotion the song seemed to be bringing out in everyone. Jake and Cass floated by, staring into each other's eyes with such intensity that suddenly, ridiculously, she wanted to cry. Without thinking, she pressed her face briefly against Andy's shoulder to stay her tears. In response, he pressed his lips against her hair, and for an endless moment she let them stay there, breathing in the scent of his aftershave and drowning in the warmth of his body against hers.

What was she doing? Twisting from his arms, she abandoned him on the dance floor and rushed back to her table.

Thankfully, her dad had returned. "Come on," she said. "Time for us to go."

Bob raised his eyebrows, smothering a

smile. "Are you sure? It looked like you were enjoying yourself to me."

"I've never been more *sure* of anything," Ellie snapped, then she felt guilty for her outburst. "Sorry Dad, I'm just tired."

"That's all right, love. You go and get your coat and I'll bring the pickup around to the front."

As she headed for the cloakroom, Ellie thought she heard Andy's voice calling her name. Increasing her pace, she stared straight ahead, ignoring him. As far as she was concerned, fickle Andy Montgomery was definitely best avoided.

It was almost dark by the time they pulled up in the yard at Hope Farm.

"I'll go and put the chickens in and look at the horses while you let Shadow out and put the kettle on," Bob said. "You can't exactly do much else in that outfit, anyway."

The young black sheepdog was ecstatic to see her. He circled around her legs, clinging close as if afraid of being abandoned again.

"It's all right, boy." Ellie grabbed hold of his ruff and rubbed the backs of his ears.

"We're home now. Come on, you need to go outside."

When Shadow refused to leave her, staring into her eyes appealingly and wriggling his whole body, she kicked off her blue suede heels, pulled on her boots and grabbed a jacket from the peg by the door.

"Okay." She sighed. "You win. If you won't go out on your own, then I'll just have to come with you."

Once outside in the velvety darkness, Shadow seemed to find his confidence. He raced off in the direction of the stables, leaving Ellie behind. She hesitated, wondering whether or not to turn back. Her dad would never forgive her if she lost Shadow, though, she realized, so she trudged on after him across the yard.

It was just as the moon slipped out from behind a silver-edged cloud that she saw it, moving stealthily along the fence line just up ahead. A big fox, ears pricked and tongue lolling from the side of its mouth. It stopped for a moment, staring right into her eyes with no sign of fear. The moon rose higher and she gasped, reveling in the moment. This was no terrified captive; this was a real wild animal in its own environment…and this, she understood, trying to capture the image in her mind, was the inspiration for her next painting.

Her dad's loud shout cut through the darkness, and with one last, leisurely look at her, lips drawn back into what seemed like a smile, the fox moved on silently, disappearing into the hedge at the end of the yard just as Shadow appeared, haphazardly following his scent with no real idea of what he was supposed to do.

Her dad appeared right behind him.

"That fox has been sniffing around the chicken coop, I know it. The hens are all jittery, and Shadow can smell it. It's a good thing we got back when we did. I should have asked Jed to lock them in."

Ellie stored the fox's arrogant expression in her memory and hurried toward him, deciding not to mention her encounter.

"There's no harm done, though," she reminded her dad. "We'll just have to make sure their door is locked a bit sooner."

"Well, I'll be out with my gun if it doesn't watch out."

Somehow, Ellie thought with a hidden smile, she had a feeling he'd be wasting his time.

CHAPTER TWELVE

THE SUN WAS already high in the sky when Ellie finally threw her bag and other gear into the back seat of her small car. She'd intended to set off early, but when she'd looked out of her window before seven and seen her dad wheeling a loaded barrow across the yard, she'd decided to give him a hand before she left. He'd told her not to bother, of course, but as usual these days, she'd ignored him. She needed to breathe in the aroma of horses and delight in their quiet company one more time before heading off to the soulless city.

Anyway, she'd come to realize, if she listened to everything her dad said, she'd still be living in Manchester. She knew, with no shadow of a doubt, that that was definitely not what he wanted, and she loved being home again. In fact, she'd slipped back into country life much more easily than she'd expected, remembering long-forgotten skills almost without noticing it. Meeting up with Andy again had been a blow she could have done without; he'd pushed her totally out of her comfort zone when he'd persuaded her to dance with him the night before. Of course, she could have said no, but that would just have been showing him he could still get to her.

She shivered, recalling the feel of his arms around her, his lips against her hair... Slamming the car door, she headed back toward the house. He *did* still get to her, if she was honest with herself. She'd never let him know that, and he only riled her up because of all the painful memories. He'd let her down, when she'd trusted him; she'd never forget that. Although it wasn't really his fault that he hadn't been there for her through all the bad stuff with her mother, it had felt like it at the time. She'd felt so alone after the diagnosis. Trying to appear strong for her mum and a million miles away from her dad, who was struggling to cope, she turned all her anger onto Andy. Survived on it in a way, she realized now.

"There's coffee for you here," her dad called from the back door. "And I've made some toast. It's time you were off, you know."

Ellie smiled at him, thinking what a long way they'd come in such a short time.

"Thanks, Dad. I'll be there in a minute."

When she walked into the kitchen, Shadow leaped up at her, white-tipped tail waving madly, and she gave him a hug, wondering why she'd stayed away from home for so long.

IT WASN'T UNTIL she was halfway to Manchester that Ellie allowed herself to think about Andy again. It had been a shock, seeing him at the wedding, although if she'd thought about it beforehand, she would have guessed that he might be there. He'd mentioned that he was working in Little Dale when he'd treated the fox cub. It hadn't occurred to her that Andy was friends Cass and Jake, but of course he must be, since he and Cass were colleagues at Low Fell.

She was genuinely glad that he'd finally become a vet. When they were young, she remembered, he'd always had his heart set on the profession. He'd gone away to start his training the year before they broke up, but back then, his ambition had been to specialize in racehorses. When had his interest in wild animals taken over? she wondered. It was a labor of love with little monetary reward. All the work he did at Cravendale was purely voluntary.

However caring and generous Andy was in his treatment of animals, though, he was totally unreliable when it came to the women in his life, and she'd had to learn that the hard way. All the things he used to say to her, the plans they used to make, had all been just words. If he'd really loved her as he once claimed, then he could never have left her like he did.

It didn't matter, though, she decided; Andy wasn't going to affect her life wherever he happened to be because she wasn't going to let him. Ellie tried to concentrate on what was truly important: the exhibition and the painting she was looking forward to working on. The big fox had looked her straight in the eyes with a bold and fearless expression on its handsome face, and she intended to re-create that on canvas.

For the next week, she was going to be busy every day at the art gallery, hopefully talking to visitors who were interested in her work, but in the evenings, she planned to paint. This piece would be a total contrast to the one of the young fox they'd set free; it would show a very different facet of the wild fox's nature. The cub's expression revealed a raw, feral ferocity, behind which lurked fear and the vulnerability of youth, whereas the big fox appeared bold as brass, cunning and clever and very sure of itself. Capturing that demeanor was a challenge that she could hardly wait to take on.

ANDY WAS HEADING back to Low Fell after a 6:00 a.m. call to a difficult calving, after which he'd gone straight to see to a horse that had been trapped in wire.

As he drove, his thoughts kept slipping back to the night before…and Ellie. Seeing her at the wedding, even though he'd expected to, had been a shock to his system. She'd looked so lovely in that blue dress. He'd assumed she would expect to see him there—he worked with Cass, after all—but the surprise on her face had been sweet. And when they'd danced and he'd held her in his arms after all this time, it had felt like traveling back in time.

She wasn't the same Ellie he'd known back then, though; *she* had been a naive teenager with a mass of blonde hair. This Ellie was chic and sure of herself, a successful painter with a dazzling career ahead of her. He was career driven, too, and he knew exactly how it felt to have a passion that overtook all else. But the feelings that bounced around in his heart whenever he was around her were for the Ellie he used to know. His head was telling him to keep well clear.

Pulling up to an intersection, he hesitated before swinging his truck to the left and putting the clinic on speaker.

"Hi Andy, what's up?" the receptionist asked.

"I'm on my way to Cravendale. Call if you need me. I'll be back for the evening clinic."

"Will do! See you later."

As the phone clicked off, Andy heaved a sigh. Working with the creatures at Cravendale always managed to clear his head and make him aware of where his priorities lay. There wasn't a woman born who'd put up with the time he dedicated to his work. He'd learned that much, at least.

IT WAS COLD in the apartment when Ellie finally arrived, cold and damp and unwelcoming. She dumped her stuff and turned up the heat, closing curtains and flicking on lights until the place finally emanated a vague sense of hominess again. That done, Ellie collapsed on a chair, her thoughts returning to Hope Farm. The horses and chickens would all be settled for the night by now, and her dad would probably be eating his supper. No doubt it would be a tin of tomato soup, which had been his staple diet before she started to cook for him. The kitchen cupboards were full of the stuff.

Thinking about supper made her realize just how hungry she was, and she rummaged in the freezer, producing a pathetic-looking microwave dinner, which she defrosted while wishing she'd stopped for groceries.

HALF AN HOUR LATER, having consumed her unpalatable meal along with a strong black coffee, her fingers were tingling to start work on her painting of the fox. She'd decided to have an early night tonight, so that she was fresh and bright in the morning, but by seven-thirty she'd set up her easel and unpacked her paints. Staring at the blank canvas, a piece of charcoal clutched between her fingers, she had a sudden rush of apprehension. What if she couldn't re-create the fox's expression? What if her memory had failed her? It was hardly a scene she could set up again. Closing her eyes for a moment, she took a deep breath, visualizing, and then she swept the charcoal across the canvas with a few sure strokes before reaching for her paints and losing herself in time.

To her surprise, the next time Ellie checked the clock, it was eleven-thirty. She put down her brush and stared at the painting with a glow of satisfaction. It was a long way from finished, but the expression was there, the exact expression she had seen the night before. Excitement flickered. She had named her first fox painting *Freedom*; this one was going to be *Bold as Brass*.

ELLIE HADN'T EXPECTED to be able to sleep, but she woke to sunshine pouring in through her window. For a moment, she thought she was at Hope Farm, and then heavy disappointment settled in as she remembered she was back in Manchester. Today, though…anticipation flared as she thought of her exhibition. Hopefully, today would give her career a boost. Smiling to herself, she jumped out of bed. She'd be happy if just a few people took an interest in her work, but Mel had assured her there would be a lot of visitors, since the main exhibitor was quite a well-known artist. Ellie hoped people coming to see his work might stop and take a look at her three paintings.

Coffee was her first priority. She padded into her tiny kitchen to put on the kettle, then walked with trepidation into the space she called her studio. Seeing a painting the day after she started it was always a revelation. Sometimes, after studying her work the next day, she would start a piece all over again.

The fox started out at her with a cunning smile, and she smiled back. Somehow, she had managed to retain its expression in her mind for long enough to do it justice. Suddenly, she couldn't wait to keep working on it. She didn't have to be at the gallery until after lunch. Glancing at her watch, fingers tingling, she reached for her painting shirt.

THE GALLERY DOORS opened at one-thirty, and Mel had asked Ellie to be there by one. She hurried along the pavement at one-twenty-five, wobbling precariously on her high-heeled shoes as she tried to run, inwardly admonishing herself for getting too carried away with her painting to notice the time... again.

The glare that Mel gave her when she appeared, pink-faced, in the entrance hall, made her squirm.

"Sorry," she mumbled.

The gallery owner raised perfectly penciled brows.

"Well, at least you're here now, I suppose."

A tall man stood next to her, trying to hide a smile behind his hand. He was in his midthirties, with a face that she'd describe as pretty, rather than handsome.

"This is Paul," Mel said, introducing the man. "And if your work ever does half as well as his has, then we'll both be happy."

"I'm sure it will," he remarked graciously, reaching out to shake Ellie's hand.

"Thanks," she responded, feeling awkward.

"Paul is going through a very difficult breakup," Mel said. "His current work reflects that. It's deep and dark."

"Do you think my current work reflects

what I'm going through?" Ellie couldn't resist asking.

Mel didn't respond right away.

"Well, I don't really know what you are going through, but…"

"Can I have a stab at that?" Paul cut in.

Ellie nodded. "Sure."

"Mel has shown me some photographs of your earlier work, and it seems to me that although your paintings have always had a contemporary slant, making them quite fresh and unusual, the three you're exhibiting today show a new depth of emotion that moves the soul. Are you also going through a difficult relationship period, by any chance?"

Taken aback by his direct approach, Ellie stumbled on her words. "No…I mean, not really. More a circumstance change, I guess. A good one, though. And I'm sorry about your girlfriend. Or is she your fiancée?"

"Fiancé, actually." Paul sighed just as the first visitors entered the gallery. "But *she*—" he raised his hands theatrically "—is actually a he."

Before Ellie could respond, Mel ushered them both forward to make introductions.

"Paul Devlin is our main exhibitor, and

this is Ellie Nelson, our newest artist. She'll take you through into the gallery to get a glass of wine, and then you can view the exhibition at your leisure. Both artists will be on hand to answer any questions you may have."

The well-dressed, middle-aged couple were only too happy to follow Mel's suggestions and happily accepted their sparkling wine before heading off to look at Paul's paintings. Ellie felt a prickle of alarm. What if no one took any interest in her work? What if it was the first and the last time she would ever get to be in a real exhibition?

By midafternoon, however, Ellie relaxed. She had no need to worry—plenty of patrons were keen to ask about her paintings.

She had just finished explaining what she was trying to achieve to two young art students when she heard a high-pitched voice right behind her.

"Oh, I just love foxes!"

She swung around to see a deeply tanned, extremely slim woman clinging excitedly to the arm of an elderly man. They were both staring avidly at Ellie's painting of the fox cub.

"It just looks so...so real," cried the woman.

"Such character," the man said, smiling adoringly at her. "Perhaps I should see if I can buy it for you, my darling."

When he looked across at Ellie, though, there was a steely glint in his eye.

"You are the artist, I believe?"

Ellie coughed nervously. "Yes...yes, I am."

"So what will you take for it?"

"I'm sorry," she told him. "But it isn't for sale."

The man frowned. "But what is the point of an exhibition if we can't buy the paintings?"

"It's about getting new artists seen," Mel answered, and Ellie glanced back in relief to see the gallery owner standing right behind her, a charming smile lighting up her face. "Ellie here will have several new paintings for sale in her next exhibition, and seeing these three will hopefully encourage people to come along."

The frown faded from the man's pale eyes and he nodded.

"Perhaps you could tell the artist here what

you might like to see," he suggested to his wide-eyed companion.

"Oh, yes," she squealed. "And then you might buy it for me?"

"Of course, my darling. If it's any good, then I'll buy it for you."

The woman squeezed her hands tightly together and Ellie smiled.

"Can I choose?" the woman asked.

"Choose?" Ellie echoed.

"Yes, choose the animal I'd like in my painting.

"Rabbits," she continued excitedly. "Or perhaps a deer with its baby."

"It's called a fawn, dear," the man interrupted, and Ellie felt an unexpected rush of sympathy for her.

"I'll do my very best for you...?"

The woman held out a small, beautifully manicured hand. "Dora," she said. "Call me Dora. And this is Dorian."

Why wasn't she surprised? thought Ellie, taking her hand and pumping it up and down. Dora and Dorian; their names fit them perfectly.

"I guess I'll see you at my next show, then," she said, smiling with genuine delight.

"And don't forget my painting," called Dora as Dennis led her away. "I'll have rabbits if that's okay?"

"Rabbits it is." Ellie smiled, raising her hand.

BY SATURDAY, ELLIE felt jaded. She'd replaced her high heels with something more comfortable that she'd rushed out and bought from the store at the end of the street, soft cream leather with a much smaller heel, but her feet still ached from hours of standing. She'd had a lot of feedback about her work, which was rewarding, and Mel had told everyone she would have a larger show in a few months, with paintings on sale. Ellie was apprehensive about that. After all, the inspiration for paintings of wild animals in real situations wasn't easy to come by.

Paul Devlin's exhibition had been very successful, with several sales, and he and Ellie had become friends in the past few days. He'd given her lots of advice on how to try and make a career out of her art, but had also warned her how hard a road it could be.

"You can be dropped like *that* if the public loses interest in your work," he told her. "Once you're *really* famous, you can ask for thousands for your paintings. The trouble is, often that doesn't happen until you're dead."

She'd laughed at the woeful expression on his face, pointing out that he was already doing well and he was a long way from dying. "It doesn't feel that way!" he'd cried, and that was when he'd given her the whole story about Harry, his ex. His advice had given her a whole new determination to be successful with her art.

The gallery opened earlier than usual on Saturdays, at ten in the morning, and didn't close until the evening. Midafternoon found Ellie in the small kitchen making drinks and taking the weight off her feet when Mel came looking for her.

"There's a man who says he'd like to meet the artist," she said. "You really must make an effort to mingle a bit more, Ellie. Success is about marketing, you know. Not just producing the work."

Irritated, Ellie hurried out to meet the person who, according to Mel, was interested in *Freedom*. He had his back to her when she approached, and she'd seen so many people over the last week that she didn't recognize him until he turned around.

"Matt!" she said, embarrassed by the rush of blood that flooded her face.

"Pleased to see me?" he asked, a quizzical expression in his gray eyes.

She reached up to give him an awkward peck on the cheek. "Yes, of course I'm pleased to see you. Although I must admit you were the last person I expected. I didn't think you did exhibitions."

"I don't, but I saw the sign outside and thought I'd come and surprise you."

"Well, you certainly did that."

The laughter in his eyes faded. "How is life in the country, anyway? Missing the city yet?"

She didn't hesitate. "No…I'll never miss city life."

"And what about me? Do you miss me?" Sadness took first place and her sense of unease faded.

"I miss what we had," she said honestly. "We were great together…"

"For a while," he finished for her. "And maybe we could be again if you ever get over this country thing."

She shook her head. "I won't. But if you

ever need me, Matt, just call, no matter what it is."

He smiled sadly, letting go of her hands.

"It's nice to know you still care…a little. And who knows, maybe I'll have to hold you to that needing thing one day."

"That's fine," she told him sincerely. "We may not be together anymore, but you're right, I do still care about you."

"Maybe I should have been a bit quicker to marry you when I had the chance." He laughed.

She shook her head slowly. "I don't think you really mean that."

The devil-may-care expression she knew so well came into his eyes.

"You could be right. Anyway, you know where I am if you need me."

"Thanks," Ellie said. "And thanks for coming."

He turned to walk away, raising his hand in farewell, and strode off into the street without a backward glance. It was only after he'd left the building that she realized he hadn't looked at any of the paintings.

That night, Ellie finally finished her painting of the fox. She was proud of the way she'd caught his exact expression and it suddenly occurred to her that she'd seen that arrogant expression somewhere else…but where?

It came to her that night, as she snuggled down in bed restlessly trying to sleep. It was Matt's expression. He had that same worldly wise look in his eyes, that same arrogant self-assurance. Bold as brass.

ANDY RAN HIS hand down the chestnut three-year-old's foreleg and stood up, turning to look at Bob Nelson. The older man pulled off his cap, clenching it in his hands.

"Well? Is it a tendon?"

Andy smiled, pushing back his hair from his forehead. "I'm happy to tell you that I'm pretty sure it's just a knock. Cold-hose it for a day or two, and give him some gentle exercise. He'll be good as new in no time."

Relief flooded Bob's features, followed by a pleased smile.

"That's great news. I've sold him, you see, for a good price. If it was a tendon, well…"

"The sale would be off?"

"Not only that," Bob said. "His career as a possible eventer would be a nonstarter, and we need these homebred youngsters to prove themselves. Hope Farm depends on it."

"By 'we' I presume you mean you and Ellie?"

"Well…yes, of course. She's back to stay, and I want her to be a real part of the business."

"But are you sure she'll stay in the country? She was engaged, after all. Perhaps she'll end up going back to her fiancé."

Bob frowned. "Of course she'll stay," he said. "She wants to be back here, and she needs to be in the country to get inspiration for her paintings. If you think about it, she has two reasons to stay around. There's been a lot of heartache at Hope Farm over the years, but now it's time to move on."

"And I suppose you think I was a part of that heartache."

"Your timing was bad, that's true…"

"I did come back to see her you know, after we broke up. I wanted to tell her that I'd made a mistake."

The ghost of a smile flitted across Bob's weather-worn face.

"And her mum sent you away with a flea in your ear, I believe."

"Made me promise to stay away from her, or else. She said that Ellie was over me and that trying to win her back was a big mistake."

"She was strong-willed, my wife—fought right up until the end. Guarded Ellie like a lioness." Suddenly, his face fell and he turned away. "Couldn't fight off the damned cancer, though."

Not wanting to upset Bob further, Andy changed the subject.

"Cass told me that Ellie has an exhibition of her paintings. Are you going to see it?

"I'm too old to be driving into Manchester," Bob replied. "And I'm sure she wouldn't really want me there."

"Course she would. I could drive you."

"You'd do that?"

Andy shrugged. "I have to stop by Cravendale anyway, and that's almost halfway there, so why not? To be honest…I wouldn't mind seeing the show, either."

"You're on, then," Bob said, reaching out to shake on it."

"You'll have to come to the animal sanctuary with me, though."

"That's fine. I'd love to see it. Ellie's told me so much about Paula and Cravendale."

"Right," announced Andy with a broad grin. "I'll be back for you after lunch."

"I'll be ready," said Bob.

SUNDAY DAWNED CLEAR and bright. Ellie decided to wear her blue dress and matching shoes for the final day of the exhibition, and to Mel's surprise, she arrived at the gallery early, in time to have a leisurely coffee and a chat with her and Paul before the doors opened. All in all, they agreed, the week had been very successful.

The morning was disappointingly quiet, with only a handful of people stopping in, but by lunchtime, the place was buzzing.

"Sunday is usually the best day," Mel informed her. "People like to drop by around midday, or just after.

To Ellie's delight, she received her first real commission. Bert Granger, a stocky man with work-worn hands, wanted a painting of his wife's horse as a surprise for her birthday. She gave him one of the cards she'd had printed for the show and he said he'd call her in a few weeks. He wanted her to visit his house in Cheshire to look at the horse and take some photos, preferably when the sun was shining and the trees were in their full autumn glory.

Commissions that perfectly portrayed the subject matter, like painted photographs, weren't what Ellie really wanted to be known for, but as Paul pointed out, she had to start somewhere, and at least it would make her some money. She was still discussing the details with him when another visitor walked through the door, causing her whole world to momentarily tilt on its axis.

CHAPTER THIRTEEN

As HE STEPPED into the gallery, Andy caught the tail end of Ellie's conversation with a tall, attentive man.

"I just hope I can finish enough good paintings to be meet the demands of a bigger exhibition," she was saying. "At least I'm back home in the country now, so there should be more opportunity to find good subjects."

Andy and Bob strode toward them across the gleaming, hardwood gallery floor. He noted her shocked expression when she saw them approaching. Was she pleased to see him, he wondered, or was her expression one of dismay? He tried not to think about what he'd overheard. *At least I'm back home in the country now, so there should be more opportunity to find good subjects.* He was glad her dad hadn't heard her say that.

"Hello, Andy," she said. "I never expected to see you here."

When Bob moved out from behind him, Ellie's mouth fell open. "Andy called in at the stud to see the three-year-old this morning—" Bob began.

"Is she okay?" Ellie asked before he could finish.

"Oh, yes. It was just a knock, thankfully, not a strained tendon after all. Anyway, I mentioned the exhibition, and as he was already traveling in this direction to go to Cravendale, he offered to give me a ride. I was intending to come on my own, but to be honest, it's a bit tough for me, nowadays, driving in the city."

"Well, thanks Andy," Ellie said politely before giving her dad a quick hug. "I'm so glad you came, Dad…and you, too, Andy. Come on, I'll give you the grand tour. It won't take long to look at my three paintings, though, I'm afraid."

Bob Nelson appeared awkward and out of place as they studied Paul Devlin's distinctive works of art, but when he saw Ellie's paintings displayed on the wall, his lined face took on a proud glow.

"Clever lass, isn't she?" he remarked to Andy, who nodded enthusiastically.

"She was always drawing and painting when we were at school," he said. "Those paintings were nothing like this though. These are…"

"Awesome?" someone suggested from behind them.

They all spun around. It was the man Ellie had been chatting with then they'd arrived.

"Ellie doesn't realize how good she is," he continued.

"Dad, Andy, meet Paul," Ellie said. "This is his exhibition, and as you can see, he does tend to exaggerate."

"Pleased to meet you," Bob said, shaking his hand. "And it's no exaggeration. My daughter *is* awesome."

As the other two walked on ahead, Andy took hold of Ellie's arm, holding her back.

"Ex-fiancé, is he?" he murmured.

She pulled away from him.

"No, actually. And what does that have to do with you, anyway?"

"Just looking out for you."

"You lost your right to look out for me six years ago."

"Sorry." He took hold of her arm again, but gentler this time. "Truce?"

"Truce," she responded, smiling up at him.

"I'll make a pact with you," he suggested.

"Okay."

"We're going to be bumping into each other quite a lot now, so let's start fresh…as friends who've just met."

"Friends who've just met," she agreed, nodding. "*Just* friends, though. Don't go thinking there might be more to it."

"Just friends," he promised. "Now what else do you have to show me? I need to get your dad back in time to do the horses."

HEADING BACK TO her flat just as darkness crept in, Ellie reflected on her conversation with Andy. She'd promised herself that she'd never forget…or forgive. So did this mean she'd already gone back on that promise? The answer came at once.

No, she would never forgive him, or forget what he'd done to her. He'd asked her if they could start fresh, as friends, and she'd agreed, but she was determined to keep him at arm's length. As far as she was concerned, they'd be more like acquaintances than friends. Otherwise, he was quite capable of wriggling right back under her skin.

CHAPTER FOURTEEN

ELLIE WAS SAD to say goodbye to Paul.

"Come and visit me at Hope Farm anytime," she told him.

"I might just hold you to that." He smiled, kissing her on the cheek. "And be careful with that handsome ex of yours."

"How did you know?"

He raised his eyebrows. "It's the eyes, darling. It's all in the eyes."

"Well, you don't need to worry on that front—we were over years ago. Anyway, it's you who needs to be careful around your ex."

Paul stared at his long, thin hands. "Actually, he called me earlier…"

"And?" she prompted.

"Let's just say that he might not be my *ex* for much longer."

"Don't you go jumping in feetfirst, though," she warned. "Think it through first."

Paul rolled his eyes. "And seeing the way your friend, Andy, looked at you, you might do well to heed your own advice."

"Rubbish," she responded, heart quickening. "We're just friends."

BACK AT THE APARTMENT a couple of hours later, Ellie felt a sudden niggle of apprehension. Tomorrow she would be handing her keys back to the landlord and officially starting a whole new phase of her life. She was looking forward to it, but saying goodbye to the place that had been her haven for the past six years was a bigger wrench than she'd expected.

She'd arranged for a mover to load up her possessions and transport them to Hope Farm tomorrow, along with her paintings from the gallery. It felt like the end of an era. She'd painted all her early pictures in this flat, and it was where she'd finally settled on her new style. Suddenly she smiled, stretching her arms above her head. What was she thinking? This wasn't the end of an era, it was a new beginning.

ELLIE'S NEW LIFE began two days later, when her alarm clock rang at six-thirty. Her dad was in the kitchen when she staggered in, still rubbing her eyes.

"I told you that you'd pay for that celebratory drink," he remarked, smiling. "Here's a strong coffee to get you started."

Gratefully sipping from her mug, Ellie tried to pull herself together.

"I only had one glass, Dad. I think I'm just recovering from all the stress of the past week." She groaned. "I was totally wiped out by Sunday. By the way, thanks for coming, even if you did bring Andy."

"He brought me, remember? Anyway, it's time for the two of you to move on. You were just kids when you went out together."

"I guess," she reluctantly agreed. "Water under the bridge, I suppose. And fortunately he knows where he is with me now."

"You sure of that?" Her dad smiled.

Finishing her coffee, Ellie got up from her chair and pulled on her jacket.

"Definitely," she declared. "Now let's go do some work."

Ellie had been helping out with the horses for the past few weeks, but today felt different. Today she wasn't just helping out; she was working at the job she'd signed up for.

It felt good, she decided, shaking out clean straw in the stable of her dad's hack, Flora. The big gray mare nuzzled her shoulder as if in gratitude before going across to her hay net.

When she went into Dennis's stable, the bay stallion was not so obliging. His ears were flat against his head and he lunged at her, teeth bared.

"What's wrong with you, big guy?" she said, ignoring his efforts to frighten her while slipping on his head collar, then she tied him up short and began scratching his neck with the fingers of one hand.

Gradually, Dennis began to relax, twisting his head and trying to groom her in return. She let him nibble her shoulder while keeping an eye on his ears.

"There now, you see," she said. "I told you we were going to be friends."

Into the Blue was a very different prospect. He sniffed her cautiously when she put on his head collar, as if realizing that she was now a permanent fixture to be assessed and slotted into the pecking order.

"Do I remind you of my mum, boy?" she murmured in his ear, remembering how ecstatic they'd all been on the day that he was foaled. Her mother had been so proud of their future sire. She hadn't known then that she'd be gone so soon.

Pressing her face against his silken neck, she allowed herself to remember. The memories washed over her like a tidal wave. Suddenly, it felt as if it happened just yesterday... that awful, unbelievable moment when they digested the results of the scan; the brief, unbearable few weeks of waiting and hoping and finally accepting the inevitable; the day of her death and the guilt Ellie felt when a sense of release had flooded in with her grief.

Flinging her arms around the stallion's neck, her tears soaking his coat, Ellie finally faced up to the memories she'd spent so long trying to avoid. The big horse stood motionless, almost as if understanding her grief.

For the rest of the morning, Ellie got on with grooming, sweeping, emptying loaded wheelbarrows and all the other daily tasks of the stable yard, content to keep to herself. At lunchtime, she made thick beef sandwiches on automatic, as if in a trance. She couldn't hide the puffiness around her eyes, but when her dad came into the kitchen he respected her privacy, quietly brewing a pot of tea and pulling his chair up to the table.

Ellie broke the silence first.

"Sorry I'm a bit…you know. It's just…"

He shook his gray head. "No, don't apologize. I know what you're going through. It took a long time for me to come to terms with it, too."

"How long?"

"To be honest…" He hesitated. "To be honest, it wasn't really until after you came home. Before that, I think I was living on bitterness and anger."

Suddenly she brightened.

"So that was why you never made me very welcome."

"You ignored me in the end, though, didn't you?"

"Best thing I ever did."

For a moment, an image of Andy's face slid into Ellie's mind. Was he one of the reasons she'd waited so long to really face up to her memories? She couldn't deny he was part of them, too. The pain of his rejection had been like a physical thing, and Ellie had felt as if he was somehow to blame for the agony of her mother's death soon after. Well, she was over him now, really over him, so much so that she'd even agreed to try being friends with him.

"I feel better for letting it all out," she said.

Her dad nodded. "It's the only way. Oh, and there's something I wanted to ask you."

"Ask away."

"You know that painting…"

"Which one?"

"The newest one, of the fox."

Guessing what was coming next, Ellie smiled.

"When did you see him?" he went on. "You must have seen him because you couldn't imagine an expression like that."

"Do you like it?" she asked.

He nodded. "I like the truth of it."

"But not the fox itself."

"The fox is just getting on with his life. I don't like what he does, but I admire his boldness."

"It was the night before I went to the exhibition," she admitted. "The night you threatened to go and get your gun."

"And you saw him just swaggering by like that?"

"He stopped and looked at me…laughed at me almost."

"Then I guess I'd better keep those chickens well locked in at night because I can't see myself ever shooting him now."

"No chance." Ellie laughed. "He's far too clever for you."

"By the way," her dad said, changing the subject. "I thought I'd better warn you—Andy's coming by later this afternoon, to give both stallions their annual flu shots."

"Doesn't bother me," Ellie said. "I don't know why it has to be him, though. He isn't even a proper horse vet… I mean, he's a qualified vet, obviously, but he isn't specialized or anything."

"He does specialize. In wild animals, though, not horses."

Ellie shrugged. "Well I suppose someone has to."

Her dad took hold of her arm. "Don't be too hard on him, love. You were just a couple of kids back then. He's a good vet, according to Jake, and he takes some convincing. The thing is, though…"

Ellie sighed, waiting for her dad to continue.

"I have to go into town this afternoon, so you'll have to deal with him."

Her response was instant. "And I will, don't worry. We've agreed to be friends."

"Well there you go, then," said her dad. "I'll leave the vaccination certificates out for him to sign."

After her dad left, Ellie brought in two broodmares from the field and brushed them off, then she went into the barn to fill some hay nets. Despite assuring her dad that Andy meant nothing to her anymore, to her own annoyance she found herself listening with a fluttering apprehension for the sound of Andy's well-used truck.

Half an hour passed, and as she emptied some bags of horse mix into the feed bins, she began to relax. Perhaps he wasn't coming today after all—not that she cared, of course. Their history made her uneasy, that was all...uneasy and irritable.

When she did finally hear a vehicle pulling into the yard its engine was quiet, like that of a small car, so it definitely wasn't Andy. She hurried out into the sunshine expecting to see Donald or maybe Cass. The brightness outside after the dusty gloom of the barn surprised her, and she shaded her eyes with her hand.

"Hello," said a very young voice. "I saw you at the wedding."

"Robbie?"

The little boy was heading toward her, holding the leash of a small brown-and-white dog that squirmed in delight as she approached.

He grinned at her.

"My dad and Cass have gone to Ireland to buy horses. I'm staying with granddad but Andy's looking after me today. I just saw a cow having its calf—Andy helped to pull it out!"

"Well that's great, Robbie," Ellie said, returning his smile. "Where is Andy, anyway?"

"Right behind you." At the sound of his deep voice, Ellie froze, taking a backward step before turning around.

"Ah," she said. "You're here. I'll just go and get the vaccination certificates."

"For someone who has just agreed to be friends, that is not a very friendly greeting," he remarked dryly.

Anger flared inside her, then died away. This was just stupid, and she had to get over it. Turning back toward him again, she shrugged, returning the warm smile in his soft brown eyes with a rueful grin.

"Sorry, I'll try again… Good morning, Andy. Does Robbie here often accompany you on your calls?"

He ruffled the little boy's dark hair. "Not as often as I'd like. I'm just looking after him because Bill has a meeting or something."

Ellie crouched down to stroke the little dog that was straining on the end of his leash.

"He's gorgeous," she said to Robbie. "Is he yours?"

"He's called Chocolate," Robbie informed her proudly. "Choco for short. Cass gave him to me when he was just a pup. She rescued him, you know."

"Well, he's a very lucky dog to have you as his master. We can go and introduce him to Shadow, if you like. He's my dad's dog and he loves to play."

"Any chance of a coffee while we watch them bond?" Andy asked with a twinkle in his eye, and she nodded, believing for the first time that this friendship thing might actually work out.

"I can make that happen. Still no sugar?"

"Does a leopard change its spots?"

"Meaning that you haven't, I suppose," she said, smiling. "Strong with no sugar it is then, just as you used to like it. So nothing has changed about you, then?"

"No," he said. "I'm still the same guy you used to be in love with."

"Used to *think* I was in love with," she added.

The same thought came back to her as they watched Choco and Shadow frolic around the kitchen. She and Andy may have called a truce, but he was right: leopards couldn't change their spots. Andy might be charming and good company, but she knew deep down that he was totally unreliable and untrustworthy when it came to women.

He's said it himself. *I'm still the same guy.* She'd do well to remember that.

ROBBIE WAS LOOKING at her appealingly, trying to get her attention.

"Can Choco come back and play with Shadow again another day?" he asked.

"Anytime you like," Ellie told him, smiling at Andy without reservation for the first time in six years. "Tell Cass and Jake that they can leave him here with me whenever they want."

Andy nodded. "Thanks, they'll be grateful for that, I'm sure. Cass is still working full-time and Jake and Bill are often busy with their building company as well as the horses."

Ellie shrugged, putting her empty cup into the sink.

"Well, I'm always here. If I'm not helping Dad, then I'll only be painting."

"Any new pieces in the pipeline?" he asked with genuine interest.

Suddenly she was very keen for him to see her painting of the fox. Andy, of all people, would tell her if it really worked, since wild animals were his passion.

"Come with me and I'll show you," she said.

Her dad had hung the painting in the sitting room above the fireplace, opposite the one of the young fox being set free. Two images of the same species, but both so different.

Andy stopped in his tracks, staring at the painting.

Ellie hopped from foot to foot like a little girl. "Do you like it?" she asked eagerly.

When he didn't respond, her heart fell.

"Well...what do you think?" she repeated.

"It's incredible," he said eventually. "A wild, bold, full-grown fox, comfortable in its own environment. Not many people get to see that."

"I think I'm beginning to get your obsession with wild animals," she told him. "I mean, they're all around us, living their everyday lives right under our noses, and half the time we don't even realize they're there."

"You really should come with me sometime when I get a call from Cravendale," he said. "It could be anything from an injured deer to a bat caught in a fence—if it needs veterinary attention, I'll be on the case. Deer are quite common because they often get hit by cars. Sometimes, they'll jump over a hedge and land right in the road. Anyway, if you come with me, you might get some really good material for your paintings."

"Thanks," said Ellie. The thought of being in close proximity with Andy unnerved her a little, but the opportunity to get new ideas for her paintings was just too good to pass up. Excitement flickered inside her. "I might hold you to that," she said. "I do paint domestic animals as well, but I'm really drawn to the wild. All animals are so natural, though— they don't pretend."

She looked up briefly, meeting Andy's eyes.

"Unlike people you mean," he said. "And by people, I guess you mean me. I know I've made mistakes, Ellie, and I'll probably make some more before I'm done. One thing I don't do, though, is pretend."

"No…" she responded. "I guess you don't. Just forget I said anything and thank you for offering to take me on call with you."

"Okay, well my offer still stands. I'll let you know next time Cravendale calls me out to help with an injured wild animal."

"I'd like that," she said. "It doesn't have to be just a wild animal, though… Any creature that needs help will give me inspiration. I have to start some new work soon. Mel wants me to meet with her at the gallery this week, to talk about possibly planning a bigger exhibition."

"Well, give me your phone number and I'll call when I'm going somewhere interesting," he told her. "As long as you don't get in the way…"

"I won't," promised Ellie.

It wasn't until after Andy and Robbie had left that Ellie realized what she'd gotten herself into, and yet she couldn't regret it. Even the professional and sympathetic way Andy had calmly dealt with the two stallions was an inspiration. He had an amazing way with animals—there was no doubt in her mind about that. If he did invite her to go with him on one of his calls, then it would be a really good opportunity for her to get new ideas. She was already thinking of Robbie with the dogs, the excitement on his face and the sheer joy displayed by Shadow and Choco; that would make a fantastic painting if she got it right.

As HE DROVE AWAY from Hope Farm with Robbie and Choco in the back, Andy remembered the conversation he'd overheard at the gallery.

He'd been so moved by her painting of the fox that he'd impulsively asked her if she'd like to go on call with him. Now he wasn't so sure. He needed total concentration when he was out in the field, and perhaps she'd be a liability. And was it wise of him to spend more

time in her company? A part of him yearned
to get closer to her, but what he'd heard made
it seem as if her reasons for coming home
might be based just as much on finding material for her work as in helping her dad out.

What if she got bored with the country?
What if she just gathered up all her ideas and
then decided to go back to her fiancé in Man-
chester? Surely not… He'd gazed at her, his
Ellie. She would always feel like *his* Ellie.
Could she have really changed that much?

CHAPTER FIFTEEN

ELLIE DROVE SLOWLY along the lane, taking in the beauty of autumn. She'd been hoping that Andy might have called before she set off for the city; that way, she'd have had more sketches and photos to show Mel what she was going to be working on. The painting of Robbie with the two dogs was coming along well, but she would have liked some ideas for wild animal paintings.

Her phone rang just as she was about to leave the country lanes behind and merge onto the highway. Glad of the excuse, she pulled over, checking the name that popped up: Andy. Typical. Just like him to call now, when it was too late.

"Hello," she said.

"I saw your dad in the village and he told me you'd set off for Manchester. I was going to ask you if you wanted to come on call with me tomorrow, but I guess I missed you."

"Like you told me, Andy, a leopard can't change its spots." She cringed. "Sorry, that wasn't fair."

She could almost see him smile. "Doesn't matter, it just shows me that missing our outing bugs you."

"And that's a good thing, why?"

"How long are you going to be away?" he asked, ignoring her jibe.

"I'm staying over tonight, and I'll be back later on tomorrow."

"Ah," he responded eagerly. "Now there's a thought. Why don't you drop by Cravendale on your way home? Paula has asked me to come in. Someone brought in a buzzard with a damaged wing. She doesn't think it's broken, but it needs checking out. She also has a young deer that she wants me to look at. I think it's injured its leg. So what do you think? I said I'd be there around four-thirty tomorrow afternoon."

Despite the fact that all her warning systems were telling her to stay far away from him, Ellie couldn't help a flicker of excitement at the prospect. After all, it was probably better than going on call with him at home, since they wouldn't be traveling together, and she'd already agreed to that.

"Okay," she said. "I'll see you there."

"It's a date," he responded.

"My days of dating you are long gone, Andy Montgomery. Just remember that."

"Can't even take a joke anymore, eh, Ells?"

As she clicked off her phone, she realized she was smiling. He always had been able to make her smile; fortunately, she told herself, there was no harm in that.

THE CITY LOOKED more appealing today, Ellie thought as she drove through the suburbs. The trees that lined the side of the road were turning a glorious shade of red and gold, and the late summer sun cast its glow on the gray buildings, giving them a kind of warmth. On impulse, she dialed Steph, her former coworker and only real friend in the city. Apart from Paul, of course, but she'd only just met him.

Steph's larger-than-life voice burst into her ears.

"Ellie! How are you? I thought you'd dropped off the face of the earth."

Ellie laughed. "No, not quite. Still just living in the country."

"What, you're not bored with all those animals and farmers yet?"

"Definitely not, but I am in town for the rest of today and most of tomorrow. I thought we could catch up."

"Why didn't you tell me you were coming? Where are you staying?"

"Well, I let my flat go, so I thought I'd just book into a hotel. It's only one night"

"Oh, no you won't," cried Steph. "You can stay with me. I'm at work later, but you can come along with me to Dom's and catch up with everyone."

"If you're sure…" Ellie said, wishing she'd waited until tomorrow to call her friend, then realizing with a surge of guilt how anti-social that was. "I'd love to."

"Great! I'm home now, so come straight over. In fact, I've been inside all day doing absolutely nothing… I'll put the kettle on."

WHEN STEPH MET her with open arms and a huge smile, Ellie felt another rush of guilt. In throwing herself into her new life, she'd turned her back on her friends and acquaintances, and there were more than just Steph. There was Ollie, for instance, the chef at Dominoes, and Louisa, a Filipino waitress she'd taken under her wing when she first came to work there. It would be nice to catch up with them all, Ellie decided, and she'd keep in touch with them, too, on Facebook if nothing else. She hadn't even logged in to a social media site since she'd made the decision to leave Manchester for good.

"We've got a new bartender," Steph said, collapsing down beside her on the sofa. When her long black hair fell, as it always did, across her face, she pushed it aside in annoyance. "I swear I'm going to get it cut into a really short, chic style."

"No, you're not," said Ellie. "You wouldn't be you without that mass of jet-black hair. Anyway, come on—elaborate. Obviously you're interested in this bartender."

Steph's pale cheeks turned pink. "It's gone a bit further than that."

"So he's your...boyfriend?"

She shook her head. "Well, not *quite* as far as that, but...well, we've been out to dinner. Oh, by the way, I don't have to start until seven-thirty tonight, so I've arranged for us to have a takeout at five-thirty...and an old friend of yours is delivering it."

"Don't tell me," Ellie groaned. "Pizza? As I remember, you used to live on pizza. And who's delivering it?"

Steph laughed. "No, it's not pizza. Or at least, I doubt it. And as to the identity of the delivery person...you'll just have to wait and see."

As Ellie got ready to go out, a bubble of excitement grew in her stomach. She was loving her country life, and she wouldn't change it for the world, but she'd forgotten what fun it was to get all dolled up for an evening out. She was looking forward to catching up with everyone. Glancing across at Steph, who was sharing the mirror, she smiled.

"Thanks for asking me to stay," she said.

Bright red lipstick held aloft, Steph smiled back. "We're friends, aren't we? I couldn't let you stay in a hotel."

"You'll have to come and visit me in the country," Ellie offered spontaneously.

Steph rolled her black-rimmed, pale blue eyes.

"Well, I don't know about that. I mean... what would we *do*?"

"Oh, all kinds of things." Ellie smiled. "Muck out the horses, brush them off, feed the chickens and collect the eggs… Do you want me to go on?"

"Maybe one day," Steph agreed, "when I'm about sixty."

Ellie zipped shut her makeup bag, surveying herself in the mirror.

"I might just hold you to that," she said.

The doorbell rang while Steph was scurrying around the room, picking up clutter and straightening cushions.

"I take it our delivery friend is a man," Ellie remarked, heading for the door.

She froze when she saw the tall figure outside holding up two paper bags.

"Matt! What are you doing here?" she eventually managed.

"Dinner," he announced, stepping inside. "Now, where do you want these?"

"On the table," Steph said from behind them. "Ellie, meet Matt. I believe you two know each other?" She giggled.

"We used to," he said, sweeping his gaze over Ellie's pink face. "Quite well, actually."

She smiled awkwardly and stood back to let him past.

"I just happened to bump into Matt," Steph explained. "And when I told him you were here, he just had to see you. The food's on him, by the way, so it's not pizza for once."

"It's Chinese," Matt said. "Your favorite, Ellie."

"I'll go and get bowls and chopsticks," Steph said. "We may as well do this right. Just put it on the table over there, Matt, and then crack open that bottle of wine—"

"Just a minute," Ellie interrupted. "How could you have bumped into Matt when you haven't been out all day?"

"Ah…about that." Steph giggled again. "I kinda bumped into him on my phone. You guys were so good together, Ellie. You should give it another shot."

"And we still are good together. Just not quite in the same zone, that's all," Ellie explained.

"Well maybe it's time you *zoned* back in, then. This country living thing of yours is all very nice, but it's not, well, permanent, is it?"

"Oh, Steph…" Ellie felt a huge rush of regret. These people had been her world for a long time, and it was weird to be back in her old life. She looked at Matt, meeting his gray eyes with affection, and when he reached out to cover her hand with his beautifully manicured, smooth brown fingers, she was sharply reminded of Andy's broad, callused palms. Matt was like a cougar, whereas Andy resembled a half-grown Labrador. She smiled at the thought.

"What you have to understand is that, for me, the country came first. It's where I was brought up, and for now at least, it's where my future lies."

Matt's grip tightened, his tone serious for once. "Have you found someone else already, then?"

She shook her head firmly. "No, of course not."

Dropping her hand, he stood up, all traces of sensitivity gone. "So, you'll still be there if I need you, then?" he said, his mouth curving into a smile. "We made a promise, remember, that day at the gallery, and maybe one day I'll have to hold you to it."

"Of course I will," she agreed, smiling back. "A promise is a promise, although you've never really needed me up to now."

"That, my darling girl, is because I don't really need anyone. And don't take any notice of Steph. She just misses her friend, that's all."

"Yes Matt," Steph butted in. "And you miss your fiancée, too. You just won't admit it."

"I'm missing the girl I used to know," he said. "But I'm loving my freedom. Now let's eat before we get even more maudlin."

To ELLIE'S SURPRISE, Matt did not accompany them to Dominoes.

"More pressing business," he told them, hailing a cab.

"No change there, then." Ellie smiled.

Reaching down, he gave her a quick hug, planting a kiss on her cheek.

"A leopard can't change its spots," he said.

Why did that saying keep cropping up? she wondered. Was it a sign?

"Come on, Ells,'" Steph said, gabbing her arm. "I'm going to be late for work."

The evening passed in a haze of good cheer, and Ellie was overwhelmed by all the people who came over to wish her good luck. She realized she'd been a bit selfish in leaving everyone without a proper goodbye. Promising to keep in touch with them all, she left Dominoes at eleven-thirty to walk back to Steph's apartment. Steph didn't finish work until at least one in the morning, sometimes even later, and she always took a cab, despite the short distance. For safety's sake, she said.

Expecting to fall asleep immediately, Ellie was surprised to find herself still wide-awake a few hours later. The same thoughts kept circling inside her head every time she started to doze off. Matt's charming, empty smile and Andy's larger-than-life approach to everything around him. Two men who had colored her life, both so very different and both so wrong for her. Somewhere, she told herself, there was someone new, someone she could really love. For just a moment, as her eyes finally drooped shut, she allowed herself to feel once again what it had been like to love Andy Montgomery. Her heart ached with the memory; his lips against her ear, murmuring secrets, the smell of his skin, the way her pulse raced when he walked into a room, the sheer intensity of emotion when their eyes met across the distance. And the way they used to talk for hours on the phone and never remember what they'd said. That was the kind of all-consuming love she wanted from the man she was going to spend the rest of her life with, and if she couldn't find it? Well, then she'd spend her life alone…with her animals and her painting.

Ellie woke to the sound of Steph snoring. She pulled the pillow over her head, pushing away her thoughts of Andy, annoyed with herself for letting the memories back in. Eventually, she crawled out of bed to make a cup of tea, then curled up under her duvet again as the town hall clock struck five.

"Come on, lazy bones."

Steph's loud voice in her ear made Ellie's head hurt.

"I thought you country bumpkins were early risers."

Ellie put her hands across her ears.

"We are usually," she croaked. "It's just…" She sat up, stretching her arms above her head. "Okay, I'm awake now."

Steph held out a steaming mug. "Here," she said. "This will help you wake up."

Ellie's nose twitched as she smelled the coffee, and she took it gratefully, blinking the sleep out of her eyes.

"Sorry, for some reason I just couldn't seem to sleep last night."

"Was that because you met a certain someone again?" Steph asked, eyebrows raised in amusement.

"No, definitely not, so don't start any getting ideas. Matt and I are still friends, but that is all it's ever likely to be."

She could tell by Steph's expression that her friend didn't believe her.

"Honestly," Ellie insisted. "Anyway, how come you're up so early?"

Steph glanced at her watch. "It's not that early. But I'm on the lunchtime shift today."

"And I'm supposed to be at the gallery by eleven-thirty," Ellie groaned, jumping out of bed.

HALF AN HOUR LATER, casually dressed in skinny jeans and a bright blue sweater that accentuated her eyes, Ellie said her goodbyes to Steph and drove into the city center. It had been wonderful to meet up with her old friends again, she thought, while carefully negotiating a busy intersection. But it definitely wasn't good to be back in the city, she decided, slamming on her brakes to miss a car that had just pushed in front of her. By the time she'd managed to find a parking space near the gallery, she was ready to scream.

When she eventually hurried in through the door, Mel was waiting impatiently, glancing in customary fashion at her expensive-looking watch.

Ellie grimaced. "Sorry...am I late? The traffic was horrendous."

"You could have tried setting off earlier, of course," Mel suggested. "Anyway, you're here now, so let's get down to business. The reason I wanted to see you was because we've had some interest in your work since the exhibition and inquiries about when you might have paintings for sale. I need to know how soon you can have enough paintings ready for a bigger exhibition."

"I've already completed two and a half," said Ellie, trying to contain her excitement. "I've taken photographs of them to show you, and I have lots of ideas for others. There are some sketches in this file here..."

Rifling through a bulging file Ellie pulled out half a dozen sheets of paper and spread them across the table.

"They're only ideas at this stage, but I'd love to hear your thoughts."

AFTER THEY'D DISCUSSED Ellie's paintings and ideas, Mel suggested spring for the new exhibition.

"That should give you plenty of time to get enough new material to make it worth both our whiles," she said. "Do you think you can deliver?"

"Oh, yes," Ellie said, cheeks glowing with excitement. "I'll make sure that I do."

Mel held out her hand. "I'll schedule you in then."

Ellie clasped her smooth fingers. "Thanks for the opportunity."

Mel smiled graciously, removing her hand from Ellie's exuberant grip.

"Without artists, I wouldn't have a gallery," she said. "So I suppose I should be thanking you."

After her successful meeting with Mel, Ellie decided to treat herself to coffee and a light lunch. She bounced down the street to her favorite café on a cloud of elation, and settled down at a corner table to nibble on a tuna sandwich and process the morning's events. Building up to a second exhibition felt even more nerve-racking than the first. Last time, she'd had no expectations, and neither had anyone else. But now...now she had to produce work that was up to her previous standard. And what if ideas failed her? What if she couldn't find the inspiration that had driven her before? She'd been dreading getting involved with Andy's work, but looking forward to it at the same time. Now she realized that it might be her only hope, for where else would she find the material she needed? She was building a reputation for her emotional and often unusual animal paintings—glimpses, said Mel, into the mind of animals. Andy dealt with emotional animals every day, and as long as she kept their relationship totally businesslike, then she didn't need to be afraid of the past coming back to bite her. Suddenly, she was looking forward to her visit to Cravendale... for all the right reasons.

CHAPTER SIXTEEN

ELLIE SET OFF back to Little Dale midafternoon, having killed some time shopping. She'd decided to try and get to Cravendale before Andy; that way, she could spend some time with Paula and maybe get some ideas by just observing the animals at the sanctuary.

The sign, still desperately needing a lick of paint, loomed out from the trees, reminding her that she'd planned to paint a new one as a gift. She'd start it as soon as she got home, she promised herself as she parked up next to an elderly 4X4—not Andy's, she was relieved to see.

She saw Paula as soon as she walked into the low stone building, breathing in the aromas of hay and feed and animals.

"Hello," she said.

Paula spun around, clutching a baby rabbit in her arms.

"Ellie!" she cried. "How lovely to see you. Where's Andy?"

Ellie frowned. "Andy?"

Paula nodded. "He said four-thirty, but I'm glad you're here early."

Ellie shook her head. "I'm not with Andy. I mean, I said I'd meet him here, but…"

"Of course." Paula placed the rabbit gently back into its soft hay bed. "I just can't help thinking what a good couple you'd make."

Ellie smiled. "Well, we're not, or ever likely to be. If you remember, though, I used to think you and he were a couple."

Paula nodded. "I can think of worse people to be married to."

"But he's so fickle," Ellie blurted. "You'd never be able to trust him."

Paula let out a hoot of laughter. "Are you sure we're talking about the same Andy?" she asked. "No one as selfless as he is with animals could ever be disloyal to the woman in his life. It follows through, you know."

"Well, I don't like to burst your bubble," Ellie said, suddenly feeling awkward. "But I happen to have information to the contrary."

"Look," Paula patted her on the shoulder, obviously unimpressed by her observation. "Let's just agree to differ, shall we? Come on, I'll show you the young badger that came in last week."

Pushing their conversation to the back of her mind, Ellie followed eagerly, already seeing the badger as her next work of art.

BY THE TIME Andy arrived, the two women had almost forgotten that he was coming. Ellie was sitting on a bale of hay with a stray pup in her arms, its hind leg, in a cast, protruding to one side as it smothered her in sloppy wet kisses.

"Why don't you take it home with you?" Andy said.

Both women glanced around, startled by his sudden appearance. For one long moment, his eyes held Ellie's and a flicker of warmth kindled the spark between them.

"We already have a dog," she said, turning her attention back to the pup.

"Shadow's your dad's dog," Andy insisted, walking toward them. "Hopeless here desperately needs some love—and, I'm guessing, so do you, if you're honest with yourself."

Ellie curbed a rush of anger. What right did he have to comment on the love in her life…or lack of it?

"You can't call a dog Hopeless," she responded, ignoring his remark. "You'd be squashing his self-confidence before he's even found any."

"He calls it Hopeless because a couple of weeks ago, I told him it was a hopeless case and asked him to come and put the pup to sleep," cut in Paula. "He was almost starved to death. He had obviously been trapped somewhere, and apart from the broken leg, he was covered in cuts and bruises. I thought it was the kindest thing to do, but Andy insisted that we try and save him."

"And look at him now," murmured Ellie, cradling the moth-eaten collie cross in her arms. "You should call him Hope, not Hopeless."

"There you are, you see, you've called *it* he and given *him* a name," said Andy. "Hope, after your stud, so you'll have to keep him now."

She allowed her eyes to linger on his face, that oh-so-familiar, friendly face that had haunted her dreams for so long…or were they nightmares?

"I guess you're right," she agreed, excitement defusing the anger that was building up inside her. "I will have to keep him. But it won't be because I lack love in my life."

"Good," announced Paula, drawing their attention. "That means I won't have to phone up all the other animal shelters trying to find him a home. Now, come on Andy, let's go and do what you're here for. The buzzard's wing is a real mess, but I don't think it's broken, but the poor young doe is a different matter. She looks as if she could have been injured by a car, and she's so terrified."

Andy reached down to pick up his bag, asking questions about his prospective patients as he and Paula walked back out into the yard. Ellie placed the pup carefully back into his bed before following them. He stared up at her with concern in his large brown eyes, slowly wagging his bedraggled tail.

"Don't worry, Hope," she said, reaching down to cradle his puppy face between her palms. "I'll be back soon…and then I'm taking you home."

The red-and-white pup whined softly, placing his front paws on the fence that surrounded his enclosure, his nose just visible over the top, as if he already knew that she was to be his new mistress.

By comparison, the buzzard sat in the farthest corner of its roomy aviary, perched upon a tree branch. It looked at them with fierce, unblinking yellow eyes.

"Any ideas on how to catch it?" asked Andy.

Paula laughed, pulling on a pair of large gloves and reaching for a pole with a net on the end.

"It's tricky," she said. "But I didn't want to put him in too small an enclosure. The poor thing's terrified enough as it is."

"Isn't it a bit dangerous?" Ellie asked, trying to imprint the buzzard's expression into her memory.

Paula nodded. "It's big and powerful and fierce and very scared, so yes…of course it's dangerous—or at least it could be, if we didn't know what we were doing."

"The real answer must be no, then," Andy interrupted. "Because Paula knows exactly what she's doing."

Opening the aviary door, Paula smiled. "Well, I've dealt with a good few birds of prey in my time," she said, walking slowly and quietly toward the huge bird.

When she eventually acted, her movement

was so smooth that it took the buzzard totally by surprise. It flapped as the net descended over it, but in just an instant, Paula was holding it firmly while Andy carefully removed the net. Its huge curved beak made little impression on her heavy gloves as Andy set about examining its injured wing.

"Did you notice how easily it could flap it?" Paula remarked. "That's what made me think it might not be broken."

Ellie reached for her sketch pad, drawing quickly. The bird's huge talons and cruel beak, its fierce, but frightened, yellow eyes…and Andy's expression as he carefully opened out its wing, so caring and yet so professional. He was as much a part of the picture as the bird, she realized, sketching the lines of his face.

"Would you pass me my bag, please, Ellie?" he asked without looking away from the buzzard. "I've already prepared a shot—can you see it?"

Ellie handed over the syringe.

"Is he going to be all right?"

Andy deftly administered the shot and handed her the empty syringe.

"Paula was right. There's no break, thank

God, but it has a nasty infection. The anti-biotics should take care of it, but it needs cleaning up."

Suddenly he looked round with a broad smile, meeting Ellie's concerned expression.

"So do you want to hold the bird, or go and get some warm boiled water so that we can clean off all the gunge?"

"It's in the kitchen just round the corner," Paula said, guessing her answer. "The kettle's already boiled…and bring that roll of gauze beside it, please."

After they'd tended to the buzzard's wound, Paula led them over to the injured doe. Having watched them deal with the bird, Ellie didn't think anything could faze Andy and Paula. The young female deer, however, was its own worst enemy.

"Terrified, you see," said Andy, glancing across at her. "So scared, in fact, that she could really do herself some damage. The way these wild deer can panic is something else—they're just so shy."

Ellie's heart rate doubled. The vulnerability and aggression in the buzzard's eyes had been one thing, but how were they going to deal with this level of raw hysteria?

"So what can you do?"

"I'll have to sedate it," said Andy, delving into his bag and retrieving another syringe.

Watching the nervous creature pressing herself up against the fence at the back of her enclosure, Ellie wondered how they were going to restrain her for long enough to administer the shot.

"Can you stand in front of it, please Ellie?" Paula asked. "Try and attract her attention. You know, talk to her or something, but try not to spook her too much. The side of the pen is shut in you see, so that we can get at her from behind without her noticing our approach."

Ellie's mouth went dry as she took up her position. The expression in the beautiful creature's huge, terrified eyes would stay with her forever.

"It'll only take a second or two." Andy smiled in encouragement. "We have done it before, you know."

"Too many times to mention," Paula added.

Ellie stared into the deer's eyes, murmuring encouragement and trying to will it to concentrate on her. In the end, they acted so quickly that even Ellie didn't see it coming.

Placing a hand through a gap in fence, Paula wrapped her arm around the doe's delicate shoulders and pulled her as hard as she could against the smooth, broad bars. In the frozen moment before she went berserk, Andy slammed the needle into her rump and the job was done. Within minutes the deer began to stagger and they moved in quickly to arrest her fall.

Once the animal was fully sedated, they acted with professional efficiency. Andy cleaned and sutured her gaping wound, then administered another shot before standing back.

"Right," he said. "The thing now is to get well out of her way before she wakes up. The fence around the enclosure is high enough and Paula has put hay bales all along the sides, but if she panics too much as she's coming out of the anesthetic, then there's no telling what damage she could do to herself."

"I'll put the kettle on," Paula said calmly, as if this was just an ordinary day. Then again, Ellie realized, for her it was.

"Yes," Andy agreed. "We should leave the poor thing alone. Anyway, we deserve a break."

By the time Ellie was on her way home, her mind was buzzing with ideas. She'd seen enough animal action and emotion in the past hour to do ten paintings, not to mention the extraordinary human studies she envisioned. In fact, although she had intended to focus her new paintings on animals alone, seeing Andy in action had made her realize that perhaps sometimes human portraits were relevant. Andy had shown such empathy as he examined the terrified deer, he belonged in the painting. The soft lines of his face as he leaned forward; the strong, bold curves of his back against the light; the contours of his hands, their sensitivity. These impressions would draw the eye to the focal point of the painting, the beautiful lines of the helpless wild creature, totally dependent on the man who tended it with such firm yet gentle efficiency.

Emotion welled up inside her as she imagined how it would be. How *he* would be. One thing was for sure, though: she must never allow herself to be sucked in to believing in him. No matter what Paula said and no matter how much he cared for his animals, that compassion did not run through to his relationships. Ellie of all people should know that.

She smiled to herself…in a way, then, she supposed, *she* was using him. She liked that idea; it made her feel more in control of her emotions.

Beside her on the passenger seat, the pup whined softly.

"Hey, Hope," she said, reaching across to scratch his ears. "We're going home to see my dad and Shadow. You're going to love them."

The pup's tongue lolled from the side of his mouth as he appeared to smile at her.

"I'm glad Andy suggested that you come home with me," she said. "Everyone deserves to be loved, and now you will be, too. In fact, maybe I can do a happy painting for once and make you the centerpiece… It's just a bit unfortunate that you look a bit like Andy."

The thought made her giggle, and a happy glow settled itself into the place that had once been filled with pain and bitterness. All her reservations slipped way. She'd done the right thing in changing her life and moving home. She knew it now.

CHAPTER SEVENTEEN

"WELL...HOW DID it go?" Ellie's dad asked as she walked in through the door. "I've missed you these last couple of days."

Her whole face lit up. "Brilliant. I have another exhibition scheduled for spring—a bigger one—so I need to get started on some new paintings."

"Which reminds me," he said, walking across the kitchen to flick on the kettle. "The guy who wants you to do an autumn painting of his wife's horse phoned."

Ellie's hand flew to her mouth.

"Oh, no...I was supposed to call him yesterday!"

"Well, I gave him your cell number, and he said he'd call you because he doesn't want his wife to find out what he's got planned."

"Well it's certainly the weather for it. Before we know it, fall will be gone...or it'll start raining and forget to stop, as usual. By the way, Dad..."

Suddenly Ellie felt uneasy; should she have asked her dad about getting a dog instead of just springing it on him?

He turned to face her, kettle suspended in midair.

"That sounds serious. By the way, what?"

Before she could reply Hope limped into the kitchen. He stopped dead when he saw her dad, splaying his forelegs and wriggling his scrawny red-and-white body.

"Well, well, well," said her dad. "What have we here?"

"He's a rescue, and he needed a home. I thought…"

Realizing she was babbling, Ellie stopped talking and watched as her dad dropped down on one knee to scratch the backs of the pup's floppy ears.

"Shadow's going to love you," he said, glancing up at her. "I presume he is staying?"

Ellie laced her fingers together, giving him her most appealing smile.

"If you don't mind. I guess I should have asked, but…"

Her dad put down the kettle and urged her to sit down. "Ellie, let's get something straight. I've been a silly old fool, but truth is, after your mum… Well, let's just say that I found it difficult to cope for a while. It's no excuse, and I know I let you down badly, but I just couldn't seem to get past it. She was my whole world and I didn't even know it until she wasn't around anymore. She brought out the best in me, I suppose, and when she died I think my worst side took over."

Ellie leaned toward him. "No, Dad," she began, but he shook his head, determined to finish.

"You know it's true," he insisted. "I should have been there to help you, not turned you away like I did. I felt angry and down all the time, blaming everyone, and when you came back to see me or even tried to contact me, you reminded me so much of your mother that I just couldn't stand it."

"And then eventually I forced my company on you…"

"Wouldn't take no for an answer." He smiled. "Stubborn just like she was. The thing is, though, once you'd been around for a few days, I realized that it was good to remember. Healing, I suppose."

"And now…" Ellie murmured, hot tears

pressing against her eyelids. "How do you feel now?"

"Now I wouldn't have it any other way. I made you a partner in the business, didn't I? It's official now, by the way. So you don't have to run it past me if you want to get a dog…or anything else for that matter." A playful smile crossed his face. "Although I will expect to have a say in who you eventually marry, you know. Speaking of, Andy called you. He's a pleasant enough guy and it'd be handy to have a vet on-site…"

Ellie jumped up, her face turning scarlet.

"He'd be the last man on earth I'd marry," she said. "And don't be fooled by his Mr. Nice Guy act. He might care about his animals, but he's nothing like that with the women in his life."

"Keep an open mind, love," her dad suggested. "That's what your mum would have said. People change, and you were just a couple of kids, after all."

"Once bitten, twice shy, as far as he is concerned," Ellie said. "And it isn't just about me. He couldn't even stay married for more than a few months. Anyway, love and marriage have no place in my scheme of things at the moment."

Her dad sighed, then shrugged. "Best get this little fella some food then," he said, changing the subject.

"Dad." Ellie reached out one hand and touched his arm. "Thanks…for putting things straight."

"Thanks for pushing me into it," he said.

WHEN ELLIE EVENTUALLY set off for Cheshire to go and check out the horse she was supposed to paint, conditions were just right. A huge autumn sun shone in the sky, and the trees were so bright they made her heart ache.

Hope sat beside her on the passenger seat. She had intended to leave him with her dad, but he'd persuaded her to take him along.

"Best set off as you mean to go on," her dad had said. "Make him your dog. Plus, he'll be good company for you."

She drove slowly, mulling over the events of the past few days. Since getting back from the city, she'd thrown herself into helping her dad, appreciating his openness with her and determined to prove that she was going to be a real asset to the business. The evenings she'd spent trying to get on with her painting of Robbie and Choco, pleased with the way it was progressing and desperate to get started on the one of Andy and the deer. She'd seen the little boy again, when he came out with Cass to visit a lame horse, and Choco had bonded with Hope so well that they'd spent a whole hour just racing around the yard playing fetch.

Robbie had followed Ellie around, asking about their horses and telling her about his new pony, Harry.

When he'd asked if she could ride, her thoughts had gone straight back to all the happy hours she used to spend with her own pony.

"Yes," she told him. "But I haven't done it in ages. I think I might start again, though."

Overhearing their conversation, Cass had suggested that she come over to Sky View to ride with her and Robbie one day. Ellie had gladly accepted the offer, but now her nerves had kicked in. What if she'd forgotten how? What if she was useless on horseback and made herself look like an idiot? According to her dad, though, Cass didn't have much riding experience when she came to Little Dale. In fact, it had been her lessons with Jake that had brought them together initially.

Suddenly feeling better about the whole idea, Ellie turned down the drive to Morton Hall, slowing down in awe as she rounded a corner and saw the house standing on its own grounds. Large, Georgian and beautifully built of mellow stone, it looked like the set of a period drama. Smooth green lawns ran down to a small lake where swans floated majestically upon the shimmering water, and to the left of it, in a perfectly fenced paddock, two gray horses grazed contentedly beneath a canopy of autumn leaves, one small and pretty with the look of a Welsh pony and the other tall, elegant and obviously finely bred.

Pulling in next to a large silver BMW convertible, Ellie climbed gingerly out of her car, feeling like an intruder. She could see why Bert Granger had wanted her to come in the fall—the colors were phenomenal. In fact, the whole place was phenomenal.

Bert himself appeared from around the back of the house as she headed for the front door. He was big and brash, but with a wide, friendly smile.

"You made it, then," he called.

"Hi," she said. "Your house is beautiful."

"Not bad, is it," he agreed, his face suffused with pride. "I'm a self-made man and I've worked hard for this. Well, we'd better get going—Amy will be back in an hour, and I don't want to spoil the surprise."

"Amy," Ellie repeated slowly. "She's your wife, I presume?"

"Yes. We've only been married a few months, and I want this painting to be really special. You'll have to deal with the horse, though," he added, handing her a head collar. "I'm not much good with animals, and our groom is off this afternoon. It's in the paddock just over there.

The gray mare proved easy enough to catch, and was really very obliging. It was the pretty gray pony that got in the way. In the end, Bert had to go and find another head collar so that Ellie could tie the pony to the fence, where it pawed the ground and whinnied.

"At least he's making Maddie look alert," Ellie remarked as the gray mare pricked her ears and raised her elegant head to watch her small friend's antics.

"Is Maddie her full name, by the way or does she have a show name?"

"Her proper name is Made to Measure," said Bert proudly. "Because Amy says she's made to measure for her. They're doing very well in dressage."

"I'm not surprised at that—she poses like a top model." Ellie laughed, taking shot after shot of the horse, the house and the trees tinged with gold and red.

Bert held tentatively to the end of Maddie's lead rope. "Amy is…well, she was," he said. "A model, I mean."

"Sounds like you're a lucky man, then— beautiful house *and* beautiful wife."

"Yes." He nodded happily. "It was my first time down the aisle and I haven't regretted it yet. She was married before, to a vet. He treated her very badly, though, by all accounts."

"A vet," Ellie said, suddenly feeling sick. Surely it was just a coincidence.

"Was he from around here?" she heard herself asking.

Bert shook his head. "No, but funnily enough, it was through him that I heard about your exhibition. Amy and I were in Manchester when we happened to bump into him. She introduced us and he told us that he was on his way to an exhibition by a talented young artist, so when she went to get her nails done, I thought I'd stop in and take a look."

"I've known Andy since school," Ellie said. "I'd heard that his marriage didn't last long."

"His loss is my gain." Bert smiled. "According to Amy, it was a disaster right from the start. They got married on a whim, seemingly, and he treated her badly, stifling all her ambition and making her lose her self-confidence. Fortunately for me—and Amy—they split up after just a few months. Anyway…"

Glancing at his watch, he ushered her across the lawn. Hope was chasing fallen leaves and he fell in behind Ellie as they strode toward her car, afraid of being left behind.

"Sorry to hurry you off, but she'll be back soon."

"But the painting," Ellie said as he opened the car door for the two of them. Hope jumped eagerly into the passenger seat and slumped down. "Did you have anything particular in mind?"

"Just a beautiful horse in a beautiful setting. Give me a call when it's done."

Usually when Ellie drove home after taking shots of her subject matter, she spent the time considering ideas for the painting. Today, however, her mind was in a whirl. What were the chances that Amy Granger was Andy's ex-wife, not to mention that he was the one who'd told Bert about her exhibition in the first place...

"What do you think, boy?" she asked Hope, who wagged his tail and smiled at her. "Exactly. You don't think anything of it at all, and neither will I."

"Did it go well?" her dad called from across the yard as she and Hope climbed out of the car.

She strode toward him. "Yes, great! I got some really good shots. It was such a beautiful place. And guess what?"

"What?"

"The guy's wife used to be married to Andy. She used to be a model..."

Bob Nelson slid his cap back on his head and then settled it into place again, smiling at his daughter. "And did that news rattle you?" he asked.

"No!" She shook her head determinedly, already walking away. "Of course not. Why would it? I'll go and get changed, then I'll help you finish off."

"Thanks," he said. "I am a bit behind. Oh, and by the way, Oscar Goulding's coming by later. He wants to take us out to dinner and talk horses."

Ellie's face fell. "I *was* going to work on Robbie's painting tonight, but I guess business comes first. It'll be a nice change to eat out."

"Especially when we don't have to pay," he reminded her, picking up the brush he'd leaned against the wall. "I've done the stables and the nets, but if you bring in the broodmares then I can get on with feeding."

BY THE TIME Ellie had caught up and brought in the four mares from the far meadow, checked them over and brushed them off, the sun was slowly slipping down behind the fell, making her realize just how quickly the nights were getting shorter.

She gave each horse a goodnight pat,

watching as they plunged their heads eagerly into their feed buckets. There was something very satisfying about caring for animals, she decided, inhaling their scent and wondering how she could have waited so long to come back to this life.

"We need to be ready for six-thirty," her dad said when she walked into the kitchen. "And it looks like you could maybe do with a shower. Here. Take this coffee up with you."

Gratefully taking the steaming mug, she grimaced. "I had a shower this morning."

"Well, after all that work you might just need another," he remarked, struggling to contain a smile.

Heading through the hallway on her way upstairs, Ellie caught a glimpse of herself in the mirror and laughed out loud. Her whole face was covered in a fine dust of mud from the horses' coats. She was far from being a glamorous model like Amy Granger. If that was really the kind of woman that Andy went for, then it wasn't surprising he'd fallen out of love with her... Staring at her reflection, Ellie breathed out a heavy sigh. It really was about time, she decided, to stop giving Andy Montgomery all this space in her head.

Dinner with Oscar proved to be far more enjoyable than either Ellie or her dad had expected. He was generous and good company, telling tales about his life and loves that had them laughing out loud.

They had elected to go to The Plough Inn, their local village pub, and when Bob introduced him to some of the local farmers, Oscar soon had them laughing, too. He was obviously a notorious businessman who had his fingers in a number of pies, from property to finance. He reminded Ellie a bit of Matt, without the smooth, well-groomed exterior. There was nothing smooth about Oscar.

After they'd finished their meal, happily glowing with good food and wine, Bob saw an old friend and excused himself to go and catch up, leaving Ellie and Oscar alone together. He told her yet another of his jokes, mercilessly making her giggle, and suddenly she looked up to see Andy appear through the front doors. She froze as they exchanged a glance, and to her surprise, she noted that his usual pleasant expression had been replaced by a dour frown.

"Would you like another drink?" asked Oscar and she nodded.

"Thanks. Gin and tonic, please."

Oscar stood and crossed to the bar, his huge frame looming over the other customers, taller even than Andy, who was standing a bit further along.

He said something to the bartender in a loud, booming voice and they both started laughing loudly, drawing the attention of everyone there—except for Andy, who just stood sipping his beer and staring into space. Eventually he drained his glass, slammed it down and strode toward the door.

As he passed her, Ellie reached out impulsively and took hold of his sleeve.

"Are you okay?" she asked.

"I see you've moved on," he responded, looking pointedly across at Oscar.

Anger rippled inside her, then rippled and swelled as she realized he was jealous, drowning out all the confused emotions that had been wreaking havoc in her head. Any right he had to be jealous of her had expired a long time ago…along with their love.

"Look, Andy." She motioned for him to sit down and he hesitated before dropping awkwardly onto the chair beside her. "If you remember, it was you who moved on, over six years ago. You left me when I needed you most, and I can never forgive you for that."

"But I didn't know about your mother," he objected.

"And that would have made a difference, would it? Anyway, that's not the point. We were in love, or at least I thought so, and you gave up on us. That takes away any right you might have had to interfere in my life now. I'm happy to be friends, but as far as I'm concerned, that's all we'll ever be."

Before he could respond, Oscar Goulding came back from the bar. He placed the drinks he was carrying on the table and turned to Andy.

"And what can I get you, young man? You're a friend of Ellie's, I presume?"

Andy caught Ellie's eye briefly. "Yes," he said. "Ellie I are old friends, and thanks, I'll have a beer, if that's okay."

"Why don't you go and order one from the bar and put it on my tab," Oscar suggested. "And if you don't mind, will you order a Guinness for Bob?"

"Oh," said Andy, looking back at Ellie. "Your dad's here, too."

"Yes, it's kind of a business meeting. Oscar

here is bringing his mare to Dennis in the spring."

Color flooded Andy's face as he went off to the bar, and suddenly Ellie felt happier in her own space than she had in a long time, as if she'd sorted out some old issues. The shock of meeting up with Andy again on the day Matt hit the fox and then again, here in Little Dale, had really messed up her head, but now she finally knew where she was with him and could close the lid on her tumultuous emotions.

She and Andy were friends—nothing more, nothing less. Perhaps now they could finally let go of the past and move on.

CHAPTER EIGHTEEN

THE LATE SUMMER sun and autumn tints were fading by the time Ellie finally finished her painting for Bert Granger. She was pleased by the way it was turning out, the brilliance of the colors and the bold, honest expression of the gray mare.

She'd taken a chance by moving away from the classic, perfect portrait so that the painting held the same emotional, atmospheric feel as most of her other latest work. She just hoped that Bert would appreciate it. This was her style now, and she wanted to become known for it. Even the recently completed painting of Robbie playing with Choco held the same feel. When Cass first saw it, her eyes had filled with tears.

"Your paintings hold such emotion," she'd cried. "Never make compromises, Ellie. Paint how *you* want to paint."

That was the moment Ellie had decided

to change her plan for Bert Granger's painting. Now, as she put down her brush and sat back to study the finished product, a happy glow descended on her. She'd captured the horse's expression and beautiful contours just as she'd intended, and the autumn tints in the trees were captivating, fading out at the edges into a blurred mass of glorious color that lifted the painting without detracting from the subject matter.

And if Bert didn't like it, it could be in her spring exhibition and she'd paint a more traditional portrait to please him.

After reaching down to stroke Hope, who was settled by her feet, Ellie raised both arms in the air, stretching to ease her aching shoulders just as her father appeared in the doorway.

"I'm going out to check on the chickens," he said. "I'm pretty sure I shut them in, but I'll never forgive myself if your darned fox gets them."

"I'll come with you," Ellie offered. "Hope needs a run, and I'm done here."

"What, you've finally finished it? Let's have a look."

For several moments, Bob stood staring at the painting.

"It's not how you intended to paint it, is it?"

"I'm not making compromises anymore," Ellie explained. "This is my style, and if people don't like it, then they can commission another artist."

"Good girl," he said, glancing proudly across at her. "Just like your mother."

A lump formed in her throat. "Am I really?" she murmured. "Like my mum, I mean?"

"More and more every day," he said. "Come on, let's go and see to these chickens."

ELLIE HADN'T SEEN Andy since they met at the pub with Oscar Goulding. In fact, she was so focused on finishing Bert's painting, she hadn't left Hope Farm in several days. To her surprise, Andy drove into the yard just as she was about to go and deliver it.

Hope was already curled up on the passenger seat, but he jumped out when he saw the new arrival and ran to greet him.

Andy clambered out of his truck.

"See," he said, dropping down to stroke the

little red-and-white sheepdog. "He remembers me."

"He's like that with everyone." Ellie laughed. "Are you here on a call? Dad didn't say anything…"

"No." He stood up, towering over her, a broad smile on his face. "I'm here to see you, friend."

"Oh…I'm just heading off to deliver a painting, I'm afraid. I promised to have it there today."

"Can I see it?"

Ellie hesitated. The canvas was all wrapped up in the back seat of her car, ready for the journey.

"Okay," she agreed. "I guess another twenty minutes or so won't hurt. Anyway, why did you want to see me?"

"I wondered if you wanted to go out on call with me sometime, like we discussed. You know, just to get new material."

Andy held the door open as Ellie gently removed the painting from the car.

"Here," he said, reaching out to take it. "I'll carry that. Well, so do you want to?"

She smiled up at him, suddenly sure. "Yes,

that would be really helpful. Just give me a call whenever."

"What about evening visits?" he asked eagerly. "You know, gloomy buildings lit by dim electric bulbs that light up the animal's face."

"I didn't know you had such an artistic streak."

"There's quite a lot you don't know about me," he said.

A shudder ran down her spine, a delicious, prickly shudder.

She took a sharp breath.

"I'm sure there are lots of things I don't know about all my *friends*," she said pointedly.

"Touché," he murmured. "And don't worry. I know where I stand."

WHEN THE PAINTING was revealed again in all its glory, Andy stayed silent for a long moment.

"It's beautiful," he said eventually, placing one broad hand on Ellie's shoulder. She squirmed but didn't move away.

"Thanks," she said, meaning it. "Now I have to go. I promised to be there by two."

"What did you say the man's name was?"

he asked, smoothing out the wrapping and handing it to her.

Ellie pulled off a length of sticky tape, staring at him intently. "You know him, actually," she said. "In fact, weird coincidence, but you used to be married to his wife…she's a model."

He frowned, and then his face lit up. "Oh yes! Not really that much of a coincidence, though. I bumped into them, almost literally bumped into them, the day I took your dad to Manchester…" He paused, as if uncertain whether he should go on. "It was a mess from the start. I only married her because…"

His voice trailed off and Ellie prompted him. "Because what?"

Picking up the painting, he turned away.

"Oh, you don't want to know," he said, ending the conversation. "Anyway, good luck with this. Not that you'll need it, of course. He'll love it."

"I hope so." She sighed, following him to her car. "Although I think he might be expecting something a bit more…traditional."

He held her gaze, and it felt as if his smile warmed her right through to her heart.

"You have to follow your vision," he said. "And if he doesn't like it, then that's his loss."

As Ellie drove out into the lane, her conversation with Andy ran through her head He really did seem to *get* her paintings. She liked that.

But what did he mean when he said he'd only married Amy *because*…because what? Surely the only reason to get married was for love. He had almost told Ellie his reason, but did she really want to know? It was none of her business. She didn't want to learn his secrets and she couldn't bear to get inside his head…or his heart. There was a time when they'd told each other everything, but where had that gotten either of them?

Why had it ended? she asked herself now. What had happened to their all-consuming teenage love? She used to go over their breakup in her mind, over and over and over until it drove her crazy. Now the question loomed again, after all this time.

He hadn't even bothered to come back and see her, or even try and explain; that was what had really hurt.

BERT GRANGER WAS waiting impatiently on his front steps when Ellie nosed her car down the drive. As she pulled up on the gravel outside the imposing house, he bounded toward her.

"About time, too," he said. "Amy will be back from the gym in an hour, and I don't want her to see it until tomorrow."

Ellie started to retrieve the painting from the car, then hesitated.

"What if you don't like it?"

"If I don't like it, then I won't be paying for it, of course. Now let's have a look."

Ellie refused to remove the packaging until they were inside the house.

"Just open it here," he said as she pulled it from the backseat.

She shook her head. "You can't just view a painting anywhere. In fact, you shouldn't really let Amy see it until it's hung...for the best impression."

"That's not bad idea," he agreed. "Come on, I'll show you where it's going to go."

The house was beautiful—tastefully and expensively decorated and furnished. Bert beamed when she commented on it.

"Daniel Bercomp is our interior designer," he boasted, leading her into a large, sunny room. "Surely you must have heard of him."

Ellie stifled a smile. "I haven't really had that much to do with interior designers."

"Amy's very good at that sort of thing," he told her, motioning toward an empty space on the wall above a marble fire place. "There, that's where the painting is going. I told her I'd sent the one that normally hangs there to be cleaned."

Ellie started to remove the packaging from the canvas. "Well, let's get it hung, and then you can see it properly."

Ellie noticed Bert making a point of averting his eyes from the painting, not wanting to see it or make a comment until it was settled into its appointed place.

"It might not be quite what you expected," Ellie warned him as they stepped back.

"A woman at the exhibition said that your paintings would be collector's items one day," he told her. "That's what gave me the idea to get one for Amy, and I wasn't disappointed. I like how the contemporary style still links to the traditional, and the emotion you display on the animals' faces is just so real."

"I didn't know you were such an expert," Ellie said in surprise.

"I'm not," he admitted, returning her grin. "I'm just quoting what I overheard."

Suddenly, he went quiet, staring at the painting.

"And looking at this," he said, "I'm glad I acted on my impulse."

Ellie felt a gasp of relief leave her lungs.

"You like it, then?"

"I love it... It's even better than I expected, and if Amy wants me to, then I might even ask you to do one of her mounted." He glanced at his watch before pushing a package into her hand. "She'll be back soon, and I want to make sure this is hidden until tomorrow. There's the money, and I'll be in touch."

"Thanks," she said, pulling out her keys as he glanced anxiously up the drive.

A brand-new silver convertible appeared, and his face blanched. He ushered Ellie out to her car.

"If she speaks to you, just tell her you're lost," he said.

Ellie had to wait until the narrow drive was clear before she could leave. The silver car pulled up next to her and a slim, leggy blonde got out, casting her an inquisitive glance. Ellie slid down her window, allowing her car to roll forward. There was something strangely familiar about Amy, she realized, if she looked beyond the heavy makeup and the lips plumped up by Botox.

"I was lost," she explained. "But this gentleman has just set me on the right track."

Andy's ex-wife nodded, looking straight through her, and Ellie felt something wither deep inside. No wonder he'd dumped *her* if Amy was really his type.

WHEN ELLIE RETURNED to Hope Farm, the first person she saw was Cass. The vet waved, walking quickly across to meet her as Ellie got out of the car.

"I'm looking for Bob," she said. "He called the clinic about a lame horse."

Ellie nodded, opening the passenger door for Hope, who jumped eagerly out into the yard. "Oh, yes," she said. "That's Mollie. Dad thinks she might have a strained check ligament. She's in that stable over there."

The bay mare stared out at them over her door, tossing her head in greeting and nuzzling Ellie for a treat as she slipped the head collar over her ears.

"I was going to ask you if you wanted to

come over for a ride," Cass said as she ran her hand down the horse's foreleg. "Jake just bought a lovely colored cob. She's as sweet as a kitten and very safe… I mean, if you haven't ridden for a while, I thought you might prefer safe."

"You thought right." Ellie smiled. "And yes, I'd love to come for a ride. But like you said, I haven't done it in ages."

"I was a bit like that when I first came to Little Dale." Cass laughed. "That's partly how I got to know Jake. He gave me some riding lessons…only he insisted I start on Carlotta, and that was a big ask."

"You got there, though."

Cass's dark eyes took on a dreamy look. "Sure did."

"Is it going well?" Ellie asked.

"It's going really great. Now let's get this mare out and watch her trot."

Cass was giving her diagnosis when Bob finally arrived on his ATV with Shadow perched precariously on the back, ears flapping and tongue out of the side of his mouth. As soon as the bike stopped, the dog hopped down and ran over to give Hope an enthusiastic greeting while Bob followed at a more leisurely pace.

"My old joints just don't bend like they used to," he groaned. "Sorry, Cass, there was a sheep stuck in the fence."

Cass smiled. "Well, I'm afraid that you were right—it's a check ligament. It's not serious, though. Keep it well hosed with cold water and rest her for a while. Walking in hand is fine."

"There's a job for me," said Ellie. "And guess what, Dad? Cass has invited me to go out for a ride with her."

Bob nodded. "It's about time you took it up again. Come to think of it, perhaps we should look around for a riding horse of your own."

Ellie's grin spread from ear to ear. "Well, I'd better practice at Cass's first, make sure I still remember how."

"It's like riding a bike," he told her. "You never forget how."

"Tomorrow, then," Cass suggested. "I'm off all day. After lunch, okay?"

Ellie nodded, surprised by her own excitement. "That'll give me time to go and buy jodhpurs first."

She'd given up riding the day her mum had

been diagnosed…the day the whole world had seemed to stop turning. Now, though, she felt as if it was almost back on its axis… almost, but not quite.

ELLIE HADN'T EXPECTED to feel nervous as she set off for Sky View. It had been over six years since she'd sat on a horse, and she wasn't quite as confident as her dad that it was just like riding a bike. But as soon as she saw the chestnut-and-white cob that Cass had already tacked up for her, she realized that she shouldn't have worried. She ran her hand down the sweet little mare's face and fell instantly in love.

"This is Nancy," Cass told her.

Ellie laughed. "You can't call a horse Nancy."

"To be honest, it's not just Nancy…it's Fancy Nancy."

"That's even worse!" Ellie said, feigning horror as she slid back the bolt on the stable door. "I'll just call her Fancy. What do you think, Fancy?"

The chunky little horse nibbled Ellie's cheek, and she ran her fingers along her velvety chestnut ears.

"You see, she likes that far better than plain old Nancy."

"Well, get her out and I'll watch you in the school first if you like, before I get my horse out."

"Thanks, that's probably a good idea," Ellie said, fastening her chin strap. "Who are you riding anyway?"

"Not Carlotta, unfortunately—she's way too precious now that she's in foal. I have a new horse that Jake bought for me a couple of weeks ago. I'm hoping to do some showing with him one day, but he's way too green right now."

Cass had insisted that Ellie bring Hope along, saying that the pup would just follow Puddle, who was becoming quite sensible. Despite her reservations, Ellie had agreed, and when she brought Fancy out into the sunshine, an over-excited Hope started running around in crazy circles.

"I'll tie him up," she suggested, but Cass was adamant.

"He'll settle down, don't worry. You've got to start somewhere, and Fancy Nancy here won't bother... Will you, girl?"

When Hope came hurtling past for the

third time, the mare totally ignored him and Ellie nodded. "Okay, I see what you mean. She doesn't seem to mind him at all."

Puddle just stood watching, wagging her plumed tail slowly.

"You know," Cass remarked. "They really do look a bit alike. They're both the same color for a start."

"Hope and Fancy." Ellie giggled.

ELLIE HAD ONLY been riding for five minutes or so when she reined in, a broad grin on her face. "Dad was right," she said to Cass. "It is like riding a bike. I can't believe I've waited so long. And Hope is already calming down. Why don't you go and get on before we run out of time."

Cass was already heading for the stables.

While she waited for Cass to come back, Ellie allowed Fancy to fall back to a walk, her mind racing with painting ideas. The deep voice that broke through her reverie made her jump.

"So, Cass has got you riding now, has she? About time!"

Ellie's stomach did an uncomfortable flip.

"Andy! What are you doing here?"

He strode toward her, tall, angular and slightly awkward in his movements but oh so familiar. Hope raced to meet him, rolling ecstatically onto his back with his legs in the air.

Andy dropped down to scratch his belly.

"Hello, friend," he said, glancing up at Ellie before turning his attention back to the dog. "He's looking so much better," he told her. "You've done a good job with him, Ells."

The sun shone on his face, bringing a golden gleam to the lock of blond hair that fell across his forehead. His warm brown eyes seemed to see into her soul as he caught her gaze.

"Still need a haircut, I see," she said.

"No time for haircuts, I'm afraid. I was up half the night with a young Hereford bull that was tangled up in barbed wire."

"Oh, no! Is it all right?"

He nodded. "It will be eventually, but it's quite a mess right now, poor thing."

"You should have called me."

Even as she said it Ellie could have kicked herself. She didn't want him to feel that he *had* to call her.

"I thought about it," he said, standing up.

Hope jumped up against him, wanting more, and he gently rubbed the backs of the pup's ears. "It was all a bit sudden, though, and I wasn't sure about the subject matter...for your painting, I mean."

"But it doesn't have to be all sweetness and light," Ellie exclaimed. "Life's not like that. I want to portray real life...real emotion."

"Next time I have an emergency, then, I'll call you," he promised.

"No matter what it is?"

"No matter what it is. Anyway, enjoy your ride. I have to go—I'm moving today."

A heavy weight settled in Ellie's chest.

"Where...where are you moving to? I thought you were here kind of permanently."

"Here," he said, raising both hands. "Sky Cottage is vacant now, and I just signed a contract to rent it for six months. By the way, Ells..." He grinned up at her. "It's good to see you on a horse again."

Ellie rode around the school, and for a mind-blowing moment she felt sixteen again...except then Andy would have been hanging on the fence, making jokes and comments every time she passed him, waiting to take her into his arms the moment she dismounted.

Biting her bottom lip so hard it hurt, she allowed her mind to dwell for a moment on those deliriously happy days when she and Andy couldn't get enough of each other's company. How could anything so good go so wrong? All the questions she had tried to fend off crackled inside her head. Was he really as bad as she thought? Perhaps it was Amy's fault that their marriage hadn't worked. Perhaps...

Perhaps he should never have stopped loving her. At that painful thought, she turned her thoughts firmly back into the present.

Cass approached, mounted on a gawky youngster with lovely conformation and a beautiful head, but a lot of growing to do. Ellie closed the door firmly on her memories.

"Why did I ever give it up?" she cried.

Cass laughed, trotting toward her. "I told you so. Come on then, let's take them up onto the fell."

CHAPTER NINETEEN

Andy walked away from Sky View stables, his heart pounding. How come Ellie could still have this effect on him, he wondered, when he'd really believed he was over her? He'd been a fool; he'd known that on the day he'd walked away from their love. Would she ever be able to forgive him for letting her down? There was definitely still a spark between them, but trust was another matter. Trust had to be earned, and he certainly hadn't earned the right to Ellie's. It had been hard to stay focused at university, when he was so far away from everything he knew, meeting new people, starting a whole new life. His friends at vet school had all been free and single, desperate to party whenever they had the chance. When they weren't partying, then they were studying. Training to be a vet was tougher than he'd expected, too. There was so much to learn, and the farther in he got, the more he realized how much he needed to concentrate if he wanted to qualify.

But it hadn't been all about the work, if he was honest with himself. He and Ellie had been together for most of their adolescence, and Little Dale wasn't exactly notorious for its nightlife. The social side of university had been a bit of a culture shock, and it had probably gone to his head.

"You've got years ahead of you for all that true love stuff. Save it for when you're thirty," his roommate used to say when he turned down date after date because of Ellie. "Live a little, why don't you, before it's too late. Tell her you need to give it a break for a while. You can always pick it up again later, and at least it'll give you the chance to make sure she's the right one."

Andy had always known that Ellie was the right one, though; there was never any doubt in his mind about that. But Josh had made the idea of taking a break seem so sensible, a chance for both of them to feel less tied down. And in the end, he'd made the phone call. He hadn't even had the decency to tell her face-to-face. Frankly, he probably wouldn't have been able to, but that was no excuse.

His hand had been shaking when he spoke to her, he remembered, going over that conversation in his head as he'd done ten thousand times already in the past six years.

"Look, Ells," he'd said. "I think maybe we should have a break for a bit. We never get to see each other, anyway, and I have so much studying to do. I need to concentrate… It's not fair on you either…"

The line had gone silent; he remembered that moment so well. She hadn't even objected, really, just reeled in shock, he guessed.

He tried again. "It's not you, Ells. It's me…I…"

"You've got someone else," she said.

Her accusation had offered an easy way out at the time, and although there hadn't been another girl, there so easily could have been. He'd convinced himself it couldn't have been true love, after all, or surely he wouldn't have even looked at anyone else. Not that he'd given Ellie any real reason to believe he'd been unfaithful. She'd just jumped to conclusions and he'd gone along with it, taken the easy option, as usual.

He'd known as soon as he hung up the phone that he'd made the worst mistake of his life. After that, she didn't answer his calls or reply to his letters, so he'd thrown himself into college life until the spring break, when he was determined to put things right.

Hope Farm was the first place he'd stopped at when returned to Little Dale, and he would never forget the excitement he'd felt at the thought of seeing her again. As soon as he'd walked through the gate, though, he'd felt a change in the atmosphere. Nothing he could put his finger on, just a stifling silence. He'd knocked on the open door, he remembered, instead of walking right in as he used to, then he'd stuck his head inside and called for Ellie… Wanting so badly to explain, to tell her how stupid he'd been. To tell her how much he loved her.

Sally, Ellie's mum, had called him in. Her voice sounded different, though. When he saw her, sitting in her chair, she appeared gaunt and exhausted, nothing like the glowing woman she used to be. His heart had turned over.

"Where's Ellie?"

The words had tumbled out of his mouth,

struggling past the shock of so much change in such a short time.

"Not here, thank God."

Her blue eyes had held a ferocity that startled him.

"Where's Ellie?" he'd repeated, desperately needing to see her.

"She's over you, Andy, way over you. In fact, you did her a favor."

He'd refused to accept it.

"No…I messed up, that's all, I've been trying to get ahold of her for weeks. I've got to see her."

"You broke her heart, Andy. She's over it now, but I will not have you screwing up her life all over again. I'm dying of cancer, as you can obviously see, and she's taking it hard. So I'm asking you…no, begging you. Stay away from my daughter and let her get on with her life."

A rush of desolation had left him reeling as he turned to blindly walk away.

"Promise me, Andy."

He'd glanced back, meeting her eyes filled with desperation and fear.

"Please," she'd said, her voice little more than a whisper.

"I promise," he'd reluctantly agreed.

That was the last time he'd returned to Little Dale before he took the position at Low Fell. He'd sent a card when he heard about her death, though he'd desperately wanted to deliver it in person. But how could he get past the plea of a dying woman? And so he'd moved on with his life, throwing himself into his work, moving from practice to practice to gain experience. That was when he'd developed a passion for helping wild animals.

And then there had been his wedding day, the day that was supposed to make everything all right. But getting married had made everything worse.

He'd only been attracted to Amy in the first place because she reminded him of Ellie. She was much taller than his first love, but there was just something about her face, the expression in her bright blue eyes, her determined streak. They'd married on a whim after dating for only a matter of weeks, and he'd quickly realized that she was nothing like Ellie at all. She was obsessed with her looks for one thing, always going to the beauty parlor or the hairdresser. All she ever wanted to do was go out clubbing, and she hated the country. They both soon discovered that they disagreed about almost everything, so when she was offered a modeling job in Manchester and announced that she was leaving and wanted a divorce, all he'd felt was relief.

Kicking a stone into the dirt, Andy stopped to look back. Cass and Ellie were riding side by side, two beautiful women laughing out loud in the autumn sunshine. And then Ellie's eyes found his across the distance and she waved.

He raised his hand and turned away.

"You were wrong, Sally," he murmured. "And now it's too late."

Perhaps, after all this time, he could be forgiven for breaking a promise to a dying woman, but it really *was* too late. Ellie didn't trust him, would never trust him again. She'd grown into a strong, beautiful woman, the kind of woman he'd expected her to be…and they could have been together if he hadn't made such a huge mistake.

Taking the front door key from his pocket, he headed down the narrow path that led to Sky View cottage. The windows twinkled in the afternoon light.

At least he had a stable job now, and a secure future. When he'd come back here, he hadn't expected Ellie to walk back into his life; that had churned everything up again. Because of his failed marriage, she gotten it firmly fixed in her head that he was some kind of unreliable womanizer. But she'd had a fiancée herself, so was she any better? She said that their engagement had fallen through, but maybe she'd only really come back home to promote her career. After all, there wasn't much opportunity to observe nature in the city, and she did seem pretty keen to accompany him on visits, even though it was obvious that she'd never forgiven him. She loved her dad; there was no doubt in his mind about that. He just hoped she'd stay around and still be involved in the stud business after she gathered enough material for her paintings. Then again, maybe be was misjudging her and basing his presumptions on Amy. She and Ellie were a million miles apart in every way.

For a moment, his mind slipped back to the days when all he and Ellie cared about was each other, and he let out a heavy sigh. Did he still care about her? he asked himself.

The answer jumped right out at him. Oh, yes, he had never stopped loving Ellie Nelson. But was she the same girl he used to know, or had time and circumstance changed her open-heartedness? One thing was for sure: he definitely wanted to find out.

CHAPTER TWENTY

CASS AND ELLIE trotted side by side across the coarse grass, stopping eventually in a small copse where rabbits scattered as they approached.

"I'll ache all over tomorrow," Ellie said, reining in.

"You definitely will," Cass agreed with a broad smile. "Let's take a breather and then we'll walk back to cool them down."

Hope and Puddle collapsed on the ground panting.

"I've finally found a way to tire him out!" Ellie laughed.

"So buy your own horse and you can exercise him every day and enjoy yourself at the same time," Cass suggested.

Ellie mulled the idea over. "Maybe I will, when I've settled in properly and done enough paintings for my next exhibition. That's my main priority right now. Come on, let's head back, I promised to help dad finish off the horses."

Cass gasped, glancing at her watch. "And Robbie will be home from school soon. We'd better hurry—I didn't realize how long we'd been out."

They jogged along the lane in silence, except for the clopping of hooves on tarmac. Hope and Puddle ran behind them in single file. When the roofs of Sky View came into view, they slowed their pace, allowing the horses to stretch.

"Thanks," said Ellie. "That was fantastic."

"So you'll keep it up?"

"If you'll have me."

"Well, there are always horses that need exercising at Sky View, you know…especially now."

Ellie frowned. "What do you mean?"

Cass hesitated. "Promise me you won't say anything to anyone, at least not yet."

"Of course."

A flush spread across Cass's cheeks.

"I'm pregnant."

"Wow! Are you sure?"

"I took a test and it was positive."

"And does Jake know?"

"Of course, but no one else does. We're not telling anyone until after my three-month scan, not even Bill or Robbie. I just *had* to tell someone, though, or I was going to burst."

"Because you're so excited! It's only natural. And he's pleased?"

"He's over the moon," Cass told her, eyes shining with love. "I know people didn't think it would work, me and Jake, but he's changed so much. It feels like this baby will be a new beginning after all the bad stuff he's been through. I just hope Robbie feels the same way, too."

"I'm sure he will," said Ellie. "He's a lovely little boy, and he obviously adores you."

"He is lovely, isn't he? He's had it tough, too, but I think he'll love having a little sibling."

They arrived at the stables and untacked the horses. Ellie brushed Fancy, then said her goodbyes to Cass.

As Ellie drove home, she couldn't help the prickle of envy that made her heart ache. She'd had two shots at love and neither of them had worked out. She and Andy... She sighed, remembering. That had been real love, unconditional and pure, the kind of love where you can't bear to be parted even for an hour, where all you think about is each other... At least, that's what she'd thought at the time. Obviously, it had been different for Andy because as soon as they were parted, he'd met someone else. So how could she ever even dare to believe in love again?

With Matt it had been much different. He'd been good company and they'd had lots of fun...and romantic times, too. But their relationship hadn't blown her away. Perhaps that was the more sensible way to love—keep a little piece of your heart back so that when it ended, it wouldn't totally destroy you.

And Andy had destroyed her; she was only too well aware of that. If he'd come back to see her, maybe explain things, or try to, then she might have been able to get her head around how easily he'd just stopped caring. But he hadn't, and that was it.

Suddenly she felt so angry with him, just as she had back then, when it had seemed as if everything was his fault...even her mother's death. As if in taking back his love he'd placed a curse on her. She knew now that that idea had been stupid, but she'd been a teenager with a broken heart, dealing with tragedy.

Pushing Andy firmly to the back of her mind, she focused on Fancy and the ride she'd enjoyed so much. It felt as if she and Cass were becoming real friends, and she was so pleased for her about the baby… even if she was a little envious. Not that she wanted children herself…not yet, anyway.

When Ellie arrived at Hope Farm, her dad was in the yard, leaning on the gate and talking to a tall young man with short dark hair. He wore a shirt and tie with a tweed jacket, corduroy trousers and shiny brown brogues.

"Hello, love," called her dad. "You'll be pleased to know that I've done the horses. Good ride?"

"The best," she cried, walking toward them. "I can't believe I waited this long."

"I told you so," he said. "This is Tim, by the way. Tim Handley. He's a land agent."

"Thus the outfit," Tim explained, looking down at his shoes. "I have to look the part. I can do casual as well, though."

Ellie smiled politely. "I'm Ellie, nice to meet you."

There was something she didn't like about

Tim, she decided, something in his eyes. No, she was just being stupid. She held out her hand, took it briefly. "I have a mare I'd like to bring to your gray stallion. Your dad and I were just discussing it."

"Perhaps you could take him over to see Blue," her dad suggested. "I have to make a phone call."

Ellie glanced over at him, noting the sheepish look on his face. He wasn't attempting a bit of matchmaking here, was he? she wondered. If he was, then he was wasting his time.

"Come on, then," she said, whistling for Hope. "He's over here."

The red-and-white pup ran eagerly toward her, jumping up, and she laughed, cradling his face in her hands as he tried to lick her cheek."

"Nice dog," Tim remarked, but she noticed that he made sure Hope did not jump up against his immaculate trousers.

"What's your mare, by the way?" she asked as he followed her across the yard.

"Three-quarter Thoroughbred. She's already bred two foals to a Welsh Section D but we—I mean *I*—wanted to try and breed a competition horse this time."

"And do you ride?"

"I used to. I don't really get much chance nowadays, though."

Blue was watching their approach over his half door. He nickered in greeting, and Ellie ran her hand across his cheek and rubbed the backs of his ears.

"Seems good-natured enough," Tim said.

"They don't come better than Blue," she replied quietly, reaching for his head collar. "Do you want to see him out?"

Tim stepped back. "Yes, thanks."

She trotted the stallion up and down the yard while Tim made the appropriate responses.

"Wonderful movement, and what conformation! My mare is a bit light of bone, but he'll more than make up for that. What exactly is his breeding, and do you have any information on what his offspring have achieved?"

"You need to speak to my dad about that," she told him.

He pulled a face. "I was going to suggest

that perhaps *you* fill me in with all the details over dinner tonight."

"Sorry." She led Blue back into his stable, hurriedly removing his head collar. "I'm not the person you need to talk to. And as for dinner, well, I'm afraid I'm busy tonight."

He raised his eyebrows, accepting her brush-off with good grace, but determined to try again. "Well, what about—" She was already walking toward the house. "I think Dad will be in the office," she said.

Her dad looked up from his paperwork with a frown when Ellie burst in on him.

"Tim wants have a chat with you about Blue's breeding," she announced, already backing out of the room. "I just need to make sure I fastened Blue's bolt and then I'll make us some coffee."

"I can do that," he began, but she was back in the yard before she heard him finish.

He followed her outside.

"Tim has invited us for a bar snack," he said. "We can chat about Blue there."

"No!" She spun around to face him. "I have to finish my painting, and I've got a bit of a headache. You go with him, though. It'll make a nice change from my cooking."

Her dad smiled. "Your cooking's better than tomato soup and baked beans all the time." He lowered his voice. "I'll happily go, but to be honest, I think it was more your company he was after."

"He'll just have to manage without it then, won't he?" Ellie said. "I'll see you later— enjoy your meal."

Ellie heard the banging as she walked past the barn to check on Blue's bolt. A loud, panicky thumping from Dennis's stable that set her alarm bells ringing.

Hurrying toward the sound, she peered over his half door to find her worst fears confirmed. The big bay stallion was cast and in a frenzy, trapped on its back against the wall of the stable after going down to roll, hooves thrashing against the concrete again and again.

"Whoa, boy," she soothed him in the calmest voice she could muster, pulling her phone from her pocket to call her dad over. "We'll have you up in no time."

The phone rang over and over in her ear, so she raced toward the house. Her heart sank as she saw Tim Handley's sporty car disappearing down the drive, and she dialed her dad's number again. She heard its jarring tones coming from the kitchen. He'd left without it, and she couldn't help Dennis on her own. She didn't even know what pub they'd gone to.

Blood pounded in her ears as she rushed back across the yard. What if Dennis thrashed around so much that he damaged himself, maybe even broke a leg? She had to stay with him and try to keep him calm, but she needed to do something to help. She'd seen her dad deal with cast horses before. He would get a lunge line around its legs and pull until it was in a position where it could scramble to it feet; easier said than done with almost half a ton of disgruntled Thoroughbred stallion to deal with, though. Changing course, Ellie ran to the tack room and grabbed a longe line; the least she could do was try.

By the time Ellie got back to the stable, the stallion had managed to maneuver himself into an even more awkward position. He was on his back, right up against the door, so that his flailing hooves made it dangerous even to try and get into his stall.

"Okay, boy," she crooned with a lot more confidence than she was actually feeling. If she could get to his head, then she could try and calm him down. "You're going to be fine. Now just stay still a minute…"

The stallion's head was over to the right of the door, his belly distended in front of her. She could see his eyes rolling in their sockets, flashing white. His coat was dark with sweat, and steam rose above him in a cloud. It occurred to her that he might not just be cast, he might also have colic or a twisted gut.

He made another violent lunge, smashing his leg against the concrete wall, and she realized she had to act. In one crazy, foolhardy move, she leaped across his belly into the stable, clambering to her feet and staying close to the back wall as she decided what to do.

She couldn't help Dennis unless she could calm him down. Crouching beside him, she gently stroked his face, talking to him in a low, soothing tone. "There, now, big guy, don't you worry. I'll have you up in no time."

After what felt like an eternity, the stallion eventually rested his head on the banked straw as he placed his trust in her, and she carefully began looping the longe line around his fine limbs, aware that he could kick out again at any moment.

As the line settled around his hind legs,

she breathed a sigh of relief, standing back to carefully draw in the slack before starting to heave. Her arms strained with the effort, and the stallion's whole body convulsed as he attempted to stand. Just as she was beginning to think it was hopeless, his feet began to find purchase on the ground.

In one huge burst, he hauled himself upright and stood shaking in the straw, sweat dripping down his legs. Ellie collapsed on the feed trough, triumph roaring inside her…a triumph that was short-lived when she noticed he was holding up one foreleg.

The big horse raised no objection as she slipped on his head collar, patting his damp neck and murmuring to him under her breath before carefully running her hand down around his cannon bone and over the tendons behind. The limb was hot and swollen and obviously very painful. The blood in her veins turned to ice. What if it was broken?

With shaking fingers, she pulled out her phone and scrolled down to "Vet."

The female voice on the end of the line was cool and professional as Ellie explained the problem.

"Just keep the horse calm, and I'll get someone out there right away."

"Right away" seemed to take forever, and she'd never been more relieved than when she heard a rattling vehicle pull into the yard.

Rushing outside, Ellie waved, stopping in her tracks as she recognized Andy's truck. Why did it have to be him? No matter; it was Dennis who was hurt, and at least she knew Andy was a good vet.

"In here," she called.

Bag in hand, he raced across the yard.

"He was cast," she explained urgently. "And I'm alone."

Andy glanced around the stable, noting the longe line.

"You got him up?"

She felt a prickle of pride at the admiration in his tone.

"Yes, but he's hurt his foreleg."

He approached Dennis carefully, speaking to him in a calm, gentle voice.

"Hey, boy...now what have you been up to? Let's take a look."

The normally fractious stallion lowered his head, allowing Andy to run a hand down his extended limb.

He glanced up at Ellie, noting the strained expression on her face.

"Don't worry," he said with a reassuring smile. "Hopefully it's not as bad as it looks."

"Do you think it's broken? He doesn't see able to put any weight on it."

"Let's not jump to conclusions. Bones don't break all that easily, you know. Severe bruising is much more likely."

Ellie watched impatiently as he carefully examined the horse's limb.

"Well?" she said as he released the hoof and stood up.

"I can't say for sure, of course, but I really don't think it's a fracture. See, he's already putting a bit more weight on it. I could go and get the X-ray machine—we do have a portable one—or we can see how he does over the next hour or so. If it's just bruising—and I'm pretty convinced that's the case, since he has a direct trauma to the back of his tendons—then the worst of the pain should subside fairly quickly. We'll cold-hose it now, and I'll pop back in an hour... Unless you'd like to make me a coffee and I'll hang around for a bit. I'm on call, anyway."

Realizing that the horse came first, Ellie

put aside her sudden flutter of panic at the thought of being alone with Andy "Okay... as long as you aren't going to charge us for your time," she joked.

"Like father, like daughter." Andy smiled. "Now where's your hose pipe?"

Andy held the stallion for ten minutes, while Ellie ran cold water over the swelling. Andy eventually declared that it was coffee time and handed her the lead rope. As she walked Dennis back across the yard to his stable, they could both see that there was already a marked improvement in the condition of the horse's leg.

"Maybe you don't need to stay after all," Ellie said.

"You promised me a coffee, remember? Or are you afraid of being alone with me?"

Ellie closed the stallion's stable door and slid the bolt, glancing up at him.

"Don't kid yourself, Andy Montgomery," she said. "One thing you don't do is frighten me."

He fell into step beside her.

"Ah, so I do *do* something for you, then?"

"Yes, you irritate me," she said, but there was a smile in her eyes.

In the farmhouse kitchen, Ellie busied herself brewing coffee while Andy lounged in a chair, flipping through the *Horse and Hound*. She glanced across at him, catching his gaze, then quickly looked away.

"I thought you weren't afraid of me," he said.

She poured the coffee, answering without meeting his eyes. "I'm not."

"Why do I make you so uneasy, then?"

"You don't…it's just a bit weird, that's all."

"Why weird?"

"Well, you and I used to be so…you know."

"Close?" he suggested.

"Something like that. And then I spent so much time learning to hate you and blame you for all the things that have gone wrong in my life."

"And now?"

"Now…" She looked him full in the face. "Now I feel as if I'm getting to know you all over again in a very different way."

"How…different?"

For a moment she hesitated, struggling with the need to be honest. "I admire you for your work with animals—I can see that you really care about them—but I think you're shallow and selfish when it comes to your relationships."

ANDY ROLLED UP the magazine he'd been looking at, a tight knot forming in his chest. How could she think that of him and where had it come from? He'd hurt her badly, he knew that, but it was her mother who'd persuaded him to leave her alone when he came back to see her that day and she knew nothing of his relationship with Amy. A dull anger filled the emptiness; she wasn't being fair.

"How can you say that? You don't know anything about my relationships. And we were little more than a couple of kids when I broke it off with you, so surely you can't still hold that against me."

Something deep inside her quivered, and she closed her eyes for a second.

"We may have been kids, Andy, but we loved each other…and I believed in us. I thought I knew you better than that. Everyone makes mistakes, and we hadn't seen each other for so long… But the Andy I thought I knew would have come to see me, to explain *why*. I thought we were friends, too, but that fact seemed to totally evade you. I think that hurt more than anything."

Andy just stared at her. *But I did come*

back, he wanted to say. *I came here to say sorry, to see you...to tell you I was wrong.*

The image of her mother's pale face flashed in his mind's eye. "Promise me, Andy," she'd said. And he had promised.

But he and Ellie were adults now, and circumstances had changed. Perhaps he could break that promise.

"I did come back," he murmured.

"Don't lie to me, Andy," she responded, her voice sharp and cold. "You never came back. You just went off, married someone else and then let her down, as well. That's why I can never trust you again."

Before he could respond, the back door burst open and her dad came rushing in, closely followed by Tim Handley.

"What's wrong?" her dad cried. "I saw Andy's truck. Is one of the animals hurt?"

"Not exactly," Andy responded. "Come on, I'll show you and Ellie can explain on the way."

They reached Dennis's stable to find him contentedly pulling on his hay net. Ellie went in to slip on his head collar, and they all watched him trot across the yard.

"You see," Andy said. "He's fine. Just a bit sore, that's all."

"I thought he'd broken his leg," Ellie admitted.

"It could have been you breaking a leg, pulling a foolhardy stunt like that," her dad said.

"More brave than foolhardy, don't you think?" remarked Andy.

Bob Nelson smiled proudly. "Aye," he said. "I reckon it was."

CHAPTER TWENTY-ONE

ELLIE WOKE NEXT the morning to find that her arms and shoulders were one burning ache.

"What do you expect if you start hauling at half a ton of horse without any help?" her dad said when she commented on it at breakfast.

She placed a brightly colored free-range egg onto his thickly buttered toast and handed it to him with a smile.

"If you'd remembered your phone, I wouldn't have had to."

"Touché." Her dad laughed. "To be honest, I'm proud of you, lass. That took guts and determination. You must have inherited them from me."

"Or Mum," she said quietly, and a shadow passed across his face.

"*More* Mum, probably," he agreed. "You know, love, since you came home, I've found it much easier to remember all the good things about her."

"I think we both stopped remembering the good things for a while, Dad."

He nodded. "Yes, and I was so angry at the world. I felt as if I didn't want to move on without her."

"And now it feels as if we're both moving on *with* her.

"Too right. Now I feel as if she's beside me every step of the way." He took an eager bite of his egg. "I'm going to fix the fence at the bottom of the fell after breakfast, by the way. I could do with a hand if you don't mind… Unless you need to get on with your painting, of course."

Ellie agreed, feeling the need for wind in her face and a wide-open sky.

"I probably should paint," she said. "But I can do it later."

When they set off for the fell twenty minutes later, Ellie realized that with everything that had been going on in her life lately—helping with the horses and getting into riding again—she'd been neglecting her painting. She needed to finish more pieces if she was going to have enough material for a proper exhibition at Mel's gallery. After yesterday, she was desperate to paint the stallion, Grand Design, focusing on the moment he leaped back onto his feet after his ordeal, declaring war on the world. She'd already done a few sketches to keep the image fresh in her mind.

Friends, the painting of Robbie and Choco playing, just needed a few finishing touches. She'd decided to give it to Cass and Jake in thanks for letting her ride Fancy, on the understanding that she could still show it in her spring exhibition. And she'd almost finished the Cravendale sign last night.

As she handed tools to her dad, holding the fence rails in position while he secured them, she decided to try and get that done first.

"That'll do," he said, standing back to survey his handiwork before glancing at his watch. "Thanks for the help. It's only just after ten and I need to check on the rest of the fencing, so why don't you go back and get on with your painting?"

"Thanks. I think I'll go and finish the Cravendale sign," Ellie said. "I suppose I could deliver it this afternoon. I can easily be back in time to help you with the horses if I set off at twelve. I'll leave you some lunch, though."

"Don't worry about me. I'll just have some—"

"Tomato soup," she finished for him, laughing out loud.

Her dad was quiet for a second, then he swallowed hard. "I'm glad you're back, lass," he said, his voice thick with emotion.

"So am I, Dad."

AT ELEVEN-THIRTY, Ellie put down her brush with a satisfied sigh and sat back. She'd managed to work so many wild animals in and around the lettering on the sign for Cravendale that just looking at it made her smile. A worried badger peered through the C, a startled deer made a leap across the V and a cute little rabbit crouched beneath the A. The outer edges of the sign showed hints of her usual style; she hadn't been able to resist blurring the trees and vegetation to draw the eye to the animals and lettering.

"Paula will love it, I think," she said to Hope, who was watching her every move with a nervous expression on his face. He jumped up, yawning, and she reached down to give him a hug, wondering how she could have ever gotten along without his loyal companionship. "Don't look so anxious, boy," she told him. "You're here for life now, you know. I won't let you down. Come on, we'll just make Dad's lunch and then we'll go to Cravendale."

The red-and-white collie wagged his tail, totally trusting. He'd rarely left his new mistress's side since she'd brought him home a few short weeks ago. How could he still put his faith in a human being? she wondered, when he'd been so badly let down in the past? Then again, maybe he had the right idea; if you didn't take love and affection at face value, then you could miss out on love altogether. She would never trust Andy enough to let him love her again, though, she was sure of that. But she could never forget what they'd once had.

"Come on, boy," she said, putting her ex determinedly out of her head. The pup jumped up eagerly, afraid of being left behind.

WHEN ELLIE ARRIVED at Cravendale a couple of hours later, she thought there was no one around, but then she heard a high-pitched squealing from the barn, and rushed over to check it out. It took a few moments for her eyes to adjust to the gloom, but her ears led her to the farthest corner, where Paula was grappling with a fat pink piglet.

Tears of laughter ran down Ellie's face as she attempted to help Paula control the wildly objecting creature, and between fits of giggles, the two women eventually managed to get it into the pen that Paula had prepared.

"How can one small pig cause so much trouble?" Paula cried.

"Or make so much noise," Ellie added as they watched the indignant little piglet strutting around in the straw. "Where did it come from, anyway?"

Paula shrugged. "That's just it—I don't know. It was wandering around the yard when I came in after lunch. Someone must have dumped it, I guess."

"They probably got it as a pet and found that they'd bitten off more than they could chew."

"I bet they couldn't stand the noise," Paula agreed. "And she must have been a pet because she came running over as soon as she saw me. It was only when I tried to get her into the barn that I ran into trouble. I thought

I could maybe ask Andy if he knows anyone who'll give her a home."

"I'd just presumed she was a he," Ellie remarked. "She isn't acting very ladylike, that's for sure. When is Andy due to come over here, anyway?"

Before Paula could respond, the piglet ran toward them, placing her front trotters on the top bar of her pen and making friendly grunting sounds. Paula scratched the back of her neck and she twisted her head up in ecstasy. "See, she's okay when we don't try and make her do something she doesn't want to."

"I guess that explains the term *pigheaded*," Ellie joked.

"Coming back to Andy, though," Paula said. "I guess he must be a bit pigheaded, too—about this place, anyway. I thought he wouldn't want to be so involved when he went to work further away, but he's here every spare minute he has. To be honest, I don't know how we'd manage if he wasn't so committed, because I'd never be able to pay for all the work he does. He's been helping with fund-raisers, too, and he has this crazy dream of setting up a proper vet clinic here one day, focusing on treating rescued animals, mainly. Any kind of animal, of course, but he wants to specialize in wild creatures."

"It's a pity he isn't so caring in other aspects of his life," Ellie said sharply.

Paula shot her an inquiring glance. "I don't know anything about that, but he did once tell me that he'd lost the love of his life and there was no chance of ever getting her back. Maybe that's why he throws everything into his work with animals."

"He must have meant his wife, then," Ellie said, ignoring the pain in her heart by turning her attention back to the piglet. "Princess," she announced, changing the subject. "That's what you'll have to call her."

"It is very fitting," Paula agreed. "She's certainly a diva. Here, Princess."

When the piglet grunted loudly in reply, almost as if she understood, both women burst into yet another fit of giggles.

"She knows her name already," Ellie said. "Oh, and by the way, I've brought something for you."

"For me?"

"Yes…well, kind of. Come on, I'll show you."

When Paula saw the sign, she drew Ellie into a tight hug.

"It's beautiful," she said, tears shining in her eyes. "Thank you so, so much. It's really too good to hang outside in the rain, though."

"I can always touch it up if it fades," Ellie offered.

"Well, what do I owe you?" Paula asked. "It must have taken ages to do."

Ellie shook her head. "You don't owe me anything. I enjoyed doing it, and I admire what you do here so much that I wanted to contribute."

"I'm very grateful, Ellie, and I will find a way to pay you back."

"You already paid for it by looking after the fox, remember?"

Paula smiled. "Oh, yes. That was one of our success stories. Unfortunately, though, they don't all turn out like that. But let's go visit our current residents."

Ellie loved looking at the animals in Paula's expert care. An old, half-starved gray pony that had been at the center for a week gazed up at her through shining brown eyes, totally nonjudgmental. The pony was so thin that the very sight of her pulled on Ellie's heartstrings, but Paula assured her that Andy had checked her over on the day she arrived and pronounced her perfectly fine.

"She just needs some food inside her," Paula said sadly. "I don't know how people can be so cruel."

"Or ignorant," Ellie added.

"I suppose anyone can go and buy an animal." Paula sighed. "Even if they don't have a clue how to care for it. Anyway, at least little Merrylegs here will soon be fat and shiny again."

They moved on to the new arrivals, which included an African gray parrot someone had found in their garden and an exceptionally friendly ferret that had obviously been very well cared for.

"Someone must be really missing him," Ellie said when the ferret snuggled happily into the crook of Paula's arm. "And I've never heard a parrot talk so well."

"I'm going to put up signs in the local shops, and the paper has agreed to do a feature on these two on Friday to see if we can find their owners," Paula told her. "They're both healthy and seem well groomed, so I assume they got out and wandered off."

"Or flown off in the parrot's case." Ellie laughed. "The thing is though, Paula …this is supposed to be a *wild* animal sanctuary, isn't it?"

Paula paused. "Well, yes, I suppose it is. What did you put on the sign, though?"

"Just Cravendale Animal Sanctuary—I didn't have room for the wild."

"There you go, then, you've made the decision for us. We do mainly treat and care for wild animals, but we never turn any animal away."

"It must be hard to raise enough money to keep a charity like this going," Ellie said thoughtfully.

Paula nodded. "We do get donations—it's amazing how kind people can be. And we run all kinds of events—sales, sponsored walks, anything really. If people adopt one of our animals, they leave us a donation, and of course we get this place for free, thanks to Harold Fawcett, the man who owns it. He used to have a small farm, but when he retired and had no need for it anymore, he kindly offered to let us use it. Trouble is…"

Her usually smiling face fell and Ellie felt a prickle of alarm.

"Trouble is what?"

"I don't know why I'm telling you this because I haven't told anyone else yet."

"Not even Andy?"

Paula shook her head. "I only heard yesterday, and it isn't definite yet, so I didn't want to worry him."

"Sometimes it's easier to share a problem with someone who isn't involved, and I won't tell anyone whatever it is...least of all Andy."

"I think we might be going to lose the center."

Ellie gasped. "But why?"

"Harold, the old man I told you about, has gone into a retirement home, and the property is going on the market. There's no way we can raise the kind of money it'll sell for, so we need to find a new location...or close down."

"That's terrible," Ellie cried. "But there must be somewhere you can go. You'll have to tell Andy!"

Paula nodded. "I know. I was just hoping I'd find somewhere else before I broke the news."

"Don't worry, I won't say anything," Ellie promised. "And I'll talk to my dad and see if he knows of anywhere. He was really impressed with this place when he stopped by with Andy on the day they came to my exhibition."

Ellie couldn't stop thinking about Paula's problem as she drove back to Little Dale. She and her volunteers did such a good job at Cravendale, and it would be a tragedy if it had to close. It was nice to meet people like Paula, people who did things because they really cared… *Like Andy,* said an inner voice. No matter what Ellie thought of him, she couldn't deny that he really did love helping animals. What had Paula said about him losing the love of his life? Well, if the love of his life was Amy Granger, then maybe he should have treated her a bit better, or fallen in love with someone more suited to his way of life.

Of course, he might not have meant Amy. The thought made Ellie feel vaguely uncomfortable. After all, *she* had been the love of his life once, or so she'd believed at the time. But if that was still the case, then why had he never even tried to get back what they once had?

For a fleeting moment, a memory of the

Andy she used to know slipped into her head, the considerate, caring Andy Montgomery who she once believed she could never live without. She would never put herself back into that needy, vulnerable position...with anyone.

"Except for you, of course, Hope," she said out loud, reaching across to the passenger seat to scratch his head. "But then again, I can trust you, can't I?"

The pup whined, licking her hand and wagging his tail as if in agreement.

CHAPTER TWENTY-TWO

ELLIE'S PHONE RANG as she was getting ready
for bed. After helping her dad finish off the
horses, she'd spent the rest of the evening
putting the finishing touches on *Friends*. She
was going to ride Fancy tomorrow afternoon,
and she wanted to take the painting with her
to give to Cass and Jake.

Now there was true love. She sighed to
herself as she ran a comb through her tou-
sled curls. It was obvious at the wedding
just how in love they were; Jake hadn't been
able to keep his eyes off his new bride. Ever
since, when Ellie had been at Sky View, it
was heartwarming to see how tender they
were with each other.

Bill Munro, Jake's dad, had once mentioned it to her when she was grooming
Fancy. He'd come into the stable for a chat
and when she'd remarked on what a lovely
couple they made, he'd nodded.

"Gives you hope, a love like that. It took a lot of years and a heap of heartache, though, before they found each other, especially in Jake's case. But it makes you realize that sometimes you have to hold out for the real deal and never settle for second best."

"I suppose some of us have to settle for second best," she'd responded with a sigh.

"And have you?" he'd asked.

She'd shaken her head firmly, changing the subject and making light of the conversation, but now his words came back to haunt her. Sometimes, she told herself, second best was safest.

Her loud, melodic ringtone broke the silence, and Andy's name flashing on the screen seemed like a sign. Talk about timing!

"Ellie, it's me. Are you still up for coming out on a call, something different?"

Her response was immediate. "Yes, of course I am. What is it?"

"Pony, up on the fell. I have to pass by your place on the way, anyway, so be out in the lane in five minutes."

Throwing her phone onto the bed, she grabbed her jeans and a warm sweater. Hope whined softly, and she leaned down to plant a kiss on his head. "I won't be long, boy. You be good, and don't disturb Dad.

"I'm going out on a call with Andy, Dad," she called as she raced past his bedroom door.

"Be careful," came his muffled reply, and she smiled to herself.

Careful of what?

It was dark outside, and the cold bite of early autumn made Ellie shiver, but at least a full moon lit up the sky with an eerie glow. She felt a flutter of nerves. It was weird to be out so late in the evening, all alone in what felt like an alien landscape. But it wasn't alien, she told herself, looking around for familiar landmarks as she ran up the lane.

She heard Andy's truck approaching, and its headlights cast their yellow beam as he came up the hill. The large vehicle lurched to a halt next to her.

"Come on," he urged, reaching across to open the passenger door.

Ellie slid in beside him, heart racing. "Is it bad?" she asked breathlessly.

He nodded, his expression grim. "I didn't give you the full story. Ray Johnston has a sheep farm way up the fell. He has Fell ponies, too, but they run pretty wild for most of the year. He checks on them, of course, but most of them have hardly ever really been handled at all, which is fine until something goes wrong. Obviously, they normally foal in the spring, so he brings them closer to home to keep an eye on them. But this year things have gone a bit wrong."

"What do you mean?"

He fell silent for a moment as he carefully negotiated a rutted, single-track lane.

"Is it right up the fell?" she asked uneasily.

"Ray said to take this turn and then keep on going until the trail runs out. After that he'll give us a ride on his ATV."

"But isn't it a bit late in the year for a foal?"

"Yes, that's what I meant. Something's gone wrong. Ray didn't even know the mare was in foal…or if she was, then it wouldn't be due until spring. He didn't tell me everything, he just said to come quick. He found her by accident, right before it got dark, and tried to get her down the fell, but there was no chance. Then all the other ponies got spooked, so he decided to stay up there until the foal was born. These tough Fell ponies usually just drop their foals all on their own with no trouble at all, but this one seems to have run into difficulties. Now she's down and she desperately needs help."

Stopping his truck at a wooden gate, he grabbed his bag and jumped out, closely followed by Ellie. She shivered, wrapping her jacket more tightly.

"It's so cold up here," she said.

"And that's another problem. They're predicting frost in high places tonight."

The roar of an approaching ATV caught their attention then, and they hurried toward the sound, relieved to see the headlights appear.

"At least I'll be able to see what I'm doing," Andy remarked.

It seemed to take forever to get to where the fell filly was struggling to give birth. The ATV lurched and bumped across the steep hillside, almost throwing both Ellie and Andy off several times, but there was no way Ray Johnston was slowing down.

"There," he eventually shouted over the bike's engine. "Just up ahead."

The headlights picked out a human figure beside a dark shape on the ground. Ray pulled up sharply, cutting the engine.

"It's my son, Thomas. He stayed with her while I came to get you."

In that instant, they were plunged into eerie silence after Ray cut the motor. Ellie gasped at the sight of a dozen half-wild Fell ponies cantering along the skyline against the silver moon. She blinked, trying to memorize the vision before turning her attention to Andy, who was already crouching down to examine the filly.

"Any chance of some light, Ray?" he called.

The ATV's headlights cast a sudden glow across the scene, making Ellie cry out in sympathy for the terrified young Fell pony that seemed to have all but given up.

"I can't leave them on long, or I'll drain the battery," said Ray. "And I don't want to keep the engine running or it'll scare her even more."

"Just leave them on for as long as you can," Andy insisted. "And if Thomas here could try and keep her head down, then she won't be able to struggle so much. We need to act quickly if we're going to save then both."

Ellie felt totally helpless, hardly able to breathe as she watched Andy work. His face, lit up by the yellow beam, held a concentration and tenderness that clawed at her heart.

Down on his knees, eyes narrowed and jaw clenched, Andy felt inside the mare to find out how the foal was lying.

"Head's back," he groaned, probing deeper, his face turning crimson with the effort. "It's only slightly to one side, though," he added with relief. "So if I can push it back into the uterus, there's a chance I can turn it around."

The mare offered no resistance as he tried to physically manipulate her unborn foal into a birthing position.

Ray Johnston leaned forward, his hands on his knees.

"And if you can't?"

"Then it's surgery, I'm afraid, and it's getting a bit late for that, even if we could do it here."

Ellie felt a sob rise up inside her, but it died away on the moaning wind. Crying wasn't an option; this was about the new life that was struggling to come into the world and the brave little mare dangling on the edge of death.

Suddenly, Andy let out a triumphant gasp. "That's it! She's too weak to push, though, so I'll just get a line around the forelegs. There..."

Sitting back, he started to pull, easy and slow, murmuring encouragement. Ray switched off the lights on the ATV and they were plunged into darkness, but Andy persisted.

"Come on, little lass," he begged. "Give me some help."

And then, when they all thought time had run out, the pony managed one huge push, and the foal slid onto the ground in a rush. Ellie felt the hot tears she had been holding back running down her face as she watched Andy jump into action, clearing its tiny nose and rubbing its chest, willing it to breathe.

Come on, little one, Ellie pleaded silently. *Don't give up yet.*

Taking in a gulp of air, the foal raised its head, following a basic instinct to try and get onto its feet as soon as possible. The little black mare's own instinct kicked in, and despite her ordeal, she leaped to her feet, reaching out her nose toward her offspring, snorting gently.

Elation surged through Ellie's veins as she witnessed the bond, and she grabbed her sketch pad, desperate to capture the elusive moment; the expression of wonder in the little mare's eyes; Andy's face, contoured by moonlight.

She moved closer, and as Andy cried out a warning, the wind caught her sketch pad, fluttering the pages. She froze, seeing the panic in the mare's eyes. The pony stepped back and then wheeled away, galloping off into the darkness.

"What have you done?" Andy yelled. "The foal desperately needs to feed, and you've chased his mother away. Don't you understand that she's half-wild? There are more important things than your stupid paintings, you know."

"She'll be back," Ray Johnson said, defusing the situation. "Her mothering instinct's way too strong for her to stay away…you'll see."

Hot tears pressed against the backs of Ellie's eyelids and she brushed them away.

"I'm so sorry," she murmured.

Andy's face softened. "Maybe I did over-react a bit. I don't really think that your paintings are stupid. But there's a time and place, Ells. Let's just hope Ray is right."

"He is right!" Thomas said, pointing. "There she is."

The little black mare stood against the skyline, staring down at her newborn foal. When she started walking cautiously toward them, they all stood stock-still, holding their breath.

"Try and get hold of her lead rope, Thomas," Ray whispered as she came within reach.

Stepping forward quietly, the boy grabbed the trailing rope. The little black mare pulled back at first, and then, almost as if she was glad to be taken under control, she gave in, moving eagerly in the direction of her baby, nickering softly.

"Mothering instinct wins out every time," Ray remarked, then he let out a low chuckle, pointing to where the foal was trying to struggle to its feet. "Will you take a look at that?"

"That's no Fell pony," Thomas exclaimed as the foal wobbled over to its mother on lanky legs, eager to suckle. "It's black-and-white!"

"That's impossible," Ray said.

"Why don't we worry about that later?" Andy suggested. "Right now, we need to try and get them both down to the farm. If you hold the foal on the back of the bike, Thomas, then hopefully its mum will follow. We'll wait until the little one's had a good feed first, though."

Fifteen minutes later, Thomas was perched on the rack at the back of the ATV, holding the foal precariously across his knees. Andy hung on to the mare's lead rope and Ray prepared to drive down the steep fell side.

"Go slow, Dad," Thomas pleaded. "This little chap is heavier than he looks."

"Actually," said Andy, "It's a filly."

"Well, that's good news," Ray said. "Even if it is black-and-white."

Ellie followed in their wake, walking well behind the mare. She still felt bad about frightening her earlier, and Andy's sharp remarks had cut deep. She'd gotten so carried away with the beauty and emotion of the scene, she'd forgotten what was important. There was no excuse for that.

Way above them, now, the Fell pony herd had gathered together, outlined by moonlight, wild and free. She took in the image, trying to memorize it.

Ellie moved closer to Andy and tugged on his sleeve.

"I really am sorry, you know," she said quietly.

He glanced sideways at her with one of his face-filling smiles.

"It all worked out," he said. "Just forget about it."

It took an hour for them to get back down to the trail, and even then, it wasn't smooth sailing. At first, the Fell pony mare was fairly calm, but as she realized she was leaving her herd behind, she began to fret. It was only her compulsion to follow her foal that allowed Andy to maintain control. When they finally entered the farmyard and Ellie shut the gate, they each heaved a sigh of relief.

Ray's wife, Ruth, was waiting. She watched as they manhandled the foal and its mother into the well-bedded stable she'd prepared, exclaiming about the foal's color before announcing that she was off to make some tea.

Ellie, Andy, Ray and Thomas stood watching the little black mare devour her feed while the foal happily suckled.

"So how come it's black-and-white, Dad?" Thomas asked.

"Belle here has given me nothing but trouble," Ray said, motioning to the mare. "Last year, she was supposed to go to the Kirby Stephen horse sale, but she bolted off and jumped a barbed wire fence. Cost me a fortune to get her stitched up, so I decided to keep her and put her in foal. I always run a stallion on the fell in early summer so that the mares foal in spring, but it looks as if some stray stallion must have got to her first."

"It's into September now, Dad," Thomas said. "So she must gotten pregnant last October or November."

"That was just after I let her back out when her wounds had healed," said Ray. "I never saw a colored stallion anywhere around, though."

"Maybe it just escaped for a few hours. It doesn't take long, you know," Andy said with a smile.

"But what if he got to them all?" Ray groaned.

"There's a good market for colored foals

nowadays," Andy assured him. "Very fash-
ionable."

Ray's eyes lit up. "You think so?"

"I know so," said Andy. "Come on, Ellie,
we need to get back."

CHAPTER TWENTY-THREE

AFTER ALL THE excitement and emotion of the past couple of hours, Ellie felt totally drained. She leaned back against the worn leather of the passenger seat in Andy's truck, reliving the evening all over again. The terror on the little mare's face as she struggled to give birth and the love she displayed when she nuzzled her newborn foal. Andy's taut, worried expression as he put all his effort into helping her. The breathtaking sight of the Fell ponies on the horizon, outlined by the silvery moonlight. So many images locked inside her head, waiting to be painted.

She glanced at Andy and he smiled at her, just like he used to when they shared everything.

"I really am sorry about scaring the mare," she said.

"I know. It's just…sometimes I worry about your reasons for coming back home."

"What do you mean?"

He stared at the lane ahead, as if deciding what to say. "Well, you only really started thinking about it after the day we met again, didn't you? After you saved the fox?"

Ellie nodded slowly. "So, what…do you think I came back here for you?"

"No, of course not," he said quickly. "But you're passionate about your painting and you're very ambitious."

"Yes, I want to be successful. That's not a crime. What are you getting at, Andy?"

He shrugged. "You don't have much opportunity to find subject matter in the city, do you? I mean, you need to see animals in real situations…"

"Like tonight, you mean? So you think my reasons for coming back home are purely selfish."

"No…of course not, it's just…"

"Just what?"

"Don't let your dad down, will you Ells?"

"Look, Andy," Her voice was brittle with anger. "I'm not the one who lets people down."

"And neither am I."

"That's not how I remember it."

They pulled into the yard at Hope Farm and he stopped his truck, reaching across to take hold of her arm as she tried to open the door. She turned to face him.

"I'm sorry, Ellie. I know you won't let your dad down and I know you didn't mean to scare the mare. Can't we just forget all this and start again?"

"Start again," she echoed.

He held her eyes with his. "Please."

For an endless moment, the past rushed in to suffocate her.

"I'm so sorry, Ells," he said.

She could feel his breath on her cheek; the heat of him.

"Sorry for what?" she murmured.

His lips were dangerously close to hers, his familiar aroma bringing a strange, heady sensation.

"For everything, Ellie," he murmured.

Suddenly, she wanted this—wanted him—so much.

She didn't resist as he pulled her into his arms, covering her lips with his, and then she was drowning in the ecstasy she remembered in her dreams.

When he eventually drew away, he cupped

her face between his palms, looking deep into her eyes.

"I am so sorry for not being there for you," he said, hesitating slightly before going on. "And for not telling you—"

She stiffened. "What didn't you tell me?"

"I knew I'd made a terrible mistake, Ells." He was speaking quickly, the words tumbling out. "As soon as I ended it, I knew that. But you didn't answer my calls, so I came back for you as soon as I could."

Her breath hitched. "You came back? When?"

He pressed his lips gently against her forehead. "All you need to know is that I never gave up on us."

"That's not true," she cried, her heart racing. "You did give up on us! I don't believe that you came back."

"Your mother warned me off," he told her sadly. "She pleaded with me to stay away. She said you were totally over me and that the only decent thing to do was leave you alone. She made me promise."

Ellie pulled away from him.

"You're lying. My mum wouldn't do that."

"I'm sorry, Ells, but it's true. And what

could I do? How could I tell you? She was so ill, and I believed her when she told me you didn't want me in your life anymore."

Ellie's face turned ashen and she struggled out of his grip, hot tears pouring down her face.

"You're lying," she said again. "My mum's *dead*. How could you make up something like that?"

"It's not a lie," he called as she clambered out of his truck, almost falling on the ground in her haste. "And you deserve to know the truth."

As ELLIE RAN toward the house, a vague figure in the darkness, Andy dropped his face into his hands. Why had he told her? Why hadn't he just let their relationship blossom slowly, as he'd intended? The answer struck him full in the chest. Deep down, he was afraid that Ellie had only come home to get inspiration for her paintings, that eventually she'd go back to her fiancé and her city life.

He'd always intended to keep Sally Nelson's wishes a secret, but he just hadn't been able to bear that Ellie believed he'd never even bothered to come back. He thought that in telling her truth, she might see him in a different, better light and maybe even give him a chance to prove that he was trustworthy. But all he had done was tarnish her mother's memory and make himself sound like a liar.

FOR HOURS, ELLIE lay sleepless in her bed, her tears soaking Hope's coat as he cuddled up against her, offering comfort. How could Andy have used her mum as his excuse? What kind of guy could make something like that up?

She must have fallen asleep, because she woke to sunlight pouring in through her window. She blinked her puffy eyes, remembering the previous night and Andy's cruel lie. She had almost fallen into his trap, but now her suspicions were confirmed—he was only looking out for himself when it came to women. Kissing him had been such a huge mistake—one she wouldn't make again.

Glancing at the clock, she leaped out of bed and ran to the window. Her dad was leading Blue across the yard to the paddock. Guilt struck her as she realized just how late it was.

"Why didn't you wake me?" she called. "It's nine-thirty, and I never sleep in."

"You do now," her dad said, shading his eyes as he looked up at her. "I hope you aren't going to make a habit of it."

"No, of course not. I—"

"I didn't wake you because I heard you coming home in the early hours and I thought you could do with the rest. Put the kettle on. I'll come in for a coffee as soon as I've turned Blue out and you can tell me all about it."

ELLIE DRAGGED HERSELF downstairs and switched on the kettle, her mind a million miles away. What should she tell her dad, that Andy had told her a terrible lie about her mum? No, she decided, that wouldn't be fair to him and she would never besmirch her mother's memory like that.

"So what happened last night?" her dad asked, walking in through the kitchen door with Shadow at his heels. Hope ran across to say hello, rolling over on to his back on the floor.

"Don't be such a softy, Hope," Ellie said, trying to hide her nerves.

Her dad smiled. "He's just a pup—he'll

learn. Now tell me all about last night. Did you and Andy go out after his shift?"

"Definitely not," Ellie said. "You know full well that we were over years ago. He may be good with animals, but I would never ever trust anything he said."

"Don't be too hard on him," her dad responded, taken aback by her harsh tone. "He's not so bad."

"That's what everyone thinks because they don't know what he's really like." Ellie took a deep breath. "It was a pretty eventful night, though."

"Did you get many ideas from it?"

"Oh yes," she said, filling him in on the details of the foal's birth. She even admitted to frightening the mare away and almost ruining the whole thing.

"All's well that ends well," he told her. "I'd like to have seen Ray Johnston's face, though, when he realized that the Fell pony foal was black-and-white. Anyway, I suppose you'll want to get all your ideas down on paper as soon as you can…but do you think you could give me a hand getting some sheep down from the fell first? The vet's coming to check them over this afternoon and I'd really appreciate the help."

"It's the least I can do," she said, suddenly feeling sick. "Which vet?

Her dad looked at her curiously. "Todd, I think…at least it was him I spoke to on the phone."

THE DAY FLEW by after its slow start. Hope was more of a hindrance than a help when it came to herding sheep, but Shadow was learning fast and they soon had the bleating ewes secured in the meadow by the farm. Cass called as they were having lunch, to ask if she wanted to come over to Sky View and ride Fancy, but Ellie declined.

"I'd love to, Cass, but I should stay here and help Dad this afternoon, and I need to do some painting later."

Her dad took the phone from her hand. "Don't take any notice, Cass," he said. "I can manage fine now, and the painting will wait. She'd love to come and she'll be there around two."

"I just want to feel as if I'm pulling my weight around here," Ellie said after he hung up and handed the phone back.

"You do pull your weight," he insisted. "The sheep are in now, and it's quiet this afternoon. I've come to learn that you have to take your opportunities when you can in this life because you don't know when they'll be gone. Look at me and your mum—we hardly ever went on vacation. 'When we're older,' we used to say. Trouble is, your mum never got older…"

Ellie reached across to squeeze his arm, tears suddenly blinding her.

"When did you get to be so sensitive, Dad? While I was growing up, you were always so busy, and then after…after mum went, you became a grumpy old stranger."

He nodded slowly.

"I suppose it was only after you came back and I realized what I'd been missing. Jake Munro played a part, too, though. After all the tragedy in his life, he finally found love again. Not that I want to find love— I'm way too old to be bothered with all that. Your mum used to say that your family is your future, and since there's only you and me, then I'd be a silly old idiot to turn you away."

"Well, whatever the reason, at least we've both come to our senses," Ellie said.

"Sure have. And that's why you can't miss out on things like going riding on a glorious day."

AS CASS AND ELLIE clattered back into the yard at Sky View after a brisk ride across the fell, Ellie realized just how right her dad had been.

"I feel so much better," she said, smiling at Cass.

"Me, too," agreed Cass. "It won't be long before Jake starts telling me to stop riding, so I have to make the most of it."

"You are feeling okay, though?"

"Never felt better, to be honest. We told Bill last night, and he's over the moon."

"And Robbie?"

A broad smile lit up Cass's face.

"He can't wait to have a brother or sister."

"And he doesn't mind which it is?"

Cass shook her head. "No, fortunately not because I don't want to know until it's born."

Ellie was thrilled for Cass and her family. The Munros had been through so much, and now they were finally where they wanted to be. Her heart clenched, and Andy's face flashed in her mind's eye. Not everyone got that chance, though, did they? Or maybe everyone got the chance but missed it by making bad decisions. Had she made bad decisions? She was sure she had, she just didn't know what they were.

ELLIE'S PHONE RANG later that evening as she was sketching, trying to clarify all the images inside her head from the night before.

Paula's warm voice in her ear made her smile.

"Ellie, thank you again for that amazing sign," she said. "Anyway, I just wanted to tell you that Andy came over today and—"

"Did you tell him about Cravendale?" Ellie cut in.

The line went silent for a second. "Yes. He was upset, but we've decided that we'll just have to find somewhere else, no matter how hard that might be. And I've given him something for you, to say thanks."

"You don't need to give me anything," Ellie insisted. "I wanted to do it."

"Too late now! And I think you'll enjoy it."

"What is it?" Ellie asked.

"You'll see," Paula said playfully. "You'll need a posh dress, though."

"What—" Ellie began, but Paula had already hung up.

At nine o'clock, she gave up trying to sketch, unable to concentrate. What had Paula meant? Unfortunately, she wouldn't know until she'd seen Andy, and right now he was the last person she wanted to come across.

As she put down her charcoal and stood up, stretching her arms above her head, her dad's head appeared around the door.

"You've got a visitor," he said. "He's waiting in the kitchen."

"Who is it?" she asked, already knowing the answer, and her heart turned over in one long flip.

Andy was waiting near the back door, moving restlessly from foot to foot, a crooked smile filling his whole face. *Filling the whole room*, thought Ellie, feeling awkward and yet so angry with him at the same time.

"I've already spoken to Paula," she said. "So I know why you're here."

He seemed taken aback. "Oh, yes. It's not just that, though… I need to talk to you."

Hope slid up behind her, pushing his cold nose against her hand and Ellie took a breath, appreciating the dog's unquestioning support.

"There's nothing you can say to me that will get past your lies."

"Please, Ellie…and then I'll give you Paula's gift."

"Is that supposed to be a bribe? I'm not a child, you know."

His mouth fell open. "At least listen to me."

"What…to more lies?"

"No, just to me saying sorry and begging you to put last night behind us. Surely we can stay friends at least?"

"I'm not sure that you and I can ever be just friends," she said, shuddering as she remembered the moments before he told her his cruel lie. "Anyway, I don't trust you, and it seems that you don't trust me. You obviously seem to think I'm here for all the wrong reasons. How can we base a friendship on that?"

He took a step toward her. "We go back too far to fall out, Ellie. Please, give me a chance to show you that I'm worth your friendship, at least…for old times' sake."

"I'll try," she agreed reluctantly. "For old times' sake. But I can't promise anything.

"By the way...I'm sorry to hear about Cravendale."

Andy frowned. "So she told you. It is bad news, but we won't give up. We'll just have to try and find somewhere else, that's all."

"So show me what Paula entrusted you with, then."

"I don't know how pleased you'll be..." He handed her an envelope.

"Why wouldn't I be pleased with it?"

"Open it and you'll see."

The card she pulled out of the envelope looked very fancy and official.

CRAVENDALE ANIMAL SANCTUARY
ANNUAL CHARITY BALL
Highfield Hall Hotel, Preston.
September 24, 2014
7:30 p.m. until late
RSVP to Paula Carr

"Charity ball?" Ellie exclaimed. It was only two days away.

"I'm just the delivery boy. The tickets cost a fortune, but she wanted to give you one in thanks for the sign. We make a lot of money that night—there's an auction and a raffle and all sorts of other fund-raising. And we're hoping someone might come forward with an offer for a new location if we ask around. Look, Ells—" He took another step forward.

Too close for comfort, Ellie thought, clinging tightly to her anger.

"Let's just forget what I said last night and start again. Please."

She hesitated, remembering how deep his lie had cut.

"My mother isn't here to defend herself. Can't you see how wrong it was for you to say those things?"

He held her gaze silently, and then he looked down at his scuffed leather boots.

"All I can say is that I'm really sorry if I spoiled your memory of your mother."

She nodded briskly. "Okay, then, I will try and forget it. I'll just have to remember never to believe anything you say again."

"And you'll go to the ball?"

"I'm still not sure about that."

"But how can you refuse when Paula has been so generous? She'd be disappointed if you didn't show up... I'll pick you up at six-thirty."

"Pick me up," she echoed, panic making her heart race.

"There isn't much point in taking two cars when we're both leaving from the same place, is there?"

"Where are you going?" asked Bob, striding into the kitchen.

"To a charity ball," Andy announced with a broad grin.

"I haven't decided yet," cut in Ellie.

"Of course you must go," her dad insisted. "You'll enjoy it."

"See," said Andy. "Even your dad agrees with me. And you can't let Paula down. Six-thirty it is, then!"

CHAPTER TWENTY-FOUR

FOR THE NEXT two days, all Ellie could think about was the ball. She'd feel bad about disappointing Paula if she didn't show up, but perhaps she could make an excuse. Mostly, she just wished she was going with anyone other than Andy. At least now he realized where he stood with her, though, and knew that she would never trust him again. If she did decide to go, she'd have to keep her distance and try to enjoy the occasion.

SEPTEMBER 24 DAWNED clear and bright, with the first slight suggestion of frost. Beyond Ellie's window, the trees—in full autumn glory now—shimmered in the morning sun. Finding a dress had been her biggest problem; she'd had no time to go to the city, so she'd spent a couple of hours in the nearby town of Kendal and found a glamorous, figure-hugging creation with a deep neckline. Just looking at it made her feel both nervous and excited. Its delicate blue color also meant that she could wear her extravagant wedding shoes again, which was a huge bonus.

Since Andy dropped off the invitation, she'd scrolled through her phone again and again, her finger hovering over Paula's number but never clicking it. After all, what excuse could she make? And then she'd scroll back up to Andy's number, wondering if she should tell him she would drive herself to the ball. But she was so nervous about the whole thing that she didn't really want to go alone, either. And now it was Friday and too late to change anything.

Her phone burst into song while she was mucking out Dennis's stable. She put down her fork and fumbled for it in her pocket, flicking it on to see Paula's name flashing on the screen.

"Hi, Ellie, I wanted to make sure you were all right for tonight."

Ellie froze; this was her moment.

"Yes, thanks," she heard herself say. "I'm really looking forward to it."

"And you're coming with Andy?"

"He's insisting on it."

Paula paused before replying. "Well, why not? You make a nice couple and you have so much in common."

"The only thing we have in common," Ellie said, "is a very bad history."

The heavy silence on the line made Ellie wish she'd kept her remark to herself.

"Sorry, I shouldn't have said that," she mumbled. "Going with Andy is fine, and I can't wait for tonight. I bought a new dress and—"

"I didn't mean to interfere," Paula interrupted. "I didn't realize you and Andy were once…"

"It's fine. Really. I don't know why I haven't mentioned it before. It was years ago, when we were very young. Teenagers. We both got over it long ago."

"I don't think you ever really get *over* your first love," Paula remarked.

The understanding tone in her voice made Ellie want to cry.

She took a deep breath. "I'll see you tonight, and thanks so much for the invite."

"Thank *you* for the beautiful sign."

The rest of the day dragged. Ellie's dad was away, delivering a two-year-old filly that he'd sold last week, so Ellie threw herself into work, meticulously mucking out and then sweeping the yard with such effort that her arms ached. Then she turned out the three broodmares, followed by Blue and Dennis individually. When all the usual chores were done, she'd intended to paint, but she found she couldn't concentrate. She headed for the chicken shed instead, armed with a wheelbarrow and shovel to clean it out.

The chickens clucked inquisitively around her feet as she worked and she chatted happily to them, enjoying their busy company and feeling better already about the evening ahead. She'd never been to a ball before, and now that she'd decided to go, she was determined to enjoy it.

Her dad came home at five o'clock. Ellie went to meet him as he parked his horsebox in the yard and climbed out of the car.

"Good day?" she asked. "Did she travel okay?"

He smiled at her, pulling a package from his pocket.

"Yes, she was as good as gold. And he paid in cash." A frown flitted across his face. "Shouldn't you be getting ready by now?"

Butterflies fluttered in Ellie's stomach. "I'll just give out the feeds first."

"You'll do no such thing," he insisted. "Go right now, young lady, and make yourself look beautiful."

Over an hour later, Ellie surveyed her appearance in the mirror. Was the dress too much? Was she wearing enough makeup? Was her jewelry right?"

Fondling the crystal on a silver chain that she wore around her neck, she thought about her mother. Sally always used to tell her that less was more, and that was the effect she'd been hoping for. The necklace and matching crystal drop earrings were simple, but they glinted with all the colors around them, like the blue of her dress.

Ellie closed her eyes, trying to feel her mother's presence, seeking her approval.

"Ellie," her dad called from downstairs. "Your ride is here."

"No going back now, Mum," she whispered, reaching for her wrap. Andy stood in the middle of the kitchen, the brilliant white of his shirt accentuating his deep tan. He froze when he saw Ellie, and she smiled impulsively, unable to take her eyes off his tall frame. He was so handsome in his tux. Drawing herself up tall, she smoothed down her blue dress, feeling self-conscious. He cleared his throat and smiled, finding his voice. "You look lovely," he said.

"She sure does," Bob agreed, looking at her proudly. "You look after her, now."

Andy held out his arm and she took it as if in a trance, feeling like Cinderella and suddenly looking forward to tonight.

"I have to be home by midnight," she said, giggling when Andy frowned. "Sorry, just my own little joke."

"Come on, then, my lady," he announced. "Or we'll be late. And don't worry, Bob. I'll treat her like a princess."

As they drove out of the yard at Hope Farm, Ellie decided to put their differences out of her head for the evening and found herself chatting to Andy way more easily than she'd expected. Or was she gibbering? She smiled to herself; somehow, it felt as if the dress had turned her into a different person, with more confidence than she usually felt.

Andy regaled her with stories about his job. The time a herd of heifers knocked him over into the mud, leaving the purple-faced elderly farmer who'd called him out demanding that they should send out a "proper" vet; the dog that ran behind him when he was trying to examine it, biting him on the backside. The way he told his stories made tears of laughter run down her face, and she had to touch up her makeup.

The trip to Preston passed by so quickly that she was surprised when they pulled up outside Highfield Hall Hotel.

"Wow!" she exclaimed, admiring its beautiful Georgian structure.

"It's even better inside," Andy told her.

"You've been here before?"

He nodded. "I came to the ball last year."

She wanted to ask who his date had been, but she bit her lip, not wanting anything to spoil this special night.

Paula was waiting in the magnificent hallway beneath a glittering chandelier, greeting everyone as they arrived. A tall, clean-cut, dark-haired man with a friendly smile stood next to her.

"Ellie, Andy!" she cried. "I'm so glad you could come. Meet my husband, Greg."

"Ah, yes," he said, reaching out to take Ellie's hand. "You must be the artist."

"And you must be the chef," she responded. "Nice to meet you, Greg."

"Likewise," he murmured, making an extravagant show of raising her fingers to his lips.

Andy scowled, but Paula just laughed.

"Don't take any notice of him," she said. "He pretends to be a flirt, but I know better. It's all for show."

Andy took Ellie by the arm. "Let's go and find our table."

"Funny, isn't it, who people meet," Ellie remarked as he ushered her across the large ballroom toward the list of place sittings. "I mean, Greg seems really nice, but he's not at all what I expected Paula's husband to be like."

Placing his hand in the base of her back, Andy propelled her to a round table near to the front, drawing back the chair for her to sit. "And what did you expect Paula's husband to be like?" he asked, taking the seat beside her.

"Oh I don't know." She laughed. "Smaller, I guess, and less...dashing."

The band began to play just then, cutting off their conversation, and other guests arrived to fill up their table. Ellie sat up straight, glad that she'd splurged on such an expensive dress since most of the other women at their table exuded wealth. Diamonds flashed and sparkled in the light of the candelabra centerpiece, and their expensive perfume filled the air.

Excitement rippled inside her, and she took hold of Andy's sleeve impulsively.

"This is so much fun," she whispered, her blue eyes sparkling. "And tonight, Andy, just for once, we're going to put all our issues aside."

"Just for tonight?" he asked softly.

"You know the score," she told him. "This is all just pretend. Nothing's changed."

"Only joking," he responded with a forced smile.

Paula made a rousing speech once they were all seated, encouraging everyone to give generously and explaining Cravendale's need for a new base.

"So if anyone has any buildings they feel would be suitable, we'd be glad to hear about it," she finished. "And thank you all so much for your continuing support of the animals."

"She's amazing, isn't she," Ellie said, and Andy nodded in agreement.

"She's so passionate about helping animals. Oh Ells…" Taking both her hands in his, he looked into her eyes, an intensity in his gaze. "I'm passionate, too—passionate about Cravendale and everything we can achieve there. I really want to make a difference."

"What do you mean?" Ellie asked.

"I'd like it to have its own veterinary clinic and become known around the country as the main center for treating wild animals. Of course, we'll take other animals as well—abused and abandoned pets and livestock, things like that. I want to work with all the animal charities, like the RSPCA and Animal Concern. We just have to find somewhere to move soon, somewhere with a bit of land and room to expand."

"And I'm sure you will," Ellie said, getting caught up in his enthusiasm.

The evening took on a magical quality after Andy's outburst. A babble of conversation filled the table as the courses came and went. Marmaduke Murray, an actor, sat on Ellie's left. He regaled her with stories about his career, but she only half listened, trying to hear what the voluptuous blonde on Andy's right was saying. The blonde leaned into him, flashing her brown eyes as she took another sip from her wine glass while he smiled the broad, crooked smile that seemed to fill up his whole face. Her bored elderly companion had a resigned expression on his face, as if this was what he always had to put up with.

Well, Ellie decided, knowing how Andy was with women, perhaps the older man wouldn't have to put up with it for much longer. But that wasn't fair. Surely even Andy would draw the line at trying to seduce someone else's wife.

The dessert was magnificent.

"It's like a work of art," Andy said to Ellie, raising his spoon reluctantly.

"It's too nice to spoil." She giggled. "Tell your friend over there to try it first."

"She's driving me crazy," he whispered in her ear. "How's yours?"

"Very nice, but very full of himself," she murmured. "He's an actor."

"Mine is a would-be model. She's nice enough, too, but all she talks about are her looks. Kind of like my ex-wife. Now eat your amazing dessert and then we can dance."

Ellie froze, feeling uneasy. Was it Andy mentioning his ex-wife or the prospect of dancing with him that had rattled her? she wondered. Couples were already beginning to drift around the dance floor, holding each other close as a moody tune played. She hadn't thought this through at all.

"I hate dancing," she told him.

Disappointment flashed across his face.

"You didn't use to…remember?"

Ellie gulped, afraid of her own emotions. Oh, yes, she remembered. That was the problem.

"I'll dance when they play something more lively," she promised.

At ten o'clock, when the tables were cleared, the MC announced that raffle tickets would be drawn in fifteen minutes. The prizes, donated by all manner of people, ranged from the amusing to the extravagant.

Andy eagerly withdrew two strips of tickets from his top pocket and laid them out on the table. "Blue or white?" he asked her. "You never know, you might win the top prize."

"And what is that, exactly?" asked Ellie, picking up the blue tickets.

He gave an exaggerated shrug, smiling broadly and splaying his palms. "I have no clue, but isn't this fun?"

For just a second, Ellie's defenses slipped, and she held his gaze.

"We used to have a lot of fun, didn't we, Andy?"

He reached across to cover her hand with his, and she didn't pull it away.

"Oh, yes," he said, his voice breaking. "The best."

Panic rose in her throat and her heart beat so hard she was sure he must be able to hear it. Grabbing her purse and muttering an excuse, she fled to the ladies' room. This was all too much, this magical atmosphere; it was making things blurry.

WHEN ELLIE GOT back to the table, the band had changed the mood and a loud, contemporary song rang out into the room.

"I'll dance to this one," she said a bit too enthusiastically, wanting to avoid conversation.

Andy followed and soon got into the swing

of the music. Within minutes they were laughing together again.

Ellie felt as if she was watching herself from afar. This rapport between them was superficial, she realized. Too much water had gone under the bridge for her to ever be able to relax with Andy again.

When the lights came up, they reluctantly went back to their seats.

"What do you think?" Andy asked, waving his strand of tickets. "Are we going to win?"

"I'm not very lucky," Ellie said. "So probably not."

"Well, you used to be very lucky. Remember when you won that trip to Blackpool?"

"We went up the tower," Ellie, said, smiling at the memory.

"And I kissed you right at the top."

A strange tingling sensation in her lips made Ellie shiver as she relived the moment, and she closed her eyes. It wasn't fair of him to drag up stories like that. Suddenly, she wished she hadn't let him persuade her to come tonight.

"Blue…three, three, one," the MC announced.

"It's yours, dear," said Marmaduke Murray, nudging her gently and pointing to one of her tickets.

"Oh, it is!" she said, standing awkwardly. "Do I just go up and get it?"

"Over here!" Andy called out, raising his hand.

Ellie's face turned crimson when everyone in the room turned to stare at her.

"Come on up," the MC said into the microphone. "You have first pick of the prizes."

She headed across the floor feeling totally disoriented. Bright lights shone in her face and a hysterical giggle rose in her throat. Perhaps it was just the whiteness of the MC's teeth that was dazzling her. He held out his hand, motioning toward the huge pile of prizes.

"We have a holiday in Portugal, a two-night stay in York at a four-star hotel, dinner for two right here in this hotel, or two tickets for the races at Haydock in a private box," he announced. "Those are the main prizes, and then there is this beautiful fox sculpture, plus bottles of spirits and wine, a picnic basket, biscuits, chocolates…just pick anything you want."

Ellie reached for the sculpture. "I'll take that, please."

The man handed it over with yet another dazzling smile and she headed back to her seat with relief.

"I thought you would have gone for the holiday," Marmaduke said in surprise as she set her prize carefully on the table.

"It's for you," she said, pushing it toward Andy.

Hot color flooded his tanned face.

"For me…but why?"

Not sure how to answer and suddenly embarrassed, Ellie shrugged.

"To thank you for helping the fox that day, I guess." She squirmed in her seat. "Shouldn't we be setting off for home soon? It's a long drive back."

"But the ball isn't over yet," Marmaduke protested. "And we're all becoming such good friends."

Andy stood and pushed back his chair, the fox firmly clutched in his hands.

"Ellie's right," he said. "We've had a great time, but we have to work tomorrow. I have surgery first thing."

"Yes," Ellie agreed, grabbing her bag and

waving in the general direction of the whole table. "It's been nice meeting you all. Enjoy the rest of your night."

"Five, six, three," called the MC.

"Here," announced Marmaduke, picking up Andy's discarded ticket. "That's your number."

"Thanks,"

Andy grabbed the ticket and walked up to the front of the room, still carrying the fox.

"It's just wine and chocolates now, I'm afraid," the MC said. "Oh yes, or the picnic basket."

Andy hesitated, and then he motioned toward the wicker picnic basket with two leather straps.

"I'll have that, please."

The MC handed it over and Andy juggled with the fox, jamming it securely under his arm before taking his prize.

He almost ran back to the table. "Come on, Ells," he said. "Let's go."

As they walked out of the brightly lit hotel into the cool darkness of the parking lot, Andy handed the picnic basket to Ellie.

"It looks just like the one my dad used to have when I was a kid," she said.

"You have it. To remember tonight. And who knows, maybe one day you'll fill it and ask me on a picnic."

Ellie found that idea disturbingly tempting. "Who knows," she replied.

ANDY'S HEART LIGHTENED. If only he could make Ellie believe what he'd said about her mum. Then, perhaps, she'd realize that she really could trust him. There was no way he would ever mention it again, though; he shouldn't have said anything in the first place.

The miles rolled by, and he glanced across at Ellie. Noticing that her eyelids were drooping, he turned down the radio, allowing his eyes to rest for a moment on the contours of her face.

Had he been right to follow her mother's request, to miss out on what they might have had? he wondered. An image of Sally Nelson's face that day slid into his mind, the desperation in her fading eyes as she begged him to leave her daughter alone.

And perhaps she'd been right. After all, he was the one who'd broken it off with Ellie, and his marriage had been a disaster. Maybe he just wasn't cut out for a relationship. He'd blamed Amy, but what if he'd been at fault and he didn't even know it?

He should never have gotten married in the first place; he'd realized that before the event, but it had seemed too late to change his mind. Amy had been so in love with the idea, she even had a photo shoot a couple weeks before the big day, posing in her wedding dress in various locations. Andy had been in the last few shots, as if as an afterthought, but he'd always wondered if he'd still be there when Amy showed the photos to modeling agencies, as she intended. She'd got work from those photos, too; two days before their wedding, she'd done a shoot for a magazine and posed for the photographs in her wedding dress. That was when he'd almost called it off. Being a traditionalist when it came to big occasions, he hadn't wanted to see her dress before the wedding day, but she'd insisted on doing the photos. Using the dress for her modeling portfolio had just seemed a step too far, in Andy's opinion, and made a mockery of the whole thing. They'd fought and then she'd cried, begging him not to humiliate her in front of her family and friends.

Her makeup had run, and when she'd wiped her face with the tissue he'd handed her, she'd looked so vulnerable and sweet... like Ellie. That was why he'd married her; he could see it so clearly now. Without all the makeup she looked just like Ellie...and that made him a shallow jerk, didn't it? So perhaps Sally Nelson had been right all along.

Reaching out, he touched her cheek gently. If only he could believe that Ellie was back home for good, not just here to get material for her paintings. The way her impulsive actions had frightened the Fell pony mare that night had made him doubt her priorities, but he wanted to trust her intentions...for her dad's sake as well as his own.

ELLIE OPENED HER eyes with a start. Where was she? Easing her cramped neck she sat up, remembering.

"Sorry," she said. "I must have fallen asleep.

Andy glanced across at her. "That's okay."

"It's weird being here with you," she murmured, feeling disoriented. "Like going back in time."

"Would you like to?" he asked. "Go back in time, I mean."

A smile flickered across her face. "I'd like to go back to when we were younger. We had good times, Andy...before you broke my heart."

Why had she said that? she wondered, mentally kicking herself.

"Of course, it's fixed now," she said, digging herself into an even bigger hole. "And it's twice as strong."

"Glad to hear it," he said, smiling in the darkness. "So I guess it won't get broken quite as easily next time."

"Turns out it wasn't broken at all, actually—just a bit dented. And believe me, that will *never* happen again."

"Glad to hear that, too," he said, swinging the wheel hard left. "Look, you're home already and I almost missed the turn."

She sat up, peering out the window at the sign for Hope Farm, suddenly fully awake. "Home already... I'm sorry, Andy, I must have been out for ages when I should have been helping keep you awake."

ANDY PULLED UP on the gravel outside the front door. He cut the engine and silence fell, deep and dark and gentle.

"Do you like living back here?" he asked. Her response was immediate. "I love it."

"And I love you."

It was out before he'd even thought about it. Three simple words that meant so much.

She looked at him through the darkness, her face outlined by the silver light of the full moon that had just burst from behind a cloud...like a sign, Andy thought.

"You gave up the right to say that a long time ago," she said quietly.

"But I never stopped feeling it—never stopped loving you. Even though I'm not sure why you're here, or if you'll stay, I still can't help loving you."

"It's too late, Andy. You don't trust me, and I certainly don't trust you. Without trust there's nothing."

"No!" He leaned toward her. "I regretted it as soon as I broke up with you, you know. I've always loved you, and I think you love me, too. Surely that's all that really matters."

WHEN HE CUPPED her face with tender fingers, tilting up her chin, Ellie knew that she was lost. It felt so right when he drew her closer, so right when he lowered his lips to hers.

Warm and soft and heart-wrenchingly familiar, they seared her soul with their touch.

"I never ever meant to hurt you, Ellie," he murmured, holding her eyes with his. "There has never been anyone but you."

Alarm bells rang deep inside her.

"But you got married," she whispered, drawing back, her heart thumping hard.

"That was a mistake," he insisted. "A big, stupid mistake. I only married Amy because she reminded me of you. But she wasn't you—she was nothing like you…"

The sirens were screeching inside Ellie's head now. What was she thinking? Suddenly she was out of the door, running across the yard. She heard his voice behind her.

"Ellie, come back. Please."

Slamming the front door behind her, she leaned against it, hot tears running down her face. She'd dropped her defenses and almost let him creep back into her life, even after the lies he'd told her about her mum. How could she have been so stupid?

When a light came on upstairs, she shrank back into the shadowy hallway.

Her dad's voice floated down from the landing.

"Ellie, is that you?"

She gulped, rubbing her face dry with the sleeve of a jacket that hung on the coat rack.

"Yes…" she croaked, emotion choking her.

His bare feet thudded softly on the stairs, followed by Hope's eager paws. Ellie crouched down to cuddle the little red-and-white dog, hiding her face in his soft coat.

"What's wrong, love?"

She shook her head, feeling stupid. "Nothing, it's just…"

He placed his hand on her shoulder. "I'll put the kettle on then and you can tell me all about it."

Ellie watched as he brewed a pot of tea and poured her a cup.

"Now," he began, handing it over. "I'm guessing this has something to do with Andy. What has he done?"

She sipped her drink, cradling the mug.

"I'll never be able to trust him again," she said. "He tells lies to get what he wants. And the way he dumped me and never bothered to contact me again? He expects me to just forget about that. He even got married!"

Her dad looked at her thoughtfully. "Well, you can't really blame him for ending things.

You were both so young, and he was away at vet school…"

"I can understand that. But I thought we loved each other so much that he wouldn't be able to leave it like that. I thought he'd at least come back and see me…to talk."

Her dad hesitated, as if considering what he was about to say. "He did come back," he told her quietly.

"What?" Ellie rubbed her eyes with the backs of her hands. "What do you mean he came back? When?"

Her dad let out a heavy sigh. "He came to see you as soon as his term finished, and—"

"And what?" Ellie already knew the answer.

"Your mother sent him packing."

Ellie felt as if the room was closing in around her. "But why?" she cried. "Why would she do that…and why did he listen?"

"She was so ill, Ellie. Maybe her judgment was impaired, but she knew how much he'd hurt you. It was her way of protecting you, I suppose. He could hardly ignore the request of a dying woman, and anyway, I think she made him believe it was for the best."

"And you were there? Why didn't you say something?"

"No, I wasn't there, but she told me all about it. She thought she was doing the right thing."

"But why didn't you tell me, Dad? All these years and you never told me?"

"My wife was dying and my whole world had turned on its head. My daughter's love life, rightly or wrongly, was not my priority then."

"And now it is?"

"Now it is, and I can see that your mum was wrong. Then again, who knows what would have happened if Andy hadn't listened to her. Maybe your life would have taken a totally different path. At least you're here, back home again. You and Andy have another chance, Ellie. Forget the past and just take it."

"It's too late. We don't trust each other. He thinks I'm only back here to help my career, and he probably even believes I'll go back to Matt when I have enough material for my next exhibition."

"And will you?" her dad asked.

"Oh, no, not you, too!" she moaned.

Her dad shook his head. "No, not me. I believe you love caring for the animals and all that this life has to offer, and I believe that you intend to stay around even when your painting career takes off."

"Thanks, Dad," she said with the hint of a smile. "But what should I do?"

"When you get a chance at love, especially with a decent bloke like Andy, perhaps you should follow your heart and not your head. This kind of opportunity doesn't come along very often—never, for some—and sometimes…" His voice broke and he paused, clearing his throat. "Sometimes it's taken away from you too soon. Look, why don't you try to find a way to prove to him that you really do care about the animals, and then maybe he'll see that you're serious about staying here. Take happiness with both hands, Ellie, and see how it goes."

"But how can I do that?"

Patting her shoulder, he headed for the stairs. "You'll find a way. Now try and get a good night's sleep—not that there's much left of it."

CHAPTER TWENTY-FIVE

IDEAS FLITTED AROUND inside Ellie's head as she went about her early-morning chores. A wintry breeze whipped across the yard, ruffling the feathers of the little red chicken that always made a beeline for the house as soon as her dad let them out. It strutted over to her, bright, beady eyes searching eagerly for food. She threw it some corn, watching its happy pecking.

"What do you think, Henny?" she asked.

"I'm not sure she's the best person to get advice from," her dad remarked, suddenly appearing around the corner of the house.

"Who knows." Ellie smiled. "Perhaps she's more intelligent than we think."

"By the way," he added. "I have an idea I'd like to run by you over breakfast."

"An idea about what?"

"You'll see," he said.

ANDY CAREFULLY PLACED the ginger kitten he had been operating on back into its cage.

"Should be as good as new in no time," he said with a satisfied smile. "And perhaps he'll have learned to be a bit more traffic-wise."

"I doubt it," said Jen, the new veterinary nurse at Low Fell. "You did a good job, though. That fracture was tricky."

Andy nodded, taking off his white coat and reaching for his jacket. "Thanks. Let's just hope that no infection sets in. Anyway, keep an eye on him. I'm off to Cravendale now."

"More injured animals?" Jen asked.

Andy frowned. "I'm not really sure. Paula, she runs the place, was a bit vague when she called me earlier. She just asked me to get there as soon as I could."

"Well, good luck, then. I'll see you tomorrow."

"See you tomorrow," he replied, heading for the door with a thoughtful expression on his face.

As he drove south toward the animal sanctuary, his thoughts kept returning to Ellie. He'd told her that he loved her, but that had been a stupid move. And he'd as good as told her that he didn't trust her—another mistake. It was obvious that she didn't trust him, either. Maybe it would be better if they went their separate ways. What if the timing was all wrong and they'd missed their chance at happiness? Ellie truly believed that he'd lied about her mother, and if she thought he was capable of making up something as cruel as that, then there wasn't any hope for them, anyway.

Paula was already waiting when he arrived at Cravendale.

He grinned at her as he got out of his truck. "I take it it's good news, if the expression on your face is anything to go by?"

"The best," she cried, clutching her hands together in excitement. "Someone has offered us a place to make a fresh start. I don't have many details yet, but it's something."

"That's great," Andy said. "But couldn't you have told me over the phone?"

Paula smiled. "There's a wounded donkey, as well. He came in this morning with a nasty cut on one foreleg, and the other swollen up like a bolster."

Andy reached inside his truck, retrieving

his bag from the passenger seat. "It must have an owner, though, unless donkeys have taken to running wild around here."

Paula chuckled. "I haven't come across any others, but who knows. A local farmer brought him in his trailer—he found the poor creature in the lane, saw he needed treatment and didn't know what else to do with him. I bet the owner will turn up soon enough."

"Well, make sure you get a donation from him before he takes it back," Andy said.

Twenty minutes later, Andy gave the sad-looking donkey an antibiotic shot after examining him.

"There, that should do the trick," he announced. "You've already done a good job of cleaning up the wound, Paula, and I think plenty of cold-hosing should sort out all that swelling. I'm guessing someone clipped him with their car and just drove off."

"Sad, but true," Paula agreed. "I'll never understand how some people can be so cruel."

Andy nodded. "Now, why don't you tell me all about this place you've been offered over a cup of coffee."

"There's not much to tell yet," she said, her face bright with enthusiasm. "It's about twenty-five miles away from here. There's some land with it, and the owner wants to get involved, too, so it all sounds very promising. I've arranged to go over there tomorrow…"

"And I suppose you want some moral support?"

She nodded happily. "I was hoping you might come. You're the one with all the big plans and ideas, after all. All that matters to me is that we have somewhere to care for animals that need help."

Andy felt a flicker of excitement. Perhaps this was just what he needed to get Ellie out of his head. "How much is the rent?" he asked.

Paula rolled her eyes. "To be honest I didn't really ask any questions. I thought we could leave all that until we get there. I'm trying not to get my hopes up in case it doesn't work out."

"Doesn't seem like you're succeeding, as far as I can tell," Andy teased. "Aren't those your hopes soaring overhead? Anyway, luckily I'm only working until lunchtime tomorrow because I'm on call tonight. So what time should I get here?"

"That's just it—you don't need to come here. I called Ellie this morning to ask if she'd enjoyed the ball—she loved it, by the way—and we got talking. She invited me to visit Hope Farm anytime, to see her paintings. Since we'll be going in that direction, I thought I'd kill two birds with one stone and stop by there first. If you get to Hope Farm for about two o'clock, then we can go check out the property afterward."

ELLIE JUMPED DOWN from Fancy's broad back, giving her a pat before turning to Jake Munro with a wide smile on her face.

"Thanks for the riding lesson," she said. "I certainly needed it, and as I thought I was just going out for a ride, it was a real treat."

"You did very well, Ellie," Cass called from over by the fence. "And since Jake won't let me ride until the baby comes, at least watching you keeps me occupied. We'll have to make it a regular thing."

Jake glanced adoringly at his wife. "It's not worth taking a risk, Cass, you know that. What if you had a fall?"

"I know," she said. "I just miss it, that's all."

"How did your scan go?" Ellie asked. "It was yesterday, wasn't it?"

"We changed our minds about not wanting to know the sex. Everything looks fine and we're having a girl," Jake announced proudly.

"That's great," Ellie exclaimed. "I'm so happy for you. What did Robbie say?"

"He's thrilled," said Cass. "He wanted a sister so badly."

The look that Cass and Jake exchanged brought a rush of envy into Ellie's heart. Would she ever share that togetherness with someone? she wondered, her thoughts going automatically to Andy.

"I'll just put Fancy away and then I'll have to run," she said. "Paula from the animal sanctuary is coming to see me this afternoon. Thanks again for the lesson, Jake."

He smiled. "You're welcome. Come back next week if you like."

"Only if you let me pay you," she insisted.

DRIVING HOME, ELLIE found her thoughts going over and over her idea. It would prove to Andy once and for all that she had no intention of running back to either the city or her ex-fiancé. A faint ray of hope loomed on her horizon, and she clung to the delicious ripple of excitement that flooded her body until doubt crept in again. Surely, if he'd really loved her, he wouldn't have let her mother influence him like that. Would she ever really be able to trust him again? Did she want to be able to trust him? The answer came at once. She would have trusted Andy Montgomery with her whole life once, and she longed to be able to do that again.

Paula's car was already parked haphazardly in the center of the yard when Ellie pulled up. Ellie found her in the kitchen, having a coffee with her dad.

"Sorry I'm late," she said, bursting in with Hope at her heels. "Have you given Paula the tour yet, Dad?"

He nodded. "Yes, but we thought we'd wait for you to come back before we show her your paintings.

The rattle of Andy's truck announced his arrival and Paula jumped up.

"Why don't you go and see Andy?" she

suggested, looking pointedly at Ellie. "Your dad can take me to the paintings, can't he?"

Feeling her legs go weak, Ellie placed one hand on the back of a chair.

"Good idea," her dad agreed. "Paula thinks your plan is great, so now all you have to do is sell it to Andy."

Andy was standing in the middle of the yard when Ellie went out to find him. He towered above her in the autumn sunshine, the light breeze lifting his hair. He pushed it back with one hand, and it flopped right onto his forehead again. Ellie gulped back a rush of nostalgia.

"I want to show you something," she said.

He stared at her, uncertainty clouding his eyes.

"I'm supposed to be meeting Paula. We have a possible new property to visit."

"She's with my dad…they'll be out in a minute."

He walked beside her across the yard, so close and yet a million miles away.

"Where are we going?" he asked.

"You'll see," she told him, resisting the temptation to take hold of his hand.

Horses' heads peered inquisitively out from their stables as they crossed the main yard and rounded the corner into what her dad always called the far yard. A sturdy gray stone building stood at the end of a large cobbled area.

"We haven't used it since dad got rid of his milk cows," Ellie said. "There's a decent-sized paddock right behind it, and another entrance so you can get to it without having to cross the yard."

Andy stopped, folding his arms across his chest, jean-clad legs splayed apart.

"What's this all about, Ellie?" he asked.

"Just humor me."

Her heart hammered in her chest as he followed her into the cool emptiness of the disused building.

She took a deep breath. "You need a place for the animal sanctuary, somewhere big enough to expand and do all the things you've dreamed of, and we—that's me and my dad—would love to be involved with it all. He was so impressed when you took him to Cravendale on the way to my exhibition."

"What?" Andy's mouth fell open. "You

mean…this is the property that Paula told me about?"

Ellie nodded happily. "I have no intention of ever going back to the city, Andy. I want my paintings to be successful, of course I do, but they're just part of my life, not the be-all and end-all."

He took a step toward her, one step that bridged six years.

"I'm so sorry, Ellie," he groaned.

She reached out to touch his hand with tentative fingers, suddenly so sure. "I don't want any more apologies, Andy. That's all behind us now, and I want to think ahead. I want us to make a brand-new start, with fresh hopes and dreams and no regrets…no matter what happens."

"Us?" he murmured, looking deep into her eyes. "Oh, I love you Ellie."

"And I love you," she whispered as he pulled her into his arms. "I've never stopped loving you."

As his lips closed over hers, so warm and soft and familiar, Ellie felt seventeen again.

"So will you take it, then?" she asked, drawing back to study his face, touching one tender finger to his cheek.

"Just try and stop me," he said. "But only if you come with it."

"Oh, didn't I tell you?" She smiled up at him. "That is one of the main stipulations."

* * * * *

LARGER-PRINT BOOKS!

GET 2 FREE
LARGER-PRINT NOVELS
PLUS 2 FREE
MYSTERY GIFTS

Love Inspired

Larger-print novels are now available...

LILPDIR13R

LARGER-PRINT BOOKS!

GET 2 FREE LARGER-PRINT NOVELS PLUS 2 FREE MYSTERY GIFTS

Love Inspired®
SUSPENSE
RIVETING INSPIRATIONAL ROMANCE

Larger-print novels are now available...

ReaderService.com

Manage your account online!

- Review your order history
- Manage your payments
- Update your address

> *We've designed
> the Harlequin® Reader Service
> website just for you.*

Enjoy all the features!

- Reader excerpts from any series
- Respond to mailings and special monthly offers
- Discover new series available to you
- Browse the Bonus Bucks catalog
- Share your feedback

Visit us at:

ReaderService.com